PENNY FILES
ALASKA STATE TROOPERS, UNFINISHED BUSINESS

Ron Walden

Alaskan True to Life Crime Writer

Ugly Moose AK
Box 1326 Soldotna, AK 99669
uglymooseak@gmail.com

Musk Ox
(mâthi-môs)
Ugly Moose

ISBN 978-1-95-726321-2
eBook 978-1-95-726322-9
Library of Congress Catalog Card Number: 2016935318

Dedication

I dedicate *Penny Files* to my most avid reader, critic, editor, friend, lover and partner. My wife has kept me in the middle of the road for all these years. If I have done anything worth mentioning in my lifetime it was due to the efforts of this wonderful and tireless lady, Betty Lou Walden

Acknowledgements

It is my goal to make each book I write believable and realistic. In order to accomplish this goal I rely on the knowledge of my many friends. My stories are true to life because of this living encyclopedia of little known facts supplied by these friends. Among these founts of information are my retired trooper friends; my publisher who keeps me to the task; and my banker who instructs me in the ways of finance. I thank each of them and the folks in my daily life for the help they provide me, not only in my writing, but in my daily life.

If a man's success can be measured by the quality of his friends then I am blessed to be in the very highest percentage.

I give a special thanks to my son, Scott, who is my electronics genius and maintains my electronic devices. Without him I would still be using the old Underwood.

I thank my readers for giving me support and supplying me with plots for new stories. Were it not for these loyal fans I would have never continued writing. I thank you all for being there when I needed you.

Chapter 1

Public Defender Ryan James sat with his client Jack Marin, watching the court proceeding. Arresting trooper, Penny Rossiter, was on the stand. Rossiter had been a trooper for six years and had been on this witness stand many times. She was small in stature, five feet three inches tall, her copper color hair was long, but tied in a knot at the back of her head. She certainly didn't look like one would think of as an Alaska State Trooper.

"Your report states you were called to a disturbance at Rainbow Bar at 8:05 p.m. within the city of Kenai. Is it usual to be called to a disturbance inside the city?" Assistant District Attorney Kevin Darby was doing the asking.

"The city officers were busy with an injury accident at the time of the call and they asked for a trooper to take the call. It was standard procedure in such cases."

"Were you alone when you responded to the call?" asked the DA.

"Yes, the report stated there was some kind of disturbance reported inside the bar. There were no other details at that time."

"What sort of situation did you find when you entered the Rainbow Bar?"

"The bartender met me at the door. She said Jack was trying to start a fight with one of the customers in a wedding party near the pool table. I could hear shouting and arguing toward the back of the room."

"By 'Jack', did you mean Jack Marin?" The DA wanted this point clarified.

"Yes, Sir, I could see from the doorway there was a confrontation happening in the area she had pointed out."

"What did you do at that time, Officer Rossiter?"

"I walked to the back of the bar where the pool table is located and stepped between one of the wedding guests and Jack Marin. I asked Mr. Marin to step back and calm down."

"Then what happened?"

"Mr. Marin took one step back and swung a closed fist at me with his right hand. The rest of the crowd moved away at that time."

"Did he strike you with his close fist?"

"No, Sir, I am trained in martial arts and stepped under his arm. I caught his right arm with my right arm and pushed him backward. When he stepped back I pushed my left knee into his left knee causing him to fall to the floor. I placed a handcuff on his right wrist and held it immobile with my right knee behind his back. I was able to grip his left arm and apply the other handcuff to it. During this time he was struggling and cursing. At this time another trooper came to my assistance and we removed Mr. Marin from the bar. He was taken to Wildwood Pretrial and booked on the charges he is in court for today."

"Were you or any other patrons injured in the confrontation, Trooper Rossiter?"

"None were reported."

"Thank you. I have nothing further, Your Honor." The DA returned to his seat at the prosecutor's table.

"Your witness, Mr. James," said the judge.

"Thank you, Your Honor." The public defender studied his notes a moment before beginning. "Trooper Rossiter, how much do you weigh?" he asked.

"One hundred eight pounds, Sir," she replied.

"You weigh one hundred eight pounds and you were able to take down my client, alone, unassisted and put him in handcuffs. My client weighs over 240 and works in the oilfields. I don't see any way that could have happened. In fact I find your story totally unbelievable. Is there anything you would like to change about your description of the incident?" asked the public defender.

"No, Sir. I told you the way it happened. There were many witnesses to the altercation. You are free to ask any of them."

"I don't think I need to ask any of them. But, I still don't believe your story." He sat down in his chair.

"You are free to step down Trooper Rossiter," said the judge.

Penny Rossiter stood and stepped from the witness box to return to the gallery and was walking toward the small gate to the seating area when Jack Marin jumped from his chair, sprang around the defense table and reached for the diminutive police officer. With his left hand he grabbed her right shoulder and spun her around. With his right fist closed he threw a round-house punch, which she stepped under, hooking his right arm with her right arm and stepped into the blow. Jack faltered backward and she dropped her left knee onto the inside of his buckling left knee. He fell. She held his arm and pulled it to his back as he fell. By the time both were on the courtroom floor she had her handcuffs in her other hand and placed one cuff on his right wrist.

The Court Services Officer reacted instantly when the defendant made his move, but Rossiter had Marin on the floor and was reaching for his left arm when the officer reached them. The Court Services Officer helped her apply the other handcuff and stand the big man on his feet.

The judge, seeing the situation was now under control, looked down from the bench at the public defender. "Mr. James, I think this was a convincing demonstration of Trooper Rossiter's ability to accomplish what she claimed in her statement. I am sentencing Mr. Marin to six months to serve with three months suspended. I expect there will be further charges from this current incident. Since I will undoubtedly be called as a witness to this incident I will be forced to recuse myself from that case. Next case!"

Jack was led from the court and taken back to jail.

Penny went to the ladies room to fix her hair and inspect for damages before returning to her office to complete the statements for the new assault charges against Jack Marin. She was leaving the court when Assistant District Attorney Kevin Darby stopped her and asked how she was after the fight in the courtroom.

"Oh, I'm fine. Like I said, I'm trained in Martial Arts. I'm not as big, but I can move quicker and have a better plan than most brawlers." In reality she was fatigued by the adrenalin leaving her system. She just wanted to go to the office and sit down.

"The Judge wanted me to check on you. He was very impressed with your skills. I think he intends to write a letter of commendation to your commander for your actions here today." Kevin took her hand and shook it gently. "I would like to add my thanks to those of the Judge."

She left the courthouse, making a stop at the Holiday gasoline station for a large, cold, sweet, cola drink. At the office she stopped to give a brief verbal account of the incident to her Captain. Once done she went to her own office to complete the report and complaint for filing with the DA.

She had always been small in stature. Her father, a paralyzed Viet Nam vet, loved his daughter very much and taught her to be a fierce competitor in everything she attempted. He enrolled her in karate classes when she was eight years old. She loved the sport and did well in all her competitions. Her father was proud of her and loved her until his passing when she was fourteen. The loss was devastating for her. Her mother was kind, but had trouble dealing with life after the death of Penny's father.

Penny continued her karate training and became more skilled as she matured. She went to college at the University of Idaho, Moscow. It was her intent to get a law degree. An ROTC unit helped her finance her education for the six years at law school. She entered the military after college and passed the bar to become a Provost Marshal and Military Justice Officer. It was there she became a jet fighter pilot, although she never flew any combat missions. She loved the flying as much as she loved the karate competitions she entered while in the military.

Upon completing her military obligation she applied for a position with the Alaska State Troopers and after demonstrating her abilities to compensate for her size she was accepted and sent to the academy for further training.

Now, six years later, she sat here at her desk, exhausted and physically drained from the events of the morning. She reviewed the reports and made copies. She had decided to take them to the District Attorney personally. She was preparing to leave the office when Captain Meadows asked her to come to his office.

"What's up Cap?" she asked as she entered.

"Have you got time for a welfare check?" he asked.

"I think so. What is it?"

"I have a friend who lives at Mile 12 on Funny River Road; he sort of looks after an old trapper who lives out near him. He called me and asked to have someone go with him to check on the trapper. Gus hasn't seen or heard from the man in several days. He lives about a half mile off the road and my friend Gus Sampson will meet you at the main road and lead you into the cabin. The trappers name is Will Goodson. Like I said, this is just a welfare check."

"Sure, I can do it Cap. I'll have dispatch send this file over to the DA and I can leave right now." Standing to leave, she asked, "You say your friend, Gus, will meet me near Mile 12?"

"Yes, I'll call him and let him know you are on the way. This is kind of a personal favor, Penny. Thanks."

"No problem, Sir, happy to do it." She stepped out of the office and into the afternoon sunshine. *It'll be a nice break*, she thought.

The pleasant drive up the south side of the Kenai River aided in her recovery. She passed mile marker 12 and moments later saw a man standing on the side of the road. He had recognized the trooper vehicle and waved his arm as she approached. He stuffed his hands in his pockets and walked to the driver side of the car.

"Hi there, Trooper, are you the one Captain Meadows sent out?"

"Yes, I am, are you the one wanting a welfare check on your friend?"

"Yup, Gus Sampson. I look after old Will Goodson most of the time. I haven't seen him in a few days and he was supposed to come to my place for dinner last night, but never showed up. Maybe he just forgot, but in the past he's never missed an offer for dinner. Normally I would have just gone in and checked on him, but he has been acting nervous and strange lately. I think something may have happened to him, so I called Ted to send someone to go in with me. I hope it's a false alarm."

"I hope so, too, Sir," she said as she opened the door of the patrol car. She reached back into the vehicle and retrieved the shotgun from the locking rack in the front seat. Checking that it was properly loaded, she snapped the safety on. She looked at him watching her. "Just a safety precaution," she said. As she slipped the sling over her left shoulder, she asked, "Which way?"

He pointed to the one-time road across the ditch. It was no longer a road, only a rutted brush filled trail. He led the way across the ditch and down the path more than a half-mile to where a small cabin occupied a small clearing in the spruce woods. Firewood was piled on the front porch. A large wood block with an axe stuck in the top sat close to the steps.

"Give him a shout to let him know we're out here," she ordered. "We don't want to surprise him and have him shooting at us."

Gus Sampson nodded. "Hey! Will! It's me, Gus. Are you in there?"

No answer, "Try again," she said.

"Will," he said in a louder tone, "Are you home?"

There was still no answer from the inside. "Step back by the trees and wait. I'm going to check the cabin."

He nodded and stepped back a few paces to the edge of the clearing.

Penny Rossiter walked cautiously up the sturdy steps. There was a large window to the right of the doorway, which she approached to get a look inside. As she neared the window she stopped short and reached for her cell phone. She could not see inside the dark cabin, but immediately recognized the odor of human death; there is no other smell on earth like it.

A voice answered her phone call. It was Captain Meadows.

"Captain, it's Rossiter, you'd better send the crime scene team out here. There's no answer at the cabin and I have a strong odor of someone dead inside the cabin. I'll have Mr. Sampson meet them at my car and lead them out here to the cabin. I'm going to try to open the door now. Hold on while I try the door."

She stood beside the door and tried the handle. The door pressed open. On the floor near the rear of the visible room lay a body. She could see a great deal of blood spatter in the room and reported the find to the captain. The odor was nauseating and she stepped back a little to allow the room to air. As she jumped down from the small porch she heard the captain's voice on her cell phone.

"The crime scene team is on the way. They should be in your area in less than ten minutes. Keep Gus away from the house and let me know what you find inside."

"Yes, sir, Cap," she said as she walked away from the cabin.

"Gus," she called, "I want you to go back to the road and send the trooper team out when they arrive. I have to stay here. I want you to go home and as soon as I'm finished here I'll come to see you."

"It's bad, huh?" he asked.

"Yeah, Gus, it's bad. There is someone inside and from your description I think it's your friend. Please, meet the troopers and then go home until I contact you."

His shoulders sagged and his feet shuffled as he walked away from the cabin.

Chapter 2

While waiting for the Crime Scene Team she walked around the clearing surrounding the cabin. It was small and it didn't take long. The only thing unusual she had seen was a piece of alder log. It was about three feet long and thee inches in diameter. The log was covered with blood leading her to believe this was the weapon used on the victim. The ground was dry and she had found no discernible footprints or other evidence. It had been almost a half hour since she called the Captain when she heard voices coming from the trail. Moments later five men carrying their equipment arrived at the clearing.

In charge of the team was a tall, thin, dark haired trooper by the name of David Haskins. He stopped at the entry to the clearing where Penny Rossiter met him. He dropped a large satchel to the ground and wiped sweat from his brow.

"You could have picked a cooler day," commented Haskins.

"The day picked me," said Penny, "and it doesn't get any better inside the cabin. I didn't enter the place. I didn't want to disturb anything and the victim was obviously deceased. I did find what appears to be the weapon lying out behind the cabin. I didn't pick it up. I didn't know if you could get fingerprints from it."

Haskins turned to the second man to arrive. "Lou, go with Penny and she'll show you where there may be some evidence behind the cabin. Winston, come with me and bring the bag." Haskins had a camera in his hand taking pictures and video of the scene. He filmed the outside of the cabin before stepping up onto the porch. He took close-up photos of the wood piled near the door and the door itself. Both investigators donned masks; they would filter the air, but could do nothing to protect them from the odor inside the cabin. Haskins took more pictures from the door before entering. Two more team members arrived and began their pre-assigned tasks. They were an efficient group working without much conversation. They gathered evidence and took more pictures. It was more than two hours before they loaded the body into a black plastic bag for transport. One of the officers was sent to the road to get a four wheel ATV and a small trailer to transport the body from the cabin. Penny Rossiter waited near the front porch while the team finished their work. Finally, Haskins came out of the cabin and removed his mask.

"What a mess," he finally commented to Rossiter. "There were two and possibly three assailants. I don't know what they wanted, but they tried to beat it out of him. From the looks of it he lasted a long time before they beat him to death. He was one tough old bird. I'm surprised they didn't burn the cabin to cover their tracks. I don't know why they didn't unless that's what they wanted all along, the cabin and property for some reason."

Penny had written notes on her pad. "Are you going to leave someone here to secure the cabin?" she asked.

"No, we'll just put crime scene tape on the doors and around the cabin. I think we have all the evidence we'll find. It was definitely a murder. The killers didn't leave much for us to go on, but I'll give you that information when we get back to the office. Are you going to interview the friend now?"

"Yes, I told him to go home and I would come see him when we finished. I'll ask him to keep an eye on the place for us. He was a close friend of the victim. Did you identify him as Will Goodson, the owner of the cabin?"

"Yes, his wallet and driver's license were on the floor next to the body. His money was still in the wallet, so robbery wasn't the motive."

"Thanks, Dave, I'll go to Gus Sampson's place and give him the bad news. I'll see you at the office when I finish. Sampson may know of any enemies or strangers asking about Goodson." She closed her notebook and began the walk back to the road where her car was parked.

In her car she started the engine and rolled down the window. She activated the air conditioning unit to cool the inside of the vehicle. During this activity she noticed the odor embedded in her uniform. It held the stench of death. It wasn't strong now, but nauseating just the same. She checked the time and made more notes in her notebook. Her attention kept coming back to the odor emitting from her clothing. She finally picked up the mike and called dispatch to let them know she was going down the road to Gus Sampson's place. With the air conditioner operating at full capacity and the window down she drove back down Funny River Road hoping to air out some of the smell collected in her uniform. It was just a mile to where the road leading to the home of Sampson came into view on the right. His home was several driveways down on the right. When she stopped in front of the house he came out onto the front porch.

He waved and asked, "Want some iced tea?"

"I'd love some, Gus, thanks," she replied. "We had better sit outside. I don't smell so good."

"Have a seat and I'll get us some tea." He disappeared back inside the house and returned moments later with two tall glasses of iced tea with slices of lemon floating on top of the ice in the glass.

Rossiter took a long drink of the tea, leaned back and uttered a loud, satisfied "Aaah. Thanks, Gus, I needed this."

Gus had a sad look. "Now and then I get a whiff of you and it ain't purty."

"It was bad, Gus. I can't give you any details, but it was bad." She took another sip of the tea.

"Poor Old Will never had an enemy in the world. Who could have done this to him?" Gus was looking at his feet and shaking his head.

"That's what I have to find out. Do you know of anyone who might have had it in for Goodson?"

"Not a clue. Everybody loved old Will. He used to be a trapper, you know. People would come out to his place and just listen to him tell stories about his trapping days." Gus' voice crackled with emotion and he took another sip of his tea.

"Whoever did this wasn't a robber; they didn't take anything as far as we can tell. Can you think of anyone who might have had a grudge against him? Did he owe anyone money? Or make anyone angry in recent days?"

"You saw his cabin. He didn't have much you could consider a treasure worth stealing. His place isn't worth much either. Wait a minute. About a week ago Will told me some guys came out to his place and wanted to buy it or lease it from him. Will told them no. He said they offered him a lot of money to rent or lease the place. Will said he wasn't moving. When he told me about it he said he 'didn't like the looks of those guys.'"

"Do you have any idea who they were?" she asked, taking a last drink of her tea.

"No, and I don't think Will knew them either. He just said he didn't like their looks."

"Well, she said standing, "I have to get back to the office. I have a lot of paperwork to catch up on. Just one more thing, Gus, do you know if Will Goodson had any relatives?"

"None I know of."

"Can I ask a favor of you?"

"Sure, anything to help," he answered.

"We put up police tape and sealed the doorway to keep anyone out, but I would appreciate it if you could keep an eye out for anyone snooping around up there. If you see anyone suspicious call me. Don't confront them alone. Just call me." She gave him a card with her cell phone number.

"Sure thing, Trooper Rossiter," as he read the name from the card.

"Call me Penny." She turned to walk to her car. As she reached the car door she looked back. "Thank you for all your help. I'll do my best to find out who did this to your friend."

Gus Sampson waved to her as she backed out of the drive.

During the 20-minute drive she kept thinking about the men who wanted to rent or lease will Goodson's property. It had power and water, but other than that it was truly basic. Why would anyone want this place? The only reason she could come up with was a drug operation of some kind—possibly a marijuana farm, which since legalization didn't seem likely.

Again she sniffed at her uniform. She would have to clean up and change into a clean uniform before anything else. Penny decided to go home to change into a different uniform. She owned a small, modest house in Soldotna which she shared with her ailing mother. The home was only about six blocks off the Sterling Highway in a mostly new subdivision. She kept the yard trimmed neatly and had no pets.

As she entered the front door of the house she heard a small voice from the kitchen, "Is that you, Penny?"

"Yes, Mom," she replied. "I have to change my uniform and take a shower. I'll only be a few minutes before I need to get to the office to finish my reports. How are you doing today?"

"I'm pretty good, Honey. I'm making a pot roast for dinner. Will you be home on time tonight?"

"I'm not sure, Mom, but I think so."

Penny Rossiter's father had been in a wheelchair the rest of his life after he returned from Viet Nam. Penny was only eight when he came home, wounded and unable to do much except sit in his chair and worship his daughter. She had always been small in stature and sometimes complained to her father she was unable to do what the bigger girls could. He had told her she could do anything she wanted to do, but she would have to work harder than the other girls. He enrolled her in karate class when she was eight years old; a class she continued to this day. Her father went to every competition she entered and cheered loudly for his daughter. Penny was fourteen when he succumbed to his war wounds. She was devastated, but continued her martial arts training to honor him.

After her father's death Penny's mother Julia began to drink and smoke heavily. Over time it took away her health. She suffered a bad liver and damaged lungs from her grief-stricken lifestyle and carried an oxygen bottle with her wherever she went. She toted her oxygen bottle on the walker she used to get around. When Julia could no longer care for herself properly Penny took her into her home.

After high school Penny Rossiter was able to get several scholarships for college because of her war-hero father. She attended the University of Idaho, Moscow, and graduated with a criminal justice degree. She spent six years in the Air Force flying fighter jets, a job she loved, but after she learned of her mother's failing health she left the military to return to law school. Upon graduating she took the bar exam and passed in the first try. This would allow her to be licensed and practice law in sixteen states.

In her last days of law school a recruiter approached her from Alaska to consider a career in law enforcement as an Alaska State Trooper. It was a tough decision but she missed the action of her flying days and thought she would become a trooper and experience the other side of the law for short while before becoming a desk-bound attorney. Alaska was one of the states she would be able to obtain a license to practice when she was ready.

Now, twenty-three years after her father had passed away, she was not ready to live in an office. She loved her life as a cop. She loved the excitement, the challenges, the risks and most of all she loved taking bad people off the streets and protecting the public from lawless acts. When her mother moved into her house she made up her mind to stay with the troopers until the time came to put Julia in a nursing home.

Penny showered and changed into a fresh uniform, stuffing the tainted one in a plastic bag to be dropped at the dry cleaners. She stopped in the kitchen to have a tall glass of orange juice and speak with her mother.

"Is there anything you need from the store?" she asked.

"No, I think we have everything, unless you want to stop and get me a bottle of wine to go with dinner."

"Now, Mom, we've talked about that. You know you can't drink wine anymore." Penny was used to the request and chided her mother each time she asked.

"I know, Honey, but it would taste so good," she admitted.

Penny finished her glass of juice, picked up the bag to be dropped at the cleaners and went out to her car. On the way to the door she called back to the kitchen, "Bye, Mom, see ya later."

"OK, Honey," answered the voice from the kitchen.

Returning to work meant she would, once again, need to shift mental gears.

Chapter 3

Rossiter pulled into the dry cleaner store on her way to the office and dropped the aromatic uniform off to be cleaned. Her next stop was at the convenience store next door for a tall, cold cola in a plastic cup. She took a long drink of the cool liquid before starting her car. After putting the large cup in the holder next to the seat, she drove to the office where her first stop was the office of Captain Ted Meadows.

Looking up from his desk as she entered, he said, "My, don't you look all new and shiny?"

"Thanks a lot, Cap. I had to stop at my house and put on a clean uniform. You sent me on a smelly errand. Has Dave Haskins been in to see you?"

"Not yet Penny, have a seat and give me an outline, I'll read the rest in the report later."

"There isn't much to tell, Captain. I met with Gus out Funny River Road and he led me to the cabin. I didn't get any answer when I knocked on the door, but could smell something bad on the inside. I sent Gus back to the road and called for the crime scene guys. They got there right away and went to work, I stayed outside. The old trapper Will Goodson had been beaten to death. Haskins found a wallet next to the body and identified the victim. While I was waiting I walked around the cabin and located a three-foot piece of wood with blood on it. That was probably the murder weapon. Haskins told me the wallet contained some cash, so robbery wasn't the motive. The cabin and land can't be worth much leaving me without a possible motive. Gus told me someone had approached Goodson about buying or leasing his property and that he had turned them down. It could be the same people, but I can't say for sure. I asked Gus to keep an eye on the place until we finish." Penny Rossiter paused a moment then said, "Gus is pretty shaken up by it all,

Cap. Right now I have to write the reports." She was sipping from the large plastic cup she held on her lap.

Captain Meadows rubbed his chin, "Hmm, I wonder who wanted old Will dead and why?" He rubbed his chin again, then his neck, stretched his back and said, "Good job, Penny. I'll call Gus in a little while. I want to talk with the crime scene team first, though."

Saying, nothing, but raising her cup in way of a salute she turned and walked to her office. A pile of reports was waiting for her, piled high in her 'in' basket.

It was an hour past her regular quitting time when she finished clearing her desk and finalizing the report on Will Goodson. She was making copies of the Goodson report when David Haskins and Lou Filson came into her office.

You seem to have trouble getting you work done in a timely manner, Penny. That won't look good on you next personnel evaluation. You should be home by now sipping a Margarita and eating pizza."

"Thanks for the encouragement, David. I just finished my report and if you'll wait a minute I'll give you a copy. I have other things to do, unlike you special team boys." She giggled a little.

"Seriously, Penny, I want to thank you for the help this morning. You handled it perfectly. There was nothing we had to eliminate as evidence because of contamination from onlookers. I wish every crime scene was as clean as this one." Haskins handed her a file folder. This is a copy of our prelientary report for you. You already know most of what's in it. One thing you may not know is how he died. The medical examiner hasn't sent the final report, but whoever did this broke almost every bone in his body except for his left hand. We think they saved it for him to sign something, but he may have died before they got the paper signed; we don't know yet."

Rossiter took the file and opened it, but didn't start reading. She placed the open file on her desk and asked, "Did you talk with Gus?"

"Yes we did," answered Filson. "He was pretty emotional about it. I felt sorry for him."

"You know this all started on a welfare check initiated by Gus. They had been friends for a long time. I asked him to keep an eye on the cabin, but that may not be such a good idea since someone killed the owner and could do the same to Gus if they found him out there without anyone to help him."

"We warned him about being caught out there alone," said Haskins.

Filson continued, "The log you found was obviously the murder weapon, but we won't be able to get fingerprints from the surface. It was in the weather too long and the surface was too far gone. We do think there will be DNA on the club from both Goodson and the person swinging it. There will be sweat or some other evidence on it. We're working on that now."

"We may have some good news for you, though," Haskins interjected.

"That would be a change," said Penny.

"I had my guys canvass the area, talking with neighbors within a mile of his property and two of them had seen an old pickup with three men, scroungy-looking men according to both witnesses, and we have descriptions of all three. No one got the license number, but we have a good description of the pickup. It looks like it's a '50's model Chevy. Rusted out and dented up. It has no tailgate and there were a lot of garbage sacks in the back of the truck. We've given the information to the highway patrol division. It should turn up soon." Haskins seemed to have ended his report.

"I'll read this in the morning," said Rossiter, pointing to the report on her desk.

"All kidding aside, Penny, thanks for a great job today." Haskins made the comment as he turned to leave the office.

Penny was placing the file in a desk drawer when her intercom rang. It was Captain Meadows.

"We have four missing hikers, Penny. Do you feel up to flying?" he asked.

"Sure, Cap, where are they supposed to be?" Lost hikers never seemed to be found in the area where they were supposed to be hiking.

"We had a call from the husband of one of the hikers. He dropped the two women and two young boys off on the Hope end of Resurrection Trail three days ago. He was to pick them up today at the Cooper Landing end of the trail. They haven't shown up and he was unable to contact them on their cell phone. Cooper Landing Trooper Finlay hiked up the trail as far as the first cabin and found no sign of them. I'd like you to fly over the trail from Hope to Cooper Landing to see if you can spot them." He continued, "I know you've had a long day and I can get someone from the Anchorage office to fly down and look for them if you're too fatigued. I don't want you getting hurt."

"I'll take the Super Cub, Cap. The Cessna 185 will be too fast for this job. I'm headed out to the airport now. Can you get me a description of the hikers before I take off?"

"I'll have a trooper bring it to the hangar. You should have it before you finish your preflight check."

She went to her locker to get the emergency pack she always carried when flying. She would also take the shotgun from the trunk of her car—just in case. It's less than two miles from the office to the Soldotna Airport and the hangar leased by the Alaska State Troopers. She opened the hangar doors and pushed the blue and white Super Cub outside and did her pre-flight check. The trooper with the description of the missing hikers arrived and handed her a sheet of paper. She read it before climbing into the little plane.

There is no control tower at this airport, but she advised any local traffic she was taking off. The small, slow-flying aircraft left the ground at less than forty miles per hour and climbed steeply toward the northwest. She climbed to 4,500 feet and flew directly to Hope before circling and flying back up the narrow canyon toward the trailhead. She decided to fly the trail from the ridgeline down to the trailhead. Flying up a mountainside is never a good idea. She dropped to about five hundred feet above the treetops and began her search by crossing back and forth over the trail, searching the woods on both sides of the popular hiking trail. She circled one of the cabins along the trail finding other hikers, but no one matching the descriptions of the hikers she was seeking.

When she reached the trailhead she turned and climbed back to the ridge and used the same search technique while flying above the trail down to the Kenai River. Again she saw other hikers at a cabin and again they were not the ones for which she was searching. She climbed back to the ridge and retraced her flight path down the mountain to the Kenai River end of the trail. Near the bottom her radio crackled. It was the Cooper Landing Trooper.

"Have you seen anything?" he asked.

"No, I saw lots of hikers, but none match the ones I'm looking for. I have flown both sides of the trail twice and I'm going back to fly it one more time. We still have plenty of daylight."

"Roger that," replied Finlay. "I have the husband here. He says his wife is never late and she is a day overdue. He is very worried. The other lady and child are the wife's twin sister and her boy. The boys are nine and seven years old. The husband wants to know if you've seen any bears along the trail."

"No I didn't, but given the number of hikers I don't think I will, although there are a lot of bears headed to the river and could be in the area. I'll watch for them. I'm going back to the top and search this end of the trail again before I go back to the other side. I have about an hour of usable fuel in the tank."

"I'll be on the radio," replied Finlay. "I'm taking the husband to Cooper Landing and getting him something to eat. He needs to calm down. He's pretty hysterical right now."

"OK, I'll let you know if I spot anything." With that as a sign-off she began to climb up to the altitude needed to begin her downhill search. Again finding nothing and sighting no bears she climbed to the top again and started down the other side toward the town of Hope. She crossed and re-crossed the trail on her descent, again seeing hikers headed for the cabins, but as before none matched the hikers she was trying to locate. In one last effort she flew up the mountainside, crisscrossing the trail as she gained altitude. At the summit several hikers waved to her as she passed at her low altitude. She had the side window open and waved back to them she began her downhill search pattern, widening the path further from the trail. Again she found nothing.

She climbed to 2500 feet and called Finlay on the radio, "I'm low on fuel and returning to Soldotna. I didn't see any bears and no sign of the hikers, although there are a lot of other hikers in the area. If they are out there and injured I would think other hikers would have spotted them by now. I'll contact the captain and see if he wants a ground search."

"Good idea, thanks Trooper Rossiter."

When she landed at the Soldotna Airport Captain Meadows met her at the hangar. She gave him a report before refueling the little plane. He helped her push the craft back into the hangar.

"I'll call Alaska Search and Rescue. They have a ground search team they will send as well as a helicopter to search the area again. Get some rest, Penny. You have had a long day and tomorrow probably won't be much better."

"I'm afraid to go home. Mom was making a pot roast and I'll bet its pretty well done by now. She is going to skin me for being late." She was giggling and said, "I love tormenting her."

Meadows smiled and climbed into his car. "See you tomorrow."

Chapter 4

Julia met her daughter on the front porch with a glass of iced tea. "I know you must have been busy, but you could have called to let me know when you would be home."

"I know, Mom, but something came up and I had to go flying for a couple of hours. I'm sorry, but it was really important," Penny explained.

"It always is," said Julia as she pushed her walker and oxygen bottle back inside the house. "Well, come on and eat before it gets any blacker."

In the kitchen the table was set for two. The salads were on the table, but the roast and vegetables were still in the oven keeping warm. Penny took off her duty belt and set it on another chair at the table. She sat at the head of the dining room table, waiting, until her mother came with the hot dishes. When Julia was seated Penny offered a quiet prayer of blessing. Once the amen was sounded she opened her napkin and studied her salad.

"Can you tell me what was so important you couldn't call?" asked Julia.

"Some of it," explained Penny, pouring ranch dressing on her green salad. "I was out Funny River Road most of the day doing a welfare check. When I came back to the office to do the report I was asked to fly up to Cooper Landing to look for some lost hikers. There were little kids with them, so I couldn't turn them down."

"Of course not, Dear, I'm sorry if I was short with you. I know your job is important. It's just that I get lonely here and want to see you come home. I don't mean to be a trial to you."

"I know, Mom, and I don't mean to run off without letting you know when I'll be back. I should have called." Penny took several bites of the delicious, crisp salad. The two women sat in silence while eating the salad course.

"Would you like to take a little ride in the car after dinner?" Penny asked her mother.

"Not tonight, Dear. I know you're tired and Jeopardy will be on channel 2 when I finish the dishes."

Penny was somewhat relieved when Julia had turned down the offer. She would change into sweats and running shoes for her evening run. She should be tired from the full day, but the time spent in the Super Cub had relaxed her; it always did.

The following morning she was at her desk an hour early. The reports on the Will Goodson death were sketchy at best. There was only a crime scene and a victim. No witnesses, few clues and no motive. Not much to go on at this point, she thought. She decided to drive out to see Gus Sampson after she had done her morning check-in. She would have to write a detailed report on the aerial search for the missing hikers on Resurrection Trail. This case, too, was in a strange state. Four people, two adult females and two children went missing on a popular hiking trail. They had a cell phone, but didn't contact anyone. Did they get lost? Did they get attacked by a bear? Were they abducted? Is the husband involved? It was anyone's guess at this point. She would wait until she saw the report from Trooper Finlay before trying to sort it all out.

The sergeant handed her a handful of tasks to investigate today. Three of the complaints were domestic violence calls from last night. That meant at least three people were waiting in jail for her to determine the facts in each case. She checked her watch and thought she had time to make a quick run out Funny River Road to visit Gus.

The early morning drive was pleasant. She passed several cars and trucks moving in the opposite direction, all of which had long handle dip nets tied to the vehicles. They were headed to the mouth of the Kenai River to join in an annual subsistence fishery where netting sockeye salmon was permitted for residents. When she arrived at the home of Gus Sampson he was in the yard with a pump sprayer killing weeds in the driveway.

"Good morning, Gus," she greeted, stepping out of the patrol car.

"Good morning to you, Trooper, good to see you up and at 'em this early," he replied, setting the sprayer on the ground.

"How was your night, Gus?"

"I went over to the cabin last night and everything looked OK. But I went over there this morning and I could see someone had driven a vehicle up the trail to the cabin. It didn't look like they went inside, but they drove around the cabin and got out. It was hard to tell, but there were two or three sets of footprints out back. They walked into the woods and came back out. I followed them as far as they went, but I didn't see where they disturbed any-thing. Now, what do you suppose they were up to?"

"That is strange, Gus. Do you want to ride over there and show me what you found?" she asked.

"If I can ride in the front seat, I don't like riding in the back seat of a police car. Did it once, didn't like it at all."

"Come on, Gus. Get in the front seat." She chuckled a little when she heard his little story. "I don't think I'll drive into the property and mess up the tracks. We'll park on the road and walk in. I think I'll take my shotgun, though; just in case."

"Might not be a bad idea, what with all the goin's on 'round here," commented Gus

About the midway on the trail there was a set of tire tracks in the bare dirt. She took several photos before calling Haskins. She described the situation and the tire tracks. She then suggested he send someone out with a kit to make plaster casts of the tracks.

"Good idea," said Haskins. "In fact I'll come out and do it myself. I should be there in about twenty minutes."

"Gus and I will walk on into the cabin and check it out. We'll meet you back here in twenty minutes. I'm leaving my trooper cap on a bush beside the tacks, but we should be back here before you arrive. See ya." She closed her cell phone.

Penny turned to Gus, "You know Gus, this might be a good spot to put a trail camera and if these folks come back we might get a description of the truck and the men."

"You're pretty bright, for a trooper," said Gus, grinning at her.

She dialed Haskins again to ask for a trail camera to place somewhere near this spot. He agreed to bring one with him.

"OK, Gus, let's go. Stay behind me and be quiet. Our culprits may have come back again and if so I want to surprise them. When we get to the clearing at the cabin I want you to stay back and out of sight—just in case." She knew the precaution was probably unnecessary, but getting a witness hurt or killed wouldn't look good on her resume.

Before entering the clearing she held her hand out to stop Gus. He nodded and stepped off the trail. She checked her shotgun to be sure there was a cartridge in the chamber. Rossiter walked slowly, keeping close to the brush line on the left side of the trail. At the edge of the clearing she stopped and listened. All was quiet. She could see the yellow police tape was still attached to the front door. She kept to the edge of the clearing and moved slowly around the cabin. She could see tire tracks around the cabin just as Gus had described. She moved forward again, slowly making her way to where the vehicle had stopped. Again, as Gus had said, footprints were visible. It appeared they exited the vehicle, walked into the woods and returned. She didn't follow them into the woods, opting to wait for Haskins. He may be able to get castings of the footprints. The two troopers would follow the prints into the woods to see what the invaders were looking for. The lush green foliage would make that task difficult. Rossiter turned around and retraced her steps once she determined there was no one there.

Gus met her back on the trail. "Did you see the tracks where they walked out back?"

"I sure did, Gus. You have a good eye. We'll go out there and see where they lead when Haskins gets here. Let's go back to where the tire tracks are and wait for David."

She cleared the chamber of her shotgun and began the walk back down the trail. When the pair arrived at the spot where her hat hung on a small bush she pulled a small backpack from her shoulder and opened it to retrieve a bottle of water. She offered it to Gus Sampson, but he refused. In order to minimize the footprints she stepped off the trail and sat on a small log drinking her water and waiting.

David Haskins arrived soon after and she continued to sit on her log and drink her water, but pointed to the spot she wanted him to cast for tire prints. He never spoke, just went to the tracks and began mixing the plaster for the casting. Once the plaster was poured he stepped off the trail and opened another bottle of water and joined her on the seat.

"You and old Gus make a good investigating team, Penny," he said, sipping the water from the bottle. "Did you walk up to the cabin?"

"Yes, I did," she replied. "It looks as if they drove to the back of the cabin and got out of the vehicle to walk into the woods. I didn't follow the tracks in case you locate some tracks to cast along with the tire prints. There is a lot of vegetation back there and I don't think there are any."

"Why don't we take a walk back there while the plaster is curing?" said Haskins, putting the empty water bottle in his pack. "Maybe we can get a clue as to why they're messing around this place."

"Do you have any idea why they would want this place?" asked Penny. "I doubt it's for a marijuana growing operation. Since they legalized it, it doesn't seem likely anyone would go to this much trouble for a small parcel of land like this one."

"Yeah, you're right about that. I've been thinking about it. The only thing I can come up with is they could be looking for a private spot to run a meth lab. This land would be good for that purpose. It's secluded and far enough from any neighbors the odor wouldn't be detected. We already know they can come and go without being noticed." Haskins removed his ball cap and wiped his face, "I can't imagine anything else that would make it all worth the effort. They killed Will Goodson for it, so it must be a profitable operation, whatever they're doing."

The two stood up from the log and began to walk, slowly, toward the cabin. Again at the edge of the clearing Penny asked Gus to wait. The two troopers walked close to the brush line to prevent trampling any tire tracks or footprints that may be visible. At the back of the cabin it was easy to spot where the group had exited the vehicle. Grass and moss were trampled, but they found no clear footprints. Gus was right, there were three of them. The troopers followed the trail into the woods for more than 100 yards where it opened into a small grassy clearing. The three had walked in to the clearing to quite thoroughly inspect it. It appeared they had walked abreast while walking to the little clearing, but went back to the vehicle in single file.

Back at the front of the cabin Haskins turned to Penny and asked, "Well, what's your take on all this?"

"I can't be sure, but your scenario about a meth lab in the woods seems plausible. I'm with you on that one. It's the only thing that makes any sense."

Haskins nodded and the trio walked back to where the plaster casts had hardened.

"I'm going to leave you, David. I have several cases I have to work this morning and I want to finish up in time to talk with Finlay about those missing hikers on Resurrection Trail. Is there anything else you need from me before I leave," she asked.

"No, but I am going to look around a little before I go. I'll check with you later."

"Thanks for coming out, David. I'll drop Gus off at his place and head back to town. Let me know if you find anything else."

He waved a short acknowledgement as she and Gus walked back down the trail toward the patrol car.

Haskins dug the two trail cameras from his pack and located two half-hidden locations to place the devices. It took only a few minutes to strap the cameras to spruce trees at the edge of the trail with a good view of the trail. He made sure the cameras were operating properly and had a clear sight of the incoming trail before leaving the property with his plaster casts in hand.

Chapter 5

It was late in the afternoon when Penny Rossiter finished with the list of cases she was given this morning. She was finishing the last of the court reports when the phone on her desk jingled.

"Trooper Rossiter," she answered.

"Trooper Findlay here. Do you have time to talk?" he asked.

"Yes, in fact I was about to call you. Is there anything new on the missing hikers?"

"Not a thing, I don't understand it. At first I thought the husband may be involved, but he was working on an oil platform in the middle of Cook Inlet until just before he called me. I checked and confirmed he was out there and came in on the morning helicopter." There was frustration in Finlay's voice.

"I checked the computer and didn't find any family disputes or incidents from the past," informed Penny. "The complaint seems to be legitimate in every respect. It doesn't seem likely a bear would attack a group of four. And if it had, some other hiker should have found the scene of the attack. This whole thing is strange. What do we know about the family?"

"It turns out I know one of the missing mothers. She and the wife of the complainant were twin sisters. They're tall, blond and beautiful. The one I'm acquainted with is a livewire. She ran the Mount Marathon Race in Seward this year. That's where I met her. She and her sister were both cheerleaders at Oklahoma State University. Ella and Ellen were their names. Ella is the wife of Tom Reed, our complainant. Ellen Baxter is married to a banker in Anchorage. He was working when this all took place. I talked to him when he came down to be with Tom. Nothing I see leads me to believe this a domestic issue gone wrong."

"Do you want me to search the trail by air again?"

"I don't think it will do any good. There are a lot of hikers on the trail and if they're out there someone should see them. The Rescue Coordination Center from Anchorage has had helicopters in the area and ground teams have been hiking the trail from both ends. So far nothing has been reported by either the ground or air search teams. Both the husbands are here in Cooper Landing waiting to hear any results of the search. As you know, waiting is the tough part." Finlay had done his homework and background checks on the victims and their families.

"You have my cell phone number, call me if anything turns up," she said. "Good luck, Finlay."

"Thanks, I'll need it."

She sat at her desk for a long time, thinking. Finally she made up her mind; she was going to do another aerial search of the entire Resurrection Trail from Hope to the Sterling Highway. She marched to Captain Meadows' office to announce her plan. She was about to speak to him when he held up his hand to silence her while he was on the telephone. He motioned for her to come in and have a seat, but continued to listen to the voice on the other end of the phone.

Finally Meadows thanked the voice on the other end of the telephone. Turning to Penny he said, "That was the RCC in Anchorage. Their ground search team on the Hope end of the trail has found two bodies. Both are blond, adult females. They match the descriptions given to us by the complainant. I'm sending Finlay over there to meet the RCC team when they come out with the bodies. I'll have Finlay look at them and take some pictures before the team loads them into the helicopter to fly them to the Crime Lab in Anchorage. Do you want to fly to Hope and take a look for yourself?"

She thought a moment, "I guess not. I was going to ask permission to fly another search of the trail, but now I won't need to do it. Finlay is a sharp guy and he'll get all the information we need and the Crime Lab will get the rest."

"I agree," commented Captain Meadows.

"Since it's nearly quitting time I think I'll drive out and check on Gus, if you don't object. I want to keep an eye on him while those men are moving around in the area. If they see him at the cabin they may want to question him like they did old Will Goodson."

"I think that's a good idea, but be careful yourself. These are dangerous people and I don't want either Gus or you to get hurt." Meadows showed genuine concern for his trooper and his friend Gus as well.

"I'll have Gus go with me and I'll check those trail cameras as long as I'm in the neighborhood."

Captain Meadows scratched his chin nervously, "Good idea, be careful, and when you finish—go home."

There was no sign of Gus when she drove to his cabin. She opened her car door and called for him. No answer, she called again. This time the screen door opened and Gus stepped out of the house.

"Howdy, Trooper," Gus said, waving from the porch.

"Hello there, Gus. Where were you?" I called and you didn't respond."

"Couldn't; I was in the bathroom. Had to finish up before I came out," Gus hung his head, embarrassed.

"Well, I'm glad you're OK, Gus. Are you busy for the next few minutes?"

"Naw, I'm just sort of resting until time to fix dinner. What do you need?" he asked.

"I thought I would go up and check the trail camera for pictures. Would you like to come along and keep me company?"

Gus rode in the front seat of the patrol car with Rossiter. On the way he had said there was no sign of the old pickup or the men inside. Things had been quiet "out this-a-way."

She parked on the edge of the road and the two walked the several hundred yards up the trail to where the cameras were hidden in the woods. She asked Gus to wait on the trail in order to minimize the amount of foot traffic to and from the camera site. There were two pictures registered on the counter. She pushed the VIEW button to see the face of a calf moose. The other photo looked like the hind legs of a moose crossing the trail. She made notes of the pictures and the times they were taken. The camera was reset and she made a small attempt to erase any sign she had been in the area.

"Only a couple of moose," she informed Gus as they made their way back to the road and her patrol car. "I think I'm going to call it a day after I drop you at home."

Rossiter was just pulling into her driveway at home when her cell phone rang. It was Finlay. He had arrived at the Hope Trail scene and taken pictures. The ground team from the Rescue Coordination Center was carrying the bodies down the mountain to the road. He reported the team would take them to the Hope Airport for transport to Anchorage.

"Is there any sign of the two boys?" she asked.

"I can't find any. We found scuff marks where it looks like the women were forced to walk off the trail and into the woods. They were found about two hundred yards off the trail in thick brush and trees," reported Finlay.

"Could you determine how they died?"

"The Lab and The Medical Examiner will have to check that out, but it looks to me as if they were both stabbed with a large knife of some kind, maybe a big hunting knife. I saw one wound in one of the women and two in the other. They are twins and I couldn't tell which was which. Unless there is something you want me to look at here, I'm going back to Cooper Landing to report the find to the two husbands. You know, the fun part of being a trooper," he remarked facetiously.

"I understand, Finlay. Do you want me to come up and go with you to deliver the news?"

"No, I don't think it'll be necessary. These are both squared away men and there shouldn't be any trouble. The news will be bad enough for them, but I can't imagine how bad they will take the news about not finding the boys. If it were my family I don't think I could take it at all." Finlay had delivered many death messages, but having to tell the fathers their children were still missing was something he wished he didn't have to do.

"They're going to want to go to Anchorage to wait for the news of the autopsy report. I don't think they should be allowed to drive after you deliver the notices. They are both going to be distraught and emotionally beaten. I can send someone up there to drive them to town if you want me to," she offered.

"That won't be necessary, Penny. I thought of that issue and I'll call my friend here in Cooper Landing who owns a flight seeing company. I'll ask him to fly them to Lake Hood in Anchorage. He'll do it for me at no charge, I think. He's a good guy with a lot of heart."

"OK, Finlay, whatever you think. I'm going off duty now, but if you need anything call me on this number. Good luck, man." She sat in her patrol car for a few minutes, thinking. How did this happen? Where are the two young boys? How did the killer separate the boys from their mothers? Who could be crazy enough to commit a crime like this? How could anyone escape the area, there is only one road in or out? So many questions with no answers, she would have to wait until tomorrow to begin getting the answers to these questions.

The following morning Rossiter was in her little office planning her day when David Haskins entered bringing her a cup of hot coffee. He sipped on one of his own. "I went out to check the camera this morning. There wasn't anything on it since you reset it yesterday. There weren't any fresh tracks on the trail. I went over to Gus Sampson's place and everything seemed in order. It was early, so I didn't knock on his door to make sure he was OK."

Penny tasted her own cup of fresh coffee, "Do you have any idea who it was out there or what they wanted?" she asked.

"Not a clue, but my men talked with the neighbors and have a description of an old Chevy pickup and the three men. Everyone who saw them say there were "seedy looking" men. No one got a license plate number, but we have a good description of the truck. It's a late '50's or '60's model. Blue over white and no tailgate. It is also without a muffler, according to two of the witnesses. I asked the sergeant to check with the road troopers to see if anyone recognized the pickup. No one had which leads me to believe they may only use this vehicle when they're doing bad things."

"I have a meeting with Captain Meadows this morning and I'm not looking forward to telling him I have no answers to the questions he is going to ask. In addition to this case I've been helping Finlay with the missing hiker case. The RCC search team found the bodies of the two women, but no sign of the small boys. I need to get out of the office and find some answers, but I don't know where to look." There was frustration in her tone.

"I have a meeting with the captain later this morning too, but I'll have my team get busy analyzing what little evidence we have to see if we can help you determine where to look. I'll let you know if the road troopers come up with anything on the old pickup. Good luck, Penny, and have a nice day," he said as he turned to leave the office.

"You too," she said, "and thanks for the coffee." An hour later she was in the captain's office.

"I have a preliminary report from Finlay," he began. "I'm sending you to Cooper Landing to help Finlay. It's summertime and he has his hands full with the fishermen and tourists in the area. You have more experience with this type of investigation. You might want to drive to Hope and ask around about any suspicious activity there. It's a small community and someone may have noticed a stranger in the little town. I want you to be extra careful if you go to Hope. Remember this may not be a stranger. Someone in Hope could have committed this terrible crime and the two boys may still be alive, held captive somehow. Watch your back and stay in contact with the office." Meadows always worried when he had to send a lone trooper to a remote area off the main highway system.

"Finlay marked the spot on the trail where the bodies were found. I would like to walk up there and see the site firsthand." She thought she could use the hike to relax and think. Also, she wanted to get a feel for the crime scene. She wanted to know how the killer managed to separate the children from their mothers. It didn't make any sense.

Chapter 6

Alaska's Kenai Peninsula is about the same size and shape as the country of Ireland. The entire east side of the peninsula is mountainous and topped with glaciers reported to have ice 1,100 feet thick. The beauty of this land is unmatched anywhere in the world. On the west side of the mountains is a vast flat plain made up mostly of glacial silt. The terrain is varied with swamps, tundra, spruce forests and lakes. The several small communities thrive on the fishing, tourism and oil industries. It has become the bedroom community for the workers on Alaska's North Slope oil fields. It is a wonderful place to live and raise a family.

Tourism spotlights the summer months. Giant tour boats come to bring city dwellers to see the wonders of wild Alaska. Their goal is met from the time they enter Alaska waters. Wildlife abounds here. Whales come here to feed in the bountiful waters. Seals and sea lions swim and frolic along the shore line. Sea otters swim close to the visitors with babies on their bellies. Exotic seabirds swim close enough to be photographed by the eager tourists. Few people leave this paradise disappointed with the view or the experience.

An estimated one million tourists visit the state each year. They come from every state in the union and every country in the world to explore the mystique of this place called Alaska. Some come to enjoy the fishing. Some come to enjoy hiking the beautiful mountains. Some come to hunt big game while others come to admire the animals they have never seen except in a National Geographic Magazine or on the Animal Planet channel. This seasonal influx swells the normal resident population of the Kenai Peninsula from 60,000 to over 200,000 souls. This influx takes a toll on the available facilities. Roads are choked with automobiles and motorhomes. Restaurants and motels are filled to capacity. Bars are full of noisy patrons. Salmon streams are shoulder to shoulder with fishermen casting their lines to reap their share of the seasonal bounty.

This annual migration of humanity taxes the limits of every law enforcement agency in the state, both local and state. Wildlife troopers are tasked with maintaining fishing bag limits as well as keeping the peace among the close-packed fishermen. There is little discord among the participants, although, arguments over fishing spot or crossed and tangled lines are quite common. Highway patrol troopers attempt to keep the heavy road traffic moving peacefully and without incident. It is a difficult task with the thousands of motorhomes and rental cars on the roads, which proves to be terribly inadequate during the summer months.

With the large numbers of visitors comes a percentage of lawbreakers; it seems criminals like to vacation also. This fact strains the ability of the investigating troopers to keep pace with the volume of incidents reported each day. Each trooper spends long hours on the job to keep up with the volume of calls. Much of this time is done without claiming paid hours because of the dedication of these hard-working men and women. They seldom have the time to fish, hunt or enjoy the summertime activities with their families and likely as not will have to spend their days off sitting in a courtroom waiting to testify in one of their cases.

Penny Rossiter enjoyed the summer drive to Hope, Alaska. It was an hour and a half to the Resurrection Trail head. Traffic was heavy and the drive was slow, but it gave her a chance to think. Living with her disabled mother was a trying ordeal. Julia was a demanding charge. She tried to help out, but had no strength to do the more physical chores around the house. Penny loved her mother and felt no resentment about her life with Julia, but sometimes it was a struggle to balance her work and her life at home. She tried to keep the two matters separated, but at times like this when she was alone for a period of time she couldn't help herself. It was times like this when her personal and professional lives collided. In the end, if the choice had to be made she would have to choose her mother over her profession. As difficult as it seemed Penny was grateful she didn't have to make that choice—yet.

It was early when she drove past the little dirt airport to the trailhead, not stopping in town on her way. The thought struck her; what if the killer had flown here rather than driven? She would stop and take a look at the airstrip when she returned from the trail. It was several more miles to where she parked her vehicle and stepped out into the sun. She took a small backpack from the trunk of her car. Strapping it to her shoulders she began the walk up the mountain. It took several minutes for her leg muscles to adjust to the steep trail, but soon her body became accustomed to the exercise and was enjoying the hike. When she reached the spot Finlay had marked she began to look for anything she might consider a clue to the crime that took place here. She walked slowly off the trail to where the murders had taken place. She saw the scuff marks, the cut branches used to cover the bodies, the markers left by the RCC searchers and the crime lab investigators from Anchorage. The area had been visited by so many people it was difficult to distinguish which marks were left by whom.

Penny spent almost an hour in the area looking for hidden clues, but found none. She still had the same question. How did the killer separate the children from the mothers? She walked slowly back to the trail, looking for clues once again as she walked. She saw nothing, but now knew where the crime took place and what it looked like. Back at her car she sat thinking about the young boys. Again the question was unanswered. How did the killer get the boys away from the mothers? With nothing to be gained here she turned the patrol car around and drove back toward the little town of Hope, Alaska. On the way, as she passed the small dirt airstrip she decided to turn in to it and take a look.

As remote airstrips go this was a pretty good one. It was long and wide and well maintained. This maintenance was done by the State of Alaska Department of Transportation. There were two aircraft parked at the north end of the airstrip, a Cessna 185 and a Piper PA-18 that looked almost new. She wrote down the numbers painted on the small planes and would check for ownership when she returned to the office. She found evidence there had been several small airplanes on the strip in recent days. She would ask some of the locals about them when she got to town. It took only a few short minutes to drive to the city of Hope. There are several residences and some summer cabins in the small town. On the edge of town there is a nice little restaurant where she planned to have a burger later. The business district is small; a general store, a library, a school, several small souvenir shops and tourists asking about gold mining. The stream flowing through the small town is clear and filled with salmon. Upstream are several concessions and mining claims where gold is found even today.

Trooper Rossiter stopped at the general store to talk with the proprietor. The store itself is old with a small wood porch on the front. Inside you step into another century. There is nothing modern, with exception to a few items for sale to the tourist trade. Locals still like to buy canned peaches and beans, cans of oil and kerosene, fishing tackle and gold pans. The owner is apt at telling folks if they can't find what they want they are welcome to drive the 90 miles to Anchorage to buy whatever they wished.

Penny had met the store owner on several occasions and knew him as an irascible sort with no patience for outsiders. "Hi there, Lenny, how's business?"

"Payin' the bills, Trooper, how have you been?"

"It's summertime, Lenny, you know how it is."

"Yeah, I know," he replied, rolling his eyes in disgust.

"I came in to ask about any strangers in town lately—outside of the regular tourist types. Has anyone been hanging around?"

"Can't think of any, but with all the campers and tourists I wouldn't know." He held up a finger in thought, "there was a plane parked up at the airstrip for a couple of days. I thought it must have been someone hiking the Resurrection Trail. Whoever it was must have hitched a ride to the trailhead. Someone must have seen him and given him a ride."

"What kind of plane was it, do you know?"

"I didn't pay much attention and didn't get the numbers, but it was a PA-12 or a Super Cub. Red and white with a black accent stripe full length. It was in really good shape." Lenny turned to walk away to another customer.

Penny made a note in her notebook and waved to him as she walked out the door. That's the way it is, she thought, one tiny bit of information at a time. She drove the few blocks to where several small shops selling trinkets to tourists were grouped. Each was manned by a local who opened their shops only in the months of June through August. In each shop she asked the same questions and received roughly the same answers. At the last shop she stepped back outside into the sunshine thinking it was time for that burger.

The owner was in the kitchen frying fast food for the other two patrons at the counter. Minutes later he came out of the kitchen to deliver the freshly made sandwiches and fries. Penny was seated at a small table by the front window.

"Trooper Rossiter, good to see you again, how have you been?" He greeted the uniformed officer.

"Hello, Mr. Lagasse, I'm fine, how about yourself?"

"You know how it is here in Hope. Never a dull moment," he commented, taking a notepad from his shirt pocket. "Can I get you something to eat?"

"It's life in the fast lane for me today, Burt. Give me a bleu cheese bacon burger and fries."

"Want coffee with that?" he asked.

"No, I don't think so; too many calories in coffee. Give me a diet Coke," she said chuckling a bit.

"You got it," he said returning to the kitchen. He was back a few minutes later with her order.

"What brings you to our town, Penny?"

"I suppose you have heard about the two women killed up on the Resurrection Trail."

"Yeah, horrible thing, that kind of stuff never happens up here," he said with a sad look in his eyes,

"I'm looking into it and I wondered if you had heard or seen anything you might consider suspicious. You know…a strange vehicle in town or a stranger who seemed out of place, anything you would consider worth looking into in connection with the killings. Two little boys have disappeared at the same time and I'm looking for them. Have you seen or heard anything?"

"I'm sorry, but no, there haven't been any unusual folks in here. There are lots of tourists this year, but nobody out of the ordinary. Too bad about those kids, the locals are worried about that and want this guy caught. We have a lot of young kids here and we don't want to lose any of them."

"Thanks Burt," she said taking a large bite of her burger. She wiped her mouth and grinned. "This is a really good burger. Don't tell my mother I had it. She would make me go get on the scales to see how many pounds I gained." They both laughed. She wiped her face again and asked, "I heard there was a strange airplane parked on the airstrip at the time of the murders. Do you know anything about that?" "Not really, but I saw it there late one night after I closed the restaurant. I think it was a PA-12. I used to have one like it. I don't remember the numbers, but the tail number ended in M. That's what makes me think it was a PA-12. It sure was a pretty one. It looked as if it had just recently been recovered and painted. Whoever owns it must love it a lot. It costs a lot of money to re-fabric and paint an airplane today. If I see it again I'll get the tail numbers for you." With that Burt turned his attention to the other customers and poured them more coffee.

Penny finished her sandwich and cola and paid her bill, leaving a good tip for Burt. She could think of nothing else to look at or people to interview here in the town of Hope. She decided to return to Soldotna, stopping in Cooper Landing to see if Finlay had returned. She also decided she would be late getting home and would have to call her mother when she was back in cell phone coverage. It would not do to have Julia angry two days in a row.

Chapter 7

Once back in radio range Penny tried to call Finlay on the trooper frequency, but had no success. When she drove into the Cooper Landing area near Kenai Lake she turned off the main highway to drive the mile to Finlay's residence, a large mobile home on a state-owned lot near the local airport. Finlay was single and no one was home at his place so she called him on the cell phone.

"Hello," he answered.

"Hi Ray, Rossiter here, where are you?" she asked.

"Oh, hi Penny, I'm just leaving Anchorage heading home. Where are you?"

"I'm sitting in your front yard. I won't wait for you. I just wanted to let you know I'm coming back from Hope and wanted to fill you in on what I learned, which was almost nothing."

"You say 'almost nothing;' does that mean you did learn something?" he asked.

"Maybe," she admitted. "Two of the locals said they saw a strange airplane at the airport at the time of the incident. Both described it as really pretty with new paint; red over white and a black full-length accent stripe. Does that ring any bells with you?"

"Hmm," he muttered, "I can't recall seeing any planes like that. What kind of plane was it, did they say?"

"Yes, both of them said it was a PA-12. Neither got the tail numbers, but one said the last of the numbers was an M. That's what made him believe it was a Piper PA-12. "They manufactured something like 14,000 of those planes. They used them in the Korean War for reconnaissance and even adapted them for use as battle field ambulances. The military devised a lift-up sort of a hood aft of the cabin, over the rear, mid and lower longerons. They could lift up the hood and put a stretcher into the rear of the cabin with the patient's legs under the hood. With the short-field capability of the PA-12 it was possible to land on a road or in a field to extract the wounded. It was ingenious really. The versatility of the "12" is what makes it popular with private pilots today. Whoever owns this one must like it a lot to put on a fresh fabric cover and give it a new paint job."

"I don't remember seeing it here on this airstrip, but I'll look around to see if it appears on any of the private airstrips in the area, perhaps at one of the strips near Moose Pass or Crown Point."

"Thanks Ray, keep your eyes open. I'm heading to the office now. I'll ask the road troopers to keep an eye out for the plane as they patrol near any private strips. I'll talk with you tomorrow." She ended her call and dropped her phone on the passenger seat. It would take an hour to drive back to the office where she still needed to complete her data-keeping chores to keep up to date and on time. The captain would be gone by the time she reached the office.

Before pulling onto the main highway she picked up the phone to call Julia. It would not do for her to come home late without notifying her mother. It would cause another family confrontation. Penny tried to be patient with Julia, but sometimes it was difficult. Julia had been in poor health for a long while. She didn't require constant care yet, but it was hard for her to be home alone all the time. The television was a help, but not a companion.

There was an answer on the third ring, "Hi Mom, how's your day?"

"Just fine, dear, when will you be home?" she asked in a pleasant tone.

"Not for a while, Mom, I'm in Cooper Landing and have to do some work at the office before I can come home. Have you started diner?" inquired Penny.

"Not yet, I was waiting to hear from you. We have some of that pot roast left over, would you like that for dinner?"

"That sounds good. I'll stop at the store and pick up some ice cream for dessert. It'll probably be two or three hours until I get home. See you then."

"All right, dear, see you then." Julia said.

That was easy enough, Penny thought. She also thought she might take a drive past the five private airstrips she knew existed in the Sterling area. They were scattered on all sides of the community, but she could see them all in about an hour, if no one stopped her to talk.

Just short of an hour later she was on her way to the office without finding the little red and white airplane. The captain had gone for the day and most of the road troopers were out of the office. Her little office was quiet and she was able to finish her reports and write a note to the captain without interruption. She was leaving the office when her cell phone jingled. It was Gus Sampson.

Penny read the caller ID and answered. "Hello, Gus. How are you?"

"I'm good, Trooper, I hadn't seen you today and wondered what you were up to." He sounded a little nervous or agitated.

"Sorry, Gus, but they gave me another case and I've been busy with that. Is everything OK out there?"

"So far, but I'm getting an uneasy feeling. There have been fresh tracks going into Will's place. I haven't gone over there, only drove to where the trail starts. There are fresh tire tracks on the side of the road and scuff marks and footprints going toward the cabin. I think it may be a good idea to check the trail cameras you set out."

"Do you think I need to do this tonight, or can we go over there in the morning, that is if you'll go with me?" Penny could hear the apprehension in his voice.

"In the morning it'll be good. The light will be better then. If they were out there today I don't think they'll waste the gas to drive out here again today." Gus seemed satisfied by talking with her.

"OK, Gus. I'll come out in the morning. Lock your doors tonight." After hanging up the phone she called dispatch and asked to have a trooper patrol out Funny River Road near Gus' cabin; just in case.

She stopped at the grocery store and bought a half gallon of chocolate chip ice cream.

The following morning, after a short interview with Captain Meadows, she drove to the cabin belonging to Gus Sampson. He was sitting on the front porch drinking a cup of coffee and waved to her as she drove into the yard. She stepped out of her vehicle and waved to Gus.

"Want a cup of coffee, Trooper? It's fresh," he asked.

"Sure, Gus, why not?"

He disappeared into the house and returned seconds later with a steaming mug of great smelling coffee. "Glad to see you," he said handing her the cup.

She sipped the hot coffee and gave him a wink, "You make good coffee, Gus." She took another small sip before asking, "You seemed a little nervous on the phone last night, Gus. Have they been bothering you?"

"No, but I expect them to start. My neighbor up the road said he saw the old pickup parked there yesterday. He said nobody was around, but the truck was nosed into the driveway. They must have walked into the property. Why do you s'pose they're still messin' around out there?"

"I don't know, but they wanted the property badly enough to beat poor old Will to death in order to get it. I'm going out there and take a look at the trail cameras. Would you like to ride out there with me? I think we should take a look at the cabin and the woods behind it to see if anything is changed or missing."

"Yeah, I'd like to ride over there with you. It's good for my reputation to be seen with a purty girl from time to time. Let me get a flannel shirt to keep the mosquitoes from drinkin' me dry." He stepped inside the house for a couple of minutes and returned wearing a plaid flannel shirt over the gray tee shirt he sported earlier. It was warm and the shirt was not tucked into his jeans, but hung loose. "OK, I'm ready," he said as he approached the patrol car.

It didn't take long to drive to the end of the drive/trail leading to Will Goodson's cabin. Penny parked on the right side of Funny River Road near the trail and stepped out of the car. She inspected the tire tracks and foot tracks, really only smudges and scuff marks, in the vegetation. It was difficult to tell, but the marks looked very recent, perhaps last night or early this morning. She couldn't tell which direction they led or how many people made them, but someone had been here recently. Staying to one side of the trail so as not to disturb the tracks she slowly walked toward the cabin with Gus following at a respectable distance behind.

When they reached the spot on the trail where the cameras were located she stepped into the woods and circled toward the camera tied to a spruce tree. She opened the first one and saw it listed several new images. She scrolled through the pictures seeing several moose one huge brown bear with two cubs and, at the end, three men walking toward the cabin. Each was wearing sweatshirts with hoods and walked with their heads down making it impossible to see their faces. It was disappointing, but confirmed there was a group of men visiting the area of the cabin. She re-set the camera and made her way back to the trail where Gus was waiting.

"We've got some pictures of the men coming in, but I couldn't see their faces. When they came out of course they were facing the other direction, but I only saw two men leaving. The other one either stayed at the cabin or took another route back to the road." She spoke quietly to Gus who only grunted and nodded his head. "I'm going on ahead. I want you to stay back in case there's someone at the cabin. I don't want you to be in the line of fire if someone's there waiting."

"OK, I'll wait here for you," he whispered. "Be careful."

She nodded an affirmative and walked slowly up the trail in the direction of the cabin. Nearing the edge of the clearing where the cabin stood she stopped. She noticed immediately the yellow police tapes had been stripped from the doors and around the cabin. She unsnapped the Glock and slipped it from the holster hanging on her duty belt.

Step by step she made her way toward the cabin staying to the right side of the trail where the trees and willows offered some cover. Still in combat stance she moved out onto the trail where she could see the cabin more clearly. There was a small chain saw on the porch with a gallon size gas can beside it. She stood motionless for several minutes watching for movement or signs of life. There was nothing. She lowered the weapon she had been holding out in front of her and stood erect deciding there was no one here right now. She took one cautious step into the open about 100 feet from the cabin.

Penny Rossiter never heard the shot. She saw a slight movement near the corner of the cabin and knew she needed to return to the cover of the trees. It was too late. The heavy shotgun slug struck her on the right side of the chest knocking her backwards. The impact caused her to lose her grip on the Glock in her right hand and it went flying over her head and fell to the ground. She landed on her back, unconscious.

The shooter came from his hiding place at the corner of the cabin to see the fallen trooper. He pointed his shotgun at her lifeless form on the ground and poked her cheek with the gun barrel. He saw no movement, but could see the huge gaping hole in her uniform shirt three inches to the right of the buttons. He stood looking at the wounded trooper trying to decide what plan of action to follow. He decided he should go back to the cabin and call his boss on the cell phone. He touched her eye with the gun barrel again deciding she was dead. He turned to walk back to the cabin.

From where he had been waiting Gus heard the shot. It sounded to him like a rifle or shotgun. He reached inside his flannel shirt to grasp the handle of his old model 1911 A, Colt .45. He pulled it from its holster and began to make his way toward the cabin and where the gunshot came from. He stayed in the woods to the left side of the trail until he neared the cabin. When he got close he saw Penny lying motionless on her back in the trail. He backtracked through the woods until he was out of sight of the cabin and crossed to the other side. Again making his way toward where Penny was on the ground. He stayed low and crawled to her motionless form to begin dragging her slowly off the trail and out of sight of the cabin. She was still breathing, but unconscious. Once he felt safe he checked for a pulse. It was faint, but she had one.

Gus picked up the speaker/microphone clipped to her lapel. He found the mike button and spoke in a half whisper, "Troopers, this is Gus Sampson, Officer Rossiter is shot. I repeat. Penny has been shot. I need more help and an ambulance right away. I am at mile 13 Funny River Road. I think the shooter is still here." He let up on the microphone button.

"Mr. Sampson, please stay on the radio. I am sending help right now." On another frequency she dispatched the news. "Officer down; officer down; mile 13 Funny River Road. The officer has been shot, repeat, the officer has been shot. All units in the Funny River and Soldotna areas respond."

After dispatching an ambulance to the scene she came back to talk with Gus. "Mr. Sampson, I have help on the way and an ambulance is on its way to your location. Are you safe at this time?"

"I don't know, but I think so. Nobody is shooting at me anyway.

Dave Haskins was in the office when the call came in. Immediately he ran to his car to speed east on Funny River Road. On the way there at extremely high speeds he called his men on the cell phone and ordered them to follow. He listened to the radio and determined at least five units were responding. Eleven minutes from the time of the call from Gus, Haskins was driving his patrol car up the trail toward the cabin. He found Penny and Gus. Positioning his patrol car between the cabin and the motionless form of Penny Rossiter he jumped from the car to assess the extent of her injuries.

"Are you OK Gus?" he asked as he leaned over Rossiter.

"Yeah, I'm fine. Whoever it is must have run off after he shot Penny."

"You did a great job, Gus, but I want you to go back to the road now. Other units will be here in a minute. I want you to tell them how to get here. Have them walk in. Send the ambulance in here. Do you think you can do that?" Haskins didn't look up, but began to unbutton the shirt of the victim. As soon as he opened the uniform shirt he saw the body armor. He breathed a sigh of relief and pulled the shirt open to see how bad the wound was bleeding—it wasn't.

Gus hurried to the road to direct the others. He sent the ambulance up the narrow trail urging them to hurry. He stood in the road still holding his Colt in his right hand. One by one other officer's arrived. Gus stood in the road watching for others and suddenly realized the shooter was still in the vicinity. Two of Haskins men arrived and he directed them to the scene and also asked them to remind Dave of the possibility of the shooter being in the area.

To Gus it seemed like hours, but it had been only about 20 minutes when the ambulance came back down the trail, red lights flashing. The men in the front seat waved to him as they passed. Alone in the road Gus wondered what he should do. He went to Rossiter's car and checked. The key was in the ignition. He opened the door and climbed inside. Gunning the engine he followed the ambulance to the hospital in Soldotna.

Chapter 8

Once the ambulance had loaded Rossiter and left the scene Dave Haskins called his men together. He mapped out a strategy for assaulting the cabin. It seemed unlikely the shooter would have stayed in the area, but no one had seen anyone leaving. One trooper was stationed on the trail to secure that avenue of escape. Two men were sent to the left side of the trail and two more to the right side. Dave and his men were all trained in situations like this and took the frontal assault position. The three men in the front line carried assault rifles and wore combat gear. The second line carried handguns at the ready. It was a slow march to the cabin. Carefully the team made their way toward the cabin. At the edge of the clearing Haskins used a battery powered megaphone to call to anyone in the cabin.

"In the cabin," he called, "Come out with your hands raised. Place your weapons on the porch where we can see them. I repeat, come out of the cabin with your hands raised. Do it now. This is Alaska State Troopers. Do it now."

There was no response from the cabin. Haskins motioned for the front line to move toward the cabin. He and the other two men held back. The three combat ready leaders moved methodically toward the cabin. The troopers on either side of the trail moved steadily to the back of the cabin, keeping in deep cover for protection. When they reached the back and had a view of the open area they waited while the three lead officers at the front approached the cabin. Tensions were high and the men were alert. No one reported seeing any sign of movement. Slowly the two flankers moved to either side of the cabin while the third stayed in the open directly in front of the cabin. The man at the front called for the occupant to come out with his hands up. There was no response from inside. The man at the front moved in slowly. The flankers stepped up onto the porch at each end. At a signal from the leader in front the flankers rushed the door, kicking it in and entering with assault rifles at the ready. A moment later one of the men came back out to report the cabin empty and the rest of the team moved in. Haskins ordered two of his second line men to check for an escape route out back and to follow the trail. He ordered the two flankers to go with them.

A half hour later the team met back at the cabin with nothing to report except that there had been activity in the woods behind the cabin. Someone was clearing an area and had begun to erect some sort of barn or building back there.

It was now time for a strategy meeting. He directed the team to begin gathering evidence from the area. He had the officers taking pictures and searching every inch of the area surrounding the cabin. The first find was a spent 12 gauge casing found near the front corner of the cabin. Searching the entire vicinity would take most of the rest of the day.

Meanwhile, Gus had followed the ambulance to town in Rossiter's patrol car. He had found the switch for the overhead red warning lights and turned them on. It amazed him how much authority he was given by drivers on the road. At the hospital the ambulance drove into the secure loading area of the emergency room entrance. Nurses and doctors were waiting to help get the officer into the hospital emergency room. The ambulance crew moved quickly to get Rossiter inside where the doctors began to insert tubes and wires. Gus was forced to wait in the entry visiting room.

Gus waited and drank coffee, pacing and waiting for word. One of the security officers spoke with him, noticing he had driven there in a State Trooper cruiser.

"Are you a trooper?" he asked.

"No, but I was with Penny when she was shot. I drove her car down here," said Gus.

"OK, take a seat out here and when the doctors say it's alright I'll come get you to go sit with her. I'll try to find out her condition and let you know."

Gus waited nearly two hours before the security guard came to speak with him. "What's your name, Sir?" the guard asked.

"Gus Sampson," he replied.

"Well, Mr. Sampson, I'm afraid the doctors won't let you in to see her today. She is in critical condition and will be taken to ICU when she can be moved. A Trooper Haskins called to find out how she was doing and I told him you were here. He said he would be here as soon as he could leave the scene. He asked me to tell you he wanted you to stay here and wait for him. There is fresh coffee in the thermos on the window sill and you can wait here. I'll check in with you when I can. If there is any news on Trooper Rossiter's condition I'll come and let you know."

"I don't want any coffee, but thanks anyway. I'll just wait here and read the paper." Gus spoke quietly, hanging his head in sadness. "Let me know how she's doin' when you can."

"My name is Vern. I have rounds to make, but I'll let you know if I hear anything. If you need anything just let me know." It was one compassionate soul talking to another.

The waiting room was a busy place with people coming and going constantly. They were relatives and friends of other patients entering the emergency room for treatment. Gus fell asleep for a short period of time, but was startled back to awareness by someone shaking his arm.

"Gus, wake up." It was David Haskins.

Gus shook his head to clear his thoughts, "Oh, hi there. I must have dozed off." He shook his head again and took a deep breath. "How is she?" he asked.

"She's still unconscious. She was lucky, though. The body armor stopped the slug. She suffered severe blunt force trauma, though. The doctors say she has two broken ribs and severe bruising. There is some internal bleeding and her liver is damaged. She is one sick lady, Gus."

"Oh, Lord, I wish I could have stopped it all from happening. I heard the shot and came as fast as I could, but she was on the ground, not moving. I got on top of her to protect her from any other shots and took out my .45 in case the guy came back to finish her off. She ain't very big but she has a lot of guts. I wish I could have kept her from bein' hurt, but she wanted me to wait back on the trail in case there was shootin.' I guess she called that one right. I don't know what I could have done, but I wish I had done somethin'." Gus had tears on his cheeks now.

Haskins placed his hand on the older man's shoulder. "Don't beat yourself up over this, Gus. This is our profession and we accept the responsibility that goes with it. We don't want to get injured, but better one of us than an innocent citizen. You did what you were supposed to do and she did what she was supposed to do. From what I saw at the scene she took proper precautions to protect herself, but the shooter was waiting to ambush anyone coming for him. It happens. It's not your fault and you're not the bad guy here."

"I know, but I like that little red-head."

"The doctors won't let either of us see her tonight. Come on and I'll give you a ride home." Haskins, too, was frustrated at not being able to be with Penny. The doctor had said that as soon as she could be moved they would send her to ICU where they would give her blood thinners to stop any blood clots from forming. The doctor also said they didn't expect her to wake up before morning and when she did she would be in extreme pain for which they would medicate her.

The next morning David Haskins was on the phone inquiring about Trooper Rossiter. Captain Meadows also inquired about her condition. Both were informed her condition had not changed. Though it was difficult for Haskins to concentrate he held a meeting with his team to discuss the findings at the scene. The shooter had not left a trail they were able to follow, but it was plain he had run out the back and into the woods. It was also plain to see he had been working on building some sort of structure in the spruce woods behind the cabin. Logic would dictate this was to be an illicit operation of some sort. Drugs were the number one choice as motive for this entire incident from the killing of Will Goodson to the shooting of Trooper Rossiter.

It was late afternoon when Haskins received a call from the hospital. Rossiter was now awake and asking for him. A wave of relief overtook him as he moved quickly to his patrol car.

He checked in with the nurse's desk in the Intensive Care Unit to find her room number.

"I'll allow you to see her because she asked to see you, but if she becomes excited or agitated I will ask you to leave. She's in a very fragile condition. We've downgraded her from Critical to Serious only because she's now awake and we can ask her how she feels. She's in a great deal of pain and on medications for it. You have five minutes."

"Thank you," he said, "What room is she in?"

"I'll take you to her room," offered the nurse. She led him to a room toward the end of the hallway. "Remember what I said, five minutes."

"Yes, Ma'am," he replied as he entered the room. He stepped around the curtain to see Penny, plugged into monitors and IV's. The head of her bed was raised a few inches and her eyes were closed. The bed sheets were pulled up to her neck and no damage was visible. He pulled a plastic chair to her bedside and sat. The sound seemed to awaken her.

"Hi, David," she spoke barely above a whisper.

"Hi, Penny," he answered, amazed at how weak she sounded.

"What happened, Dave, I can't remember? I remember sneaking up to the cabin and I remember seeing a muzzle flash, but that's it. I never heard a shot. What happened?"

"It's no wonder you can't remember. You were shot with a 12 gauge shotgun slug. The doctors found the sabot inside the fabric of your vest. The armor stopped the slug, but you got beat up pretty good when it happened. We found the shell casing, but the shooter was gone. When we got there old Gus was laying on top of you with a 1911 Colt in his hand."

"The doctors tell me I'm in pretty bad shape. They are afraid of blood clots and my liver is bruised or something. All I know is that I don't feel very good. I asked when I could go back to work and the doctor just laughed. He said six months to a year. Six months to a year, Dave, six months to a year. I can't be off the job that long." She was sobbing now.

Haskins reached out to wipe away the tears, "Hey, hey, none of that now. Doctors don't know everything. Besides, you're getting paid for laying here in bed. Your job now is to get well."

"They say I may not be able to go back to work as a trooper." She was crying again, "I don't know what I'll do. I still have to take care of my mom."

"The department will take care of you and your mom, Penny, don't worry about any of that now. We just want you to get well." Haskins lowered his head a moment, "I'm sorry I upset you, Penny. The nurse is going to throw me out of here any minute, is there anything I can bring you or do for you?"

"Just go by and tell Julia I'm OK and not to worry." She slid one hand out from under the sheets to place over his as it rested on the bed. "Thanks for caring, Dave." Her voice was weaker now.

"I'll let you rest now, but if there is anything I can do for you call me. I'm praying for you, girl." Her eyes closed as he rose to leave. She looked pitiful and frail lying there. His tough professional crust was beginning to crumble. He needed to get out of there.

On his way back to the office he stopped at Rossiter's home. He tapped on the door and in a minute Julia answered. He explained her condition and said he would come back to check on her. He also said he would take her down to the hospital as soon as the doctors said she could visit.

"Is there anything I can get for you while I'm here, Julia?" he asked.

"Not unless you can bring me a nice bottle of Riesling," she said.

"Now, Julia, you know I can't do that," he said as he turned to leave.

Chapter 9

Two and a half weeks after she was admitted Penny Rossiter was released from the hospital. The doctors were now comfortable with her progress. The extreme bruising was beginning to fade, diminishing the chances of blood clots in her system. The damage to her liver was not healing as well as the doctors had hoped, but it was healing. She was able to walk without assistance and was taking physical therapy to restore her mobility. She was still having difficulty lifting her right arm because of the damage to her ribs although the images showed they were beginning to heal. Because of the medications she had been in Intensive Care the entire time she was in the hospital. Dosage for these medications had now been reduced to a level she could manage on her own.

David Haskins had been in to visit her almost every day of her stay. This morning he came to drive her home. "Good morning, sunshine," he greeted her when he entered her room.

"Easy for you to say," she replied.

"Come on, lady, you get to go home today. Get ready. The doctor told me he was having the nurses ready your release papers and letting you get dressed. Don't just sit there, let's get going." He was trying to be as cheerful as possible, but it wasn't working.

"What am I going to do when I get out of here, David?" she asked, her head hanging low.

"You are going to do whatever it takes to get back to being a real person. You have a long way to go, but you don't have to do it alone. I'm going to be alongside you all the way. Julia will do the domestic chores and I'll do the running for you. All you have to do is get well. We know you're going to have to take it one step at a time and we'll be there to help in any way we can. The rehab and healing process will be up to you." He was trying to sound cheerful and encouraging, but didn't know if it was doing any good.

"Do you know they have me scheduled to come to the hospital for physical therapy five days a week? How am I going to manage that? I can't even drive." Tears were forming in her eyes.

"I've taken care of that. I'll drive you to and from your sessions and when I have to be away I'll have another trooper drive you. It's taken care of, now get dressed."

She was sobbing now, "Did I tell you they may never let me go back to work?"

"We'll cross that bridge when we get to it. Now what about all these flowers? Are you taking them home?" he asked, prodding her along.

"OK, OK, get out of here so I can get dressed." She wiped her cheeks and seemed resigned to her fate to remain a patient, albeit an outpatient.

The nurses came with medications, prescriptions and instructions. It was difficult for her to get dressed because of the limitations of her right arm. She struggled with the clothing Julia had sent with David, but managed to dress. She combed her hair and applied a small amount of makeup to offset her pale hospital look. Finally, after almost two hours of struggle she was loaded into a wheelchair and taken to the front entrance of the hospital where he was waiting in his private vehicle, a large silver color Dodge pickup. She needed assistance from a nurse to climb into the cab and considered it a major victory when she was strapped into the passenger seat.

At home Julia was amazingly helpful and pleasant. She kept the house clean and dusted as well as making the meals and doing the laundry. She reminded Penny when it was time to take her medications and chided her when she failed to follow orders. Julia was taking her role as mother very seriously. These responsibilities had changed her completely.

Penny was driven to the hospital each morning to attend her therapy sessions and taken home again after, usually by David Haskins, but some days another officer would come to act as taxi. Each day when she returned from therapy she would rest for an hour before going for a long hike on the street. The first few days the hike was limited to a few hundred feet, but the distance began to lengthen each day as the pain diminished and her ribs healed. After two weeks she tried to expand her exercise to include some of her karate regimen. The limited use of her right arm and the pain in her ribs along with the ache and nausea from her damaged liver made it impossible. Still, every few days she would try again, always without success.

Captain Meadows had called periodically to check on her progress and today he called again. "How are you doing?" he asked.

"The hospital folks say I'm doing well and improving, but it sure is slow. How are things at the office?"

"That's why I called today. I want you to come down to the office tomorrow morning for a meeting with me about your future. Is 11 a.m. good for you?" the captain asked.

"Yes, I'm done with my therapy and had a shower by then. I can make it." She had been dreading this meeting for she was certain she was about to get the axe. The department wasn't known for paying officers to stay at home and lounge around.

"I'll have David pick you up and bring you to my office at 10.45. See you in the morning." With that short note he hung up leaving Penny feeling the heavy omen of doom as she sat in her living room.

The following morning after her visit to the hospital she showered and dressed in her uniform. 'This may be the last time I get to wear this trooper uniform and I want to look good when I get fired,' she thought to herself as she readied for the ride to the office.

At 10:45 the front bell rang and David Haskins stood on the porch. "Are you ready?" he asked when she opened the door.

"I'm ready, but not looking forward to being fired from the job," she said in a soft voice.

"They might put you on paid leave, but I don't think they will fire you. You're too much of an asset to the department for that kind of treatment. There are a lot of officers who deserve firing, but you're not one of them. Come on, we have an appointment."

They entered the officer's door of the office and went directly to Captain Meadows' office. There was another officer in the office when they arrived. She recognized him when he turned to greet her. It was the Colonel, Commander of the Alaska State Troopers. She saluted him with her left hand as her right wouldn't reach the bill of her cap.

"Sit down, Penny, I don't want this to get too formal," the Colonel said as he shook her hand. "How are you feeling?"

"Not quite up to par yet, Sir, but I'm getting there," she replied.

He and Captain Meadows seated themselves and again turned to Trooper Rossiter. The Colonel was the first to speak. "I have been in contact with the doctors and the hospital. I have been given a full report on your condition and progress. It is my sad duty to inform you that the doctors will not release you to return to regular duty. The injuries you received are going to heal, but not to the extent they will allow you to indulge in extreme activities required of an Alaska State Trooper. I have spoken with the Governor and the Attorney General for the state and we have come up with a plan I hope you will find agreeable. First the bad news, the Governor has set your termination date for December 15th. That is three months from today. It saddens me to lose such a valuable and dedicated officer." He nodded at Captain Meadows.

"Trooper Rossiter," he began, "It is my pleasure to promote you to the rank of Captain, effective this date." He handed her a small box containing a set of captain's bars. Haskins reached out to take the box. He opened it and pinned the bars on her collar.

The three men applauded as she stood in amazement.

"You are not being terminated, Penny, you are being medically retired at the rate due a captain. This retirement will take place December 15th. Because of the nature of your disability the Governor has given special dispensation in the matter of your insurance coverage. He has arranged for you to receive 100% coverage on all illness and injuries for the rest of your life. He knows this will never repay you for the injuries you received but should defray any future costs ailments were caused by your injury." The Colonel was speaking again.

"I don't know what to say. I thought I would just be terminated. Thank you all. Thank you." She looked at David Haskins, "You dirty dog, you knew about this didn't you?"

The Colonel was speaking again, "Penny, I said we had spoken with the Attorney General and he has offered you a position in his department. We all know you have a law degree and have passed the bar. The Attorney General said if you want to fall back on your legal training he would arrange for you to be a law clerk for the Superior Court Judge here in Kenai. This is a position which could allow you to refresh your legal knowledge and prepare you for advancement in the court system. You have until January 15th to accept or reject this offer. There is no way to repay you for the service you have given this department. I just want to give you my personal thanks." He held out his hand to shake hers. "Congratulations, Captain."

"And you have my congratulations also, Captain Rossiter. We have a photographer in the outer office waiting to take some pictures when you're ready." Captain Meadows took her hand and pressed it gently.

Haskins was grinning like a crazy man, "I guess, technically, I now work for you." He, too, shook her hand.

"I don't know what to say," she said to the group.

"I'll buy lunch for the group after we finish taking pictures," said Captain Meadows. "After lunch the Colonel has to fly back to Anchorage."

The four met at Louie's Restaurant in Kenai for their lunch. Penny had ridden with Haskins in his big Dodge pickup. She ordered a shrimp salad the others all had cholesterol building sandwiches. She was able to eat her salad with her ailing right arm without straining it too badly.

After lunch the Captain took the Colonel to the airport to catch his flight back to Anchorage while David returned Penny to her house in Soldotna. He said his goodbye from the pickup and backed out into the street leaving her to break the news to Julia.

Penny was excited and apprehensive about what had taken place in the hour's prior. She was now a captain in the troopers and would be unemployed in three months. She knew the Colonel had stuck his neck out to get her promoted and she appreciated the gesture. The uncertainty of the future was what weighed heavily on her thoughts.

Julia was excited to hear the news and see the new bars on her collar. This would mean her daughter would be home with her, at least for the next several months while she was in physical therapy. If she took the job as clerk for the superior court judge she would have regular hours and be home at the end of the day. No more late nights all summer and no more testifying on her off days. There should be no more call-outs in the middle of the night. Yes, Julia was excited about the prospects of her retirement.

Penny, on the other hand was not as thrilled with her future prospects. She loved her job, a job she had been very good at for so many years. She knew she would have a retirement income that rivaled her work wages taking security out of the question. The promise of enhanced health insurance was a bonus and represented a huge wage increase, making her future even more secure. Most officers would be envious of her position, but Penny Rossiter didn't think she was ready for retirement.

There would be time to consider all her options over the next three months. She was certain her physical condition would have a great deal to do with her final decision. She was met with frustration and indecision as she changed clothing to go out for her run—which today would be only a walk. Her arm ached and her stomach was upset from eating all the greenery in her salad, but mostly she was uncomfortable with her future prospects.

It had been many years since she left law school and that side of the criminal justice system. It would take a lot of study to bring her skills up to those of her would-be peers in the court system. She had always enjoyed studying, but now it wasn't a grade she was shooting for it was her entire career.

She had no hint what would become of the cases she had been working. She wanted to know who killed Will Goodson, who shot her and why did they want Goodson's little cabin so desperately? Who had killed the two young mothers on Resurrection Trail and what had become of the two young boys? How had anyone taken them without alerting any of the locals? There were only questions without answers and she would not be here to find those answers.

All this made her press harder as she walked down the sidewalk forcing her to increase the pace. She swung her right arm vigorously attempting to increase its range of travel. It only increased the pain.

Chapter 10

Three months ago the three men had cleaned up all the materials and tools from the lot on Funny River Road and moved it to another hidden spot on Scout Loop Road near Sterling, Alaska. The leader of the trio was a bully named Terry Boyette. His two stooges, Kenny Pierce and Bobby Gunther willingly took his orders. When they refused they were met with a sound punch in the gut from the big man.

"Why in the world did you shoot that trooper?" Boyette had asked Kenny Pierce. "We needed that piece of property. Now we have to come all the way out here and on a public highway. I don't like it out here in Sterling. Too many people see us coming and going."

"She was nosing around and coming right to the cabin. I had to do something. The saw and gas can were on the porch. She knew someone was there. It was just easier to shoot her and clear out." Pierce was never a deep thinker, but he was loyal to Boyette and liked the excitement of the drug manufacturing business more than he liked the money he made. He was a simple soul; violent and simple.

"Well, it's done now. This time be more careful and don't shoot anybody on the new lot." Terry Boyette chided his underling. Bobby Gunther sat in the front seat of the old Chevy, listening but not wanting to get involved in this dispute. All three men wore beards and old clothing, but Gunther couldn't grow a proper beard and looked like a fugitive from Gilligan's Island or a Scooby Doo cartoon. "Let's try to get the new building finished today and get to cooking."

Winter had set in hard. It was now below zero and there was a foot of new snow on the ground. The snow made it difficult to hide the fact they were there working. The good news was the trail to the lot was on a dirt street with no houses and almost no traffic. The three men parked the old pickup on the street and walked the several hundred yards to the simple barn structure they had constructed. It was well insulated and warm inside. A generator provided electricity when they were in the building and a converter hooked to a small bank of batteries provided power for the ventilation fan when they were out. Cooking meth is hazardous at best and breathing the toxic fumes was dangerous.

The men were skilled in their trade and had a name for making quality product. Business was good and dealers were anxious to buy any amount the product the men could produce. It was back-breaking work to bring all the canisters and barrels to the barn, but as of this time, no one had questioned them. The word on the street was that someone was manufacturing product, but the troopers had no idea who or where it was being done.

December 15th was an eventful day for Penny Rossiter. It was her retirement day. The party was held at Froso's Restaurant in Soldotna. It had very good food, very good atmosphere, and for their use tonight, an excellent bar. Froso, the beautiful Greek lady who owned and managed the restaurant made certain everything went according to plan. Tables were decorated and behind the head table was a small dais for the speakers wishing to tell a story or joke at the expense of the retiring captain. Every seat in the room was filled with well-wishers. At the head table was the guest of honor, Captain Penny Rossiter, Captain Ted Meadows, the Colonel, Commander of the troopers, David Haskins and Julia Rossiter. Haskins had hired a limo to drive Penny and Julia to the party. When they entered there was a loud applause and a standing salute while some announced the entry of the retiring Captain. When she arrived at her seat at the head table she raised her bad arm to salute the standing officers. The gesture drew another round of applause from the crowd.

Captain Meadows was the emcee for the gathering. He gave a short speech praising Penny for her years of service and dedication and presented her with her duty badge and her duty weapon as a gift from the department. Next he introduced the Colonel who presented her with a plaque and a letter from the Governor thanking her for her service. The Colonel also added his praise and thanks for her untiring devotion to the department.

David Haskins led the list of speakers who mostly roasted the honoree. When he came back to his seat he leaned over and whispered in her ear, "I love you, Penny Rossiter."

Penny was shocked by the comment, but pleased to hear it. Leaning toward David she smiled and whispered, "We'll have to talk about that in more detail later."

Julia had sat quietly all evening, smiling and nodding at all the nice comments about her daughter. When the crowd began to leave the dining room one by one, Julia was sipping her third glass of wine discreetly supplied by David Haskins, knowing Penny would be furious.

One of the last to leave was the Colonel. He would return to Anchorage on the last scheduled flight of the day. He and Captain Meadows left together, obviously discussing business as they went out the door.

Haskins volunteered to drive Penny and Julia home. Once Julia was inside and headed for bed Penny stepped up in front of David, stood on her tip-toes, wrapped her one good arm around his neck and kissed him passionately. Haskins looked her in the eye, smiled and returned the kiss.

"What brought this on, David?" she asked.

"My old fashioned ethic, I guess. I could never tell you as long as we worked together, but now you're retired and it seemed to be the right thing to do." he explained, rather shyly.

"I have to admit I never allowed myself to think of you as anything other than a fellow officer, but tonight it seems right. I think I'd like to get better acquainted, if you think it could work."

"I think it can work. We can give it a try." He kissed her again.

"Whew," she said, "This has been some evening." She pulled at the collar of her uniform, "This is the last time I will be wearing this," she said. "I'm going to miss it."

"I have to ask, have you made up your mind about taking the job with the judge?"

"I haven't told them yet, but I need to work somewhere and this is where I live and an opportunity to brush up on my legal skills, as the Colonel said. It will be a big change for me, but with this bad arm I think it's the thing for me to do. At least I'll be able to take care of Julia—which reminds me, Mr. Haskins, what gave you the idea you could give her a glass of wine. You know she doesn't like to stop once she starts." They were sitting on the couch with her staring him in the eye.

"I know, and I'm sorry if it upset you, but she deserved a little celebration once in a while. I promise, I won't do it again," he said.

"I'll hold you to that." She was smiling and stepped closer. "Now kiss me again and get out of here. The neighbors will begin to talk if you stay later." She snickered a little and he pulled her close.

For the next month at the rehab center she worked like a person possessed. Her chest was healing and her arm was beginning to regain some strength. Her nausea from the liver trauma continued, but it was diminishing too. She had gained back some of the weight she had lost during her recovery and could now jog part of her morning walk. The doctors were still telling her she should be watchful of extreme exercise because of the damage to her liver. They warned her over and over again of the dire consequences she could suffer if she were struck in the same area for a second time. She promised to be careful.

On the morning of January 15th she had an appointment with the Superior Court judge, Nelson Bartolis. She walked through the front entry of the court house at 8 a.m. She was met by the judge's clerk, Nancy Riddle, a middle aged, well preserved blond. Riddle was all business and handled all the affairs for which the judge had no time. She recognized Penny as she entered and went through the security checkpoint inside.

"Ms. Rossiter?" she asked.

"Yes."

"My name is Nancy Riddle. The judge asked me to meet you and show you the way to his chambers. Please come with me."

Penny followed the blond lady through one of the many doors in the lobby of the court building. It led to a long hallway with a door at the far end. She opened it and they were in the private sanctum of judges and their staff. This area is only visited by those invited by the judges or for juries who used one of the rooms for deliberations. The area was deathly quiet, no music, no voices, no phones ringing, none of the hubbub she was she was accustomed to in her last office. She was led to a door a few feet down the hall. The two ladies entered.

"This is my office," Nancy announced. "As the judge's clerk I am responsible for everything that happens back here. If you have any questions or reasons to meet with Judge Bartoli you will make an appointment with me. It may sound harsh, but I assure you, the judge is extremely busy and cannot be disturbed while he's working. If you accept this position your title will be Law Clerk, but it's much more important than that. You will be the special assistant to Judge Bartolis. He will rely on you to do his research and investigating. I'm told you have been out of the legal profession for some time and need to refresh you knowledge and study court rules. This position will give you ample opportunity to do both. The Judge has read your resume and told me he was very impressed with it. Judge Bartolis is not easily impressed, so you must be an exceptional person. Have a seat over there and I'll tell the judge you're here.

To Penny the clerk seemed a little self-important, but ran an efficient office. Penny sat on one of the four chairs in the office and waited. Within two minutes Nancy Riddle returned to escort her into the plush office of Judge Nelson Bartolis, Superior Court, State of Alaska, his official title given courtesy of the large brass nameplate resting at the front of his desk.

"Have a seat, Ms. Rossiter. The judge will be with you in a minute." She turned to march out the door, but the judge only read the file resting on his large oak desk. Soon he began to nod his head and finally closed the file and looked up at his guest.

"How do you do, Ms. Rossiter, I'm Nelson Bartolis. As long as we are alone in chambers you may call me Nelson. In court or in public you should refer to me as Judge or Your Honor. This protocol is common and must be observed. If you will permit it we'll be on first name basis while in this office. Your being here tells me you will be accepting the position and accept all the responsibilities associated with it. By accepting, you place yourself in a unique position. We in this office are just people like anyone else, but we are held to a higher standard because of the power we have over the daily rights and privileges of the citizens of this country. While you are associated with this office you will not be involved in any type of scandal either public or private. You must not associate with anyone convicted of a crime. You must not associate with anyone having a case heard by this court. You must maintain a good financial standing within the community. It is imperative you maintain a personal life in keeping with the tenets I have described. Do you understand the importance of this doctrine?"

"Of course I do, Sir. They are not much different from those maintained by peace officers. I'm sure you've checked and found there has never been an issue with my personal or professional life." She was a little put out with this sort of introduction.

"You're right. We did investigate your background and found nothing that would prevent us from hiring you for this position." He was grinning now. "OK, Penny, now that the warning label has been read let's get down to business as it really is." He held out his hand to shake hers, "Welcome aboard Rossiter. We're glad to have you. How about some coffee?"

"Yes, Sir, I'd love some." She began to relax a little. "I was beginning to think you didn't want me here."

"It's a standard speech I give all new employees, but quite frankly, I've never given it to a person I wanted working this office more than I do you. You are an exceptional person and I am looking forward to working with you." He punched an intercom button and ordered Riddle to bring two coffees. "I need an assistant. I've had some paralegals, but they never seemed to grasp the importance of their work. I don't want you to think you are a paralegal. By no means! I want you to be my legal aide. I want you to research my cases and to help me decide outcomes and verdicts. Your influence in this office will be second only to mine."

The door opened and Nancy Riddle entered with a tray of three cups of hot coffee. She put the tray on his desk and sat in the other chair in front of his desk.

"Rossiter, meet Nancy. She will assist you in any way you wish. You can count on her knowledge and advice. She is my pathway to reality."

"Hi, Penny. The stiff neck attitude is what greets all outsiders in this office. Back here in the Lord's office we sometimes act almost human." She shook hands with Rossiter before sipping her coffee.

"I was beginning to think no one in this office was friendly, but I'm beginning to see through all that now. Thank you for being so kind." Rossiter sipped her coffee now. "I think I'm going to enjoy working here. I must warn you, though. It's been a long time since I spent any time in the law books. I am pretty well versed in the state statutes and basic federal laws, but it will take a while before I can recite them with statute numbers, case references and legal doctrine. I promise to study all of that and bring myself up to date as quickly as possible. I promise I'm going to make mistakes and I will appreciate any advice you can give."

The judge put his coffee cup on the desk, "I think we are going to make a good team. How about you Nancy? Do you like her?"

"I sure do, Nelson. I think you're right. This is going to be a good team."

"How about it Penny? Do you have any questions before you begin filling out all the mandatory forms?"

"No, I think I'm ready to get my feet wet."

"OK then, take her to her new office, Nancy. Find out what supplies she needs and fix her up. Show her where the coffee pot is located and give her all the paperwork she needs to sign. I think the two of you are going to get along just fine. Now get out of here and let me get to work."

Chapter 11

Kenny Pierce was on the cell phone ringing Boyette. He was parked in the parking lot at the city of Kenai library. Boyett answered on the third ring.

"Yeah, what do you want now?"

Pierce tried to hold his temper, "I'm in Kenai delivering the last order. I was driving by the court house and I saw that lady trooper I shot. She was coming out of a side door in the court building. She was dressed in civvies, not in a trooper uniform. I don't know what she was doing there, but this is the first time I've seen her since I shot her. I just thought you'd want to know."

"Don't let anyone see you over there. I don't want any of us tied to that shooting. Did she look like she had any health problems? Like limping or anything?" asked Terry Boyette.

"No, in fact she was looking hot. I mean really hot. She was carrying a briefcase when she came out. The strange thing is she came out the side door, you know, where the juries usually come out."

"Hmmm, that is strange. That side door goes to the judge's chambers. I don't know what she was doing there either, but she wasn't there to see the DA. His office is across the street. My guess is that this has nothing to do with us," opined Boyette.

"Do you want me to follow her and see where she goes?"

"No, I need for you to go to the warehouse and bring back those two tanks we filled yesterday. And fill the gas can for the generator. The wind is kicking up and we need to do some cooking tonight. Get back as soon as you can. We need to get to work. Pick up Bobby on the way back."

"OK, Terry, I'll see you in about an hour." As he finished his call Penny drove by, turning left toward Soldotna. He followed as far as the traffic light on the Spur Highway where she turned left and he drove across to Bridge

Access Road. He would return by way of Kalifornsky Beach Road where the warehouse rented by the trio was located.

After obtaining the items from the warehouse he drove toward Sterling. On the way he stopped at a run-down old mobile home. Junk, old furniture, a parted out old four wheel drive pickup and plastic garbage bags littered the front of the property. Pierce stepped up on the small, shaky, front porch and banged on the door. There was no answer so he banged again and shouted, "Come on, Bobby, get up, we gotta go to work." Pierce then heard noises from inside.

In a few moments a shirtless, disheveled figure appeared at the door. "Come on in Kenny. Give me a minute. I need to go to the bathroom and comb my hair. I'll be right out."

"I'll wait in the truck. Hurry it up," said Pierce, shaking his head and stepping off the porch.

Fifteen minutes later the two men were traveling east on a slippery road, headed to the barn off Scout Lake Road. The men were unloading their supplies when Terry pulled in to join them. They each made two trips in and back to take all the chemicals and supplies to the little barn. Terry had purchased plastic hazmat suits to wear when they were working in the lab. They also wore full face air filters to protect themselves from the fumes and particulates in the small barn. Brewing Meth is a hazardous business and Boyette wanted to protect his crew. They worked in the confined area for over two hours before leaving for the day. They closed the inner door and changed out of their protective gear in the small entry room they had named the mud room.

Out in the fresh air again Bobby Gunther opened a pack of cigarettes and stuffed one in his mouth. As he reached for his Bic lighter Boyette screamed at him.

"Don't light that thing in here," he shouted. "You could blow this whole place up. I preach to you all the time about how dangerous this business is and you stand outside the door and try to light up a smoke. Don't ever do that again."

"Sorry Terry, I wasn't thinking."

"You've been told this shack is one huge bomb waiting to blow. Don't ever light up while you're here." Terry Boyette was more than angry, he was frightened. "Kenny, I want you and Bobby to go to the garage where that Gilmore kid works. He owes me two grand and I want you to collect it. He said he would pay me a month ago and he has been avoiding me since. I can't afford to have that kind of money hanging out. If he won't pay then convince him he should and by this weekend or it will get worse."

"How bad do you want me to hurt him?" asked Kenny.

"Just don't kill him until he pays me," answered Boyette.

"Come on Bobby, we can go out to North Kenai and have some fun. I'll let you smoke in the truck."

"I gotta stop at the house and get another coat so's I can leave the window open." He followed Pierce to the truck and jumped into the passenger seat. "Can we stop at McDonalds for a burger?"

Boyette was shaking his head as the pair drove out of the little side road toward the main Scout Loop Road. Many times he had questioned his own judgment for hiring this pair of intellectual derelicts. They were loyal and could be counted on to do any job he asked, but they could never be trusted to think for themselves or make important decisions on their own. It was the heavy labor and the enforcement qualities for which they were hired that he kept them around. Kenny loved to hurt people and was good at it. Proof of that was the shooting of the trooper. It was stupid, but it was his answer to taking charge of the situation. Luckily, no one had seen him at the scene and he was smart enough not to leave any identifying evidence lying around.

Checking to make sure the ventilation system was working by watching the fumes and heat escaping from the tall chimney atop the little barn he picked up a small athletic bag and tossed it into the backseat of his truck. This was his new inventory and he was now off to visit his customers and distribute the new product. Manufacturing Meth is a dangerous and unhealthy occupation, but the rewards are worth the risk. With his building locked and secured he turned his truck toward the town of Soldotna to make the rounds of willing customers.

Penny Rossiter had come home a little early today because she had to take Julia's oxygen generator to the pharmacy to be serviced. She was in particularly good spirits today and offered to ride along on the short trip.

They had just turned into the parking area at the drug store when her cell phone rang. "Rossiter," she answered.

It was David Haskins, "I see you have quit calling yourself 'trooper'," he commented.

"Don't be a smarty, David. What do you want?"

"If you promise not to be grumpy I'll take you and Julia out for dinner tonight. Do you want to go?"

"Let me ask her," she turned to Julia and asked. Julia nodded her head enthusiastically. "It looks like we'll go. What time?" she inquired.

"I should finish up here around six thirty, how about I pick the two of you up at seven?"

"Remember your promise, David. I'm holding you to it." She was referring to his not buying any wine for Julia.

"I promise, Penny. I do understand but that was a special occasion. I'll pick you up at seven. You figure out where you would like to go for dinner. See you then."

She was still wearing the gray business suit and red blouse she had worn to work this morning when she opened the door, but looked as if she had just taken it from the closet. "Would you like to come in before we go to Froso's?" she asked.

"No, not now, but I will for a few minutes when we come back from dinner, perhaps." He looked past her shoulder. "Where's Julia," he asked.

"She said she had changed her mind and wanted us to have the evening together. Intuitive of her wasn't it?" She smiled and stepped out the door and past him to walk to the truck.

"I'm beginning to like her more all the time." He walked to the driver's side and climbed inside. "Froso's it is, then."

David ordered deep fried halibut and a beer while Penny ordered a Greek salad and a white wine. They passed small talk while in the restaurant, but conversation began to attain a personal aspect when they returned to the truck.

"I think I could get used to having dinner with you on a regular basis," commented Haskins.

"I like it too, David. Do you think we could make this a less formal and more personal relationship?" She turned in the seat to face him. He reached out and kissed her warmly.

"I think that's a wonderful idea," he said, kissing her again.

"You do understand I have Julia in my life and for me she is an important obligation."

"Of course, I recognize that. I'm willing to take it one step at a time, but I would like to spend some time with you, just you and me."

"I don't know what kind of hours I will be working. This new job is a whole new arena for me. The judge is a nice guy and a dedicated practitioner. I'm guessing I'll be putting in a lot of hours, but I think there will be time for us. I certainly hope there is. I'm becoming very attached to you." She leaned forward to kiss him now.

It was at this inopportune time his cell phone rang. He took time to finish the kiss anyway, "Haskins," he answered.

It was Lou Filson, his second in command at the crime scene investigations unit. "Dave, it's Lou… we need you. We just got a call from one of the troopers and there has been a fatal assault out on the North Road. Someone beat one of the mechanics to death at the trucking company garage. Do you want to come with us to take charge of the scene?"

"I'm not in uniform, but I'll meet you there. I'll be there in fifteen minutes." He shut off his phone and looked Penny Rossiter in the eye, "You remember how it is, right?"

"Yes, I remember, call me tomorrow evening." She was sad to see him leave, but knew his work was important. She stood in the drive until he was out of sight.

Julia was waiting for her when she came inside.

Penny smiled and said, "I'm not in high school now, Mom. You didn't need to wait up for me."

"Oh, that's not it at all. I wanted to know what he said tonight."

"Why, you old gossip, what makes you think I'll tell you?"

"Because I'm your mother," said Julia, shaking a finger at her daughter. "He told me he wanted to see you alone tonight and I just thought he might have something important to say to you. Being your mother I have a right to know."

"You have no such right, mother. I am long past needing your permission to stay out late or date whomever I wish to date."

"I knew it. He kissed you, didn't he?" Julia was excited.

"As a matter of fact, he did. Now, are you satisfied? You know all my secrets." Penny feigned indignation. "And he asked me to go steady," she added smugly.

Julia was grinning broadly now. "Good, I can go to bed happy now. I hope he makes an honest woman of you."

"Things haven't gone that far yet, Mom."

"Why did he leave in such a hurry?"

"He's a trooper, Mom. He had a call and had to go to a crime scene. Don't ask me what it was, because I don't know. He can't talk about his cases to me and I can't talk about my cases to him. That's just the way the system works. And before you ask, I can't talk with you about my cases either."

"Hmph," Julia uttered. "If that's the way you're going to be I'm going to bed." Pushing the walker holding her oxygen tank she walked to the hallway humming *Here Comes The Bride*.

Penny just shook her head and went to the kitchen to fix a cup of hot cocoa before she went to bed.

Chapter 12

When Haskins arrived the entire area around Wildwood Drive was alive with red and blue flashing lights. A City of Kenai patrolman checked his identification and let him through to the scene. Four of his crime scene team were already on scene. Team member Don Winston met him in the huge parking area. They were surrounded by large trucks and trailers. Three trooper cars were in the lot and two City of Kenai patrol vehicles were in the lot. Their officers directing traffic while one of their sergeants assisted the troopers gathering evidence from the scene.

"Lou is out back with the body, Dave. The victim is a mess. Beaten to death it looks like. They're behind the garage. So far it looks like someone parked out back and stopped him when he came out of the garage where he worked." Winston recited the information and led Haskins to the back of the large shop where the company repaired their trucks.

"Thanks, Don, I'll find Lou, you go back to what you were doing." Winston gave a sort wave of his hand and walked away. Haskins surveyed the scene while walking slowly to where the body lay on the dirt. The parking lot was well lit in order to dissuade thieves from pilfering goods and fuel from the trucks. It was easy to see the scuff marks in the area near the body. Haskins judged there were two assailants from these marks in the dirt. Lou was talking with the Kenai Police Sergeant when David approached.

Lou Filson had heard his footsteps behind him and turned as he approached. "I hope you were having a nice time when I called," said Lou.

"I hope you have all the work done so I can go back to doing what I was doing when you called."

"Not quite, David. This is Sergeant Bill Dunham with KPD," Filson introduced the bystander.

Haskins reached out to shake his hand, "Hi, Bill, it's been a while since we have worked a case together."

"Hello, David, good to see you again. Yeah, that was some case. That nutty car-bomber, is he still in jail?"

"The Department of Corrections sent him out to Arizona to do his time and he got cross-threaded with one of the big drug kingpins down there. They found him lying in the exercise yard. He had been stabbed 31 times. Of course nobody saw it happen." Haskins explained what little he knew of the incident.

He turned to Lou, "What do we have here, Lou?"

"You can see they keep this area plowed pretty well. The marks in the dirt tell me there was quite a struggle and fight. It looks like two attackers. See, over here?" Lou pointed to several sets of foot tracks. "Two sets were face to face with this guy when it started. From the tracks they must have talked for a couple of minutes before the two jumped this guy. His name is Wade Gilmore, by the way. One of the other mechanics said he was a meth user. He didn't see the fight, but knew Gilmore owed some dealer a lot of money."

"Have you found anything unusual on the scene?" asked Haskins.

"Not yet, we're still looking, but I did see something familiar, and you're going to love this," Lou quipped.

"What would that be?"

"Remember the old guy out Funny River? The one Penny found in the cabin?"

"Yeah, I remember, Will Goodson. What about it?"

"The condition of the body, it's the same brutal style as Goodson. We haven't seen a weapon, but it looks like he was beaten with a club or pipe or something like it. They broke his legs and one arm after they had beaten him until he could no longer stand. It looks like he has internal injuries and broken ribs. The medical examiner will have to look at those. There's a lot of blood. The other mechanic didn't hear or see anything, but he said the radio was playing loud in the shop so he didn't hear the fight." Filson was a thorough and competent investigator and knew what to look for.

"It looks like you have everything under control here. Is there anything you want me to do for you tonight?" asked Haskins.

"I don't think so, David, I can take it from here. I'll see you in the morning at the office unless I find something I think will amaze you."

Haskins chuckled. Filson had a sense of humor no matter the circumstance. His entire crew was a pleasure to work with. It meant the horrifying crime scenes and viscous assaults on innocent victims could be viewed and dealt with without personal attachments. Even so, viewing these scenes day after day made this an occupation not many people could endure. David understood how special his five man team really was. He walked back to his pickup, made some notes in his notebook and drove back to his home in Soldotna.

At this same time Kenny Pierce and Bobby Gunther were at the home of Terry Boyette. Boyette was not happy to see them. He had other business to on his mind. "What do you two want? Did you take care of the job I gave you?" The three moved inside the house where papers were scattered over the surface of the kitchen table and the kitchen countertops.

"We took care of it, Terry, but there was a problem," announced Pierce.

"What kind of problem? Did you get my money or not?"

"That was the problem, Boss. He said he didn't have the money so we sort of beat him up a little. Then he started to cuss us out and said he was never going to pay. That's when Bobby grabbed his arm and I hit him in the gut with my fish bonker. That little baseball bat looking club has knocked out a lot of big fish. He was screaming and cussing and swinging his other arm at me, so I smacked his free arm with the fish bonker. I hit it kind of hard and I think I broke it. He screamed again. I was afraid someone was going to hear him and kicked him in the gut. He went down and was layin' on the ground, cussin' and tryin' to kick me so I stomped his leg and heard it snap. He tried to kick me with his good leg so I stomped that one, too. Bobby kicked his arm and backed off. That's when he spit a mouthful of blood at me and I kicked him in the head. He went out like a light. I tried to wake him up, but he wasn't breathing. He had a partner inside the garage and we were afraid he would come outside and see us so we climbed in the truck and left to come here."

"You killed him?" a shocked Boyette screamed. "You idiots, he owed me money. A dead man can't pay. He owed me about two grand. That's coming out of your take this week. What's the matter with the two of you? The last thing I told you was 'don't kill him'."

"I'm sorry, Boss. It was business, it just happened. We didn't mean to." Pierce was trying to justify his act, but it only made Boyette more angry and loud.

Bobby Gunther was frightened by the confrontation and began to back toward the front door. Boyette saw his move and screamed for him to "get back in here."

"You two are beginning to cost me more than I can afford. One more screw-up like this one and I'll have someone take the two of you out." Boyette was sweating and his face was beet red from the anger, "Now, you two get out of here before I kill you myself."

The two underlings wasted no time making their exit. Boyette kicked the door closed behind them. When he saw the headlights back out of his drive he went to the kitchen and poured a very large glass of Jack Daniels whiskey. He tipped it up and drank it down. He poured another and sat down to finish the papers he had been working on when the two stooges had come to interrupt him. He sipped the second glass of whiskey, becoming less agitated as he drank. He had been working on a financial statement to be used to purchase another rental property, this one a four-plex in the heart of town. He found he could not concentrate now and refilled his tall whiskey glass. He went to the living room to watch the ten o'clock news while drinking his third drink.

It had been a tense evening for both men. Bobby went to his trailer and lit up a joint, smoked it to a stub and lit another. Kenny Pierce went to his house and heated a syringe full of heroine, which he injected into the vein of his left arm. Now, he too, was feeling mellow.

The following morning as Penny entered the courthouse to begin another day of training in her new position as legal aide to Judge Bartolis, David Haskins was in a meeting with Lou Filson. Lou had drafted a preliminary report outlining the evidence found and the condition of the body in last night's murder investigation. Under the heading of WITNESSES was a list of one name, Kevin Morse. In truth there were no witnesses as Morse had neither seen nor heard anything at the time of the killing.

There had been scuff marks, but no clear shoe prints. There were tire marks, but no clear tread prints. There was one bit of evidence; officers measured the tire tracks as well as the axle width and the wheel base length of the vehicle that had been parked at the scene. Officers were still researching the measurements to determine the make and model of the vehicle.

The body had been sent to the crime lab during the night. The scientific investigators would be on the job now attempting to ascertain the extent of the injuries the victim had suffered and if there were drugs in his blood stream. Other tests would be done, such as ultra-violet light to see blood spots and spattering patterns. By late this afternoon there would be a call from the trooper captain in charge of the crime lab.

Haskins read the report again, making notes on a yellow legal pad. "There isn't much to go on, Lou. What's your plan?"

"We have the victim's address and I'm sending three of the team over there as soon as it's daylight. The victim had a string of keys on his belt and we're hoping one of them is the key to his home." Filson spoke to his supervisor about the plan of the day while David made notes on his yellow pad. "I mentioned it last night, but did you see a similarity between the way this guy died and the injuries to Will Goodson?"

"I know your guys searched the area for a weapon, did they find one?"

"No, but I'm going out to the garage this morning and look around in the daylight. Do you want to come along?" asked Lou.

"Sorry, Lou, I can't this morning. My schedule is filled until at least three this afternoon. I can't get out of this office. Call me here if you find anything out there. And tell your men at the victim's house to call me if they find anything there."

Haskins picked up his notepad and walked down the hall to the office of Captain Meadows. The captain was on the telephone when he arrived. Meadows motioned for him to come in and take a seat. Meadows mostly listened to the call without making any comments. Finally, after several minutes, he said, "Thank you, Sir, I will," and hung up.

"The colonel," he said, greeting his investigator. "I heard you had another murder last night, just one victim?"

"Yes, Sir, a mechanic out on the North Road, he was working nights with another mechanic and went outside to take a smoke or something and the assailants were waiting for him. They really worked him over. Lou says the injuries remind him of the assault on old Will Goodson a few months ago. I saw the body and I think he may be right, although I can't think of anything Goodson and this victim had in common. It looked to me as if this mechanic was a druggie. It's possible he owed the dealer some money and they came to collect. That would make the Goodson killing and this one similar. I think both men were meant to be warned, but the beatings got out of hand and both victims died. Only speculation mind you, we have no evidence to substantiate any of this."

"Well, keep at it," the Captain said. "You know how I hate open case files."

"I'll be in the office all day, Cap. I have several cases to follow up on and I expect the crime lab will be calling later today." Haskins stood to leave the office.

"I heard you had a date with Penny Rossiter last night," the captain noted.

"How do you learn all this gossip, Captain?"

"I'm a Captain, that's how. When you're able to learn these things we'll make sure you become a Captain, too."

Chapter 13

Penny had been spending far more time at her desk doing case research than she had expected. Looking back she should have known it's the nature of her job description. She was standing at her desk stretching her back when Nancy Riddle came in.

"Is your body rebelling at the amount of time you spend at your desk?" she asked in a friendly way.

"I guess I'm not as healed up as I thought I was."

"At least you have an excuse for the aches and pains of sitting. Most of us can't claim an old gunshot wound for our creaking bones. Come on, Penny. Let's go to Louie's for lunch. I'll buy this time, but next time it's your turn."

"That sounds like a good idea to me," Rossiter said as she reached for her purse.

Both ladies ordered chef salad and iced tea. Riddle opened the conversation while they waited. "I know you have only been on the job a short time, but how do you like it so far?"

"Mostly, I like it a lot. The hours are great and I like the people I'm working with, even you." Penny tried to make light of this conversation. "I guess I'm an adrenalin junkie at heart. I miss the excitement. I miss being out there on the street and taking care of business. I miss protecting the underdog and saving victims. This is a whole new world to me. I know that with my injury I'll never be able to do those things again, but I miss it."

"Can I tell you a secret?" asked Riddle.

"Of course," Rossiter answered.

"I envy you. I envy the things you've done. I envy that you had the courage to do all the things you've done. Most of us only dream of doing something like that, but you did it. You lived the life. You put your life on the line while helping other people. I admire you for what you have done in your lifetime." She was about to say something else when the waitress brought their lunch.

Rossiter was pouring dressing on her salad as she answered. "You can thank my father for all that. He made a tomboy out of me. He said since I was so small I needed to learn how to protect myself. I had good teachers and I liked it. In fact I took pride in beating opponents who were bigger and older than me. Even today, after my military career and my years as a trooper, I have always had to prove myself. I've loved doing it. The real problem will be if I'll be able to stop doing it?"

They both ate lunch without conversation, but while sipping their tea, Riddle made a flattering comment, "I just wanted you to know how much I admire you. I hope you stay with our office forever. You are so much fun to work with. The Judge has hired some other stuff-shirts, fresh out of college and knowing it all, they were so arrogant and self-centered I hated working with them. You're different, even the judge says so, you are a perfect addition to our office. My best advice is, don't let it overwhelm you. There are no dumb questions in our office. If you have questions, ask them. And don't be afraid to ask questions or offer opinions with the judge. He is always willing to hear a different point of view and wants to know both sides of an argument when he is considering a case."

Rossiter sipped her tea and smiled, "I hope I can live up to your expectations, and for what it's worth, you have been a great help to me in the short time I've been here and I appreciate your pointers, thanks."

Nancy glanced at her wristwatch, "That concludes this meeting of the mutual admiration society. We have to get back to the office."

Late in the afternoon Terry Boyette was in the courthouse to file some paperwork with the clerk of the court on a property he had bought. While he was in the clerk's office a short, pretty, red haired lady entered. She had a handful of papers she presented to another clerk in the office.

"The Hostettler case, from Judge Bartolis," she informed the clerk.

"Oh, yes, thank you. I have been waiting for this." The clerk thumbed through the papers, checking the signatures and dates. "This looks good Ms. Rossiter, thank you." She tapped the end of the pages on the tall counter top. "You're doing a great job, Penny. How do you like working for the judge?"

"He's wonderful to work with. And tolerant, he hasn't fired me yet." Penny commented as she turned to walk back to her office across the hallway.

Terry Boyette had listened carefully to the comments of the court clerk and to the reply from Judge Bartolis' new aide. He was surprised to finally see the tiny ex-trooper Kenny Pierce had shot all those months ago. He was puzzled by what he saw. This petite little law clerk didn't seem so much of a threat that she deserved to be shot with a 12 gauge shotgun, much less be able to withstand the shooting and survive. Terry was beginning to think his number one enforcer was getting too enthusiastic about his work. It may be time to do something about him. This new incident with the mechanic seemed an extreme measure and now, seeing his last victim, was this the time for him to make a change in personnel? Bobby was a loyal and trusted employee, but could never do what Peirce was capable of doing. This was going to require some thought. His hangover was interfering with his thought process right now.

Boyette was a modern entrepreneur, of sorts. In his business he manufactured and sold crystal meth, cocaine, heroin, marijuana, spice and any other illegal substance he could make a profit selling. He never sold to the public, only dealers. This had been the secret of his success. He was a wholesaler. Boyette had made a great deal of money in the drug business and had invested his earnings wisely. He owned three duplex apartments, one four-plex, several single family dwellings he rented and several out-lying lots where he could set up shops like the one on Scout Loop Road in Sterling. He was attempting to buy the cabin and acreage thirteen miles out Funny River Road when Kenny Pierce went crazy and killed the owner. At the time he considered it an accident, but after the shooting of the tiny trooper and now the death of the mechanic who owed him a great deal of money he determined Kenny was just crazy. He liked killing people. His actions had drawn too much attention in his direction and he didn't like it. He could hire laborers like Bobby any time, but to find someone to do his collecting and enforcing was another thing. Boyette had made many contacts in the drug world and decided he would ask around about someone to replace Pierce.

Boyette owned a small warehouse on the outskirts of Soldotna where he stored chemicals and supplies. The old blue and white Chevy was parked inside, out of sight. It was only used when he needed a vehicle he could afford to lose. When he arrived at the small building Bobby Gunther was waiting.

"I called Kenny and he said he was on his way down here." Bobby was an obedient and loyal employee who didn't do well when asked to think on his own.

"Thanks Bobby, we have to go out to Sterling and fuel the generator. I want to take those two drums of chemical out there when we go. You'll need the small Akio sled. Unhook it from the snowmobile; we can tow it by hand today. Don't take the snowmobile this time. Take those four plastic cans of gasoline for the generator. We won't be working with the chemicals today, but suit up when you get there anyway. I don't want you to get sick. I need you on the job." Terry Boyette liked Bobby and relied on him to get the labor portion of most jobs accomplished.

Bobby had just finished loading the last of the containers in his own truck when Kenny Pierce showed up. "You're just in time, Kenny," Bobby said oozing sarcasm, "I've got everything loaded and ready to go."

"Get off my back, Bobby. I have more things to do than to babysit you." Pierce spoke in a nasty and threatening tone.

"Knock it off, you two. We have work to do. Bobby, you get going and we'll follow behind. Kenny, you ride with me. I have some things we need to talk about." Boyette was barking orders.

"I'm on my way, Boss," said Gunther.

Terry was driving his own small truck with Pierce in the passenger seat. Once out of the downtown area Pierce asked, "What did you want to talk with me about, Boss?"

"I'm getting a little worried about you, Kenny. I saw that lady trooper you shot. She was at the courthouse today when I was filing some papers. It baffles me to understand how that little hundred pound woman could have been a threat to you. Why didn't you just leave?"

"She looked a lot bigger when she was carrying a .40 caliber Glock and sneaking up on the cabin. I was just protecting myself and your business."

"I'll accept that, Kenny, but what about the old man in the cabin? Was he a threat, too?"

"No, but each time he said no we upped the pressure. He kept it up until he couldn't take it any longer and died. We didn't mean to kill him, it was an accident."

"OK Kenny, how about the mechanic? Did he just keep saying no until he died?" Boyette was now becoming impatient.

"You sent me out there to collect from him and he wouldn't pay. It was that simple. We beat him up pretty bad and while he was down he tried to slug me. I kicked him in the head. I thought I just knocked him out, but he was dead. I can kill 'em, boss, but I never learned how to bring 'em back." Pierce was now very agitated.

"Don't get smart with me, Kenny. I pay you to get the job done and lately you have failed. You are bringing a lot of attention this way in the process. I don't want any attention. You had better understand that now or I'll replace you. I pay you a lot of money to do the job the way I tell you and you will do it my way, understand?"

"Yeah, I understand. I understand you're getting might uppity for a guy who operates entirely outside the law. Don't tell me how to do my job, Terry. I know too much."

Boyette turned to look him in the eye for an instant. It was time for Kenny to go. "OK Kenny, if that's the way you want it, but don't come to me asking for favors any more. If you like a paycheck you do things my way. If not, pack up and move on." Terry had made up his mind. His enforcer would have to be replaced. He knew a man in Anchorage who could recommend a good replacement.

As they drove to the end of the trail leading to the little barn Bobby was attempting to wrestle a large drum of chemicals into the Akio.

Two hours later the chemicals were inside and the generator refueled. Kenny helped his buddy Bobby load the little sled into his truck for the return to town. Boyette had told the men to meet him here the day after tomorrow to make another load of product. They would begin at 10 a.m., "Don't be late," he ordered.

Alone in his truck and returning to Soldotna he called his acquaintance in Anchorage. "Eddie, I need some advice and help. Do you have time to meet me later this afternoon?"

"What time," asked Eddie.

"I'll get a flight up and we can meet, then I'll take another flight back. What time is good for you?"

"Can you be here around six? We can have dinner and talk a little business." Eddie had been in the business for a long time and knew every dealer, associate and hit man in the state of Alaska. He also supplied much of the chemical Terry used in his manufacturing process. Eddie no longer dealt in processing himself, but supplied anyone who wanted to do so. He had helped Terry corner the market on the Kenai Peninsula. He distributed to distributors.

Eddie picked up Terry at the Ted Stevens International Airport. Eddie's car was a large Hummer, black with tinted windows. On the way to the restaurant Terry outlined the problem and asked if he knew a replacement for Kenny.

"It seems Kenny has become a distraction," explained Terry Boyette.

The discussion went on while they ate in a bistro on the south side of town. Satisfied that Terry's quest was legitimate he finally agreed to introduce him to someone who might be interested. The two men remained in the restaurant, drinking Christian Brothers Brandy until the third man arrived.

His name was Conrad Dooley. He preferred Connie as a nickname. He was a neat appearing man with a calm demeanor. Eddie made the introductions and left the two men to their business. Dooley had agreed to take Terry back to the airport when the business was finished. The discussion went on for almost an hour discussing pay, duties, safety, chain of command and other details. In the end Dooley agreed to come to work for Terry Boyette. Both agreed his first order of business would be for Kenny Pierce to have an accident.

Boyette agreed to rent him an apartment until he could find a better place, somewhere more private, to live. Dooley agreed to be in Soldotna in three days. He would call Boyette when he arrived.

Chapter 14

Conrad Dooley had called his new boss as he entered Soldotna. Terry gave him directions to one of his duplexes and was waiting there when Connie arrived. He unlocked the door for his new tenant and stepped inside with him to discuss his plan.

"If you aren't familiar with the area, I think you should spend the rest of the day driving around and acquaint yourself with the city. When you think you're ready to deal with our employee problem give me a call and I'll help you set it up." He reached into his pants pocket and produced a roll of bills. He counted out a couple of hundred dollars to give to the new man. "This should get you some groceries and supplies to set up housekeeping. I need to go out to the Sterling site for a while. One of my clients wants a large delivery and I have to make some up. My two employees will be there with me most of the afternoon. Do you have any questions or need anything else?"

"I don't think so. I'll get set up and then go drive around the area. I've been here a few times and know some of the main roads. I'll call you later."

Terry Boyette liked the new man. He was friendly, competent and non-confrontational. Eddie had described him as a good man to have on your side and a bad man to be against. Terry would soon see if his dark side was as dangerous as advertised.

It was 15 degrees and a light wind blowing. The sky was clear, but the forecast was for snow this evening. Terry and his two hired men worked all afternoon preparing a fresh batch of product for the dealer with an impressive order. Included in the order were several kilos of marijuana and several slips of heroin. A large safe in the little barn contained enough old stock to supply the meth order, but depleted his inventory making it necessary for him to cook up new stock. The imported supplies were stashed under the front seat of his truck. The three men had gone about their chores without much conversation for most of the afternoon. As they closed up for the day Kenny came to him and asked for a couple of slips of heroin, personal use, he had said.

"You know the rules, Kenny, don't use it in public," cautioned Boyette.

"Yeah, yeah, I know. I'll see you here tomorrow."

"You had better steer clear of Kenny tonight, Bobby. I think he is about to get mummified this afternoon," Terry warned his other employee.

"Yeah, I know how he is when he's usin,'" Bobby replied as he went to his own truck for the return to his home. It was now dark in the late afternoon, though the days had begun to gain several minutes of daylight.

Boyette was in his own home when the phone rang. It was Dooley.

"I guess I'm ready," he said.

"Good, meet me at the warehouse. I have an idea. It may help you out. I'll be there in five minutes."

The two men walked to the warehouse together and Terry opened the locked door. "Come into my office," he said to Connie.

Inside, Terry sat at his desk while Dooley stood in front of it. Boyette took a small vial from a desk drawer and handed it to Dooley. "Kenny hit me up for some "H" when he left work today. I think he'll be at home sticking a needle in his arm. Take this and make sure he has an accidental OD. It will be tragic, but those things happen when you use illicit drugs."

Connie took the vial, "I've heard that happens."

Boyette handed the man an envelope filled with papers and pictures. He explained how to get to Kenny's place and assured him there was a picture of his house, his truck and a picture of Kenny inside the envelope. There is also a key to his front door. Kenny is no dummy and he's a dangerous person. He likes to kill and won't hesitate to take you out if he catches you. If my thinking is correct, though, he'll be out of it when you get there, but be careful, like I said, he's dangerous."

"I'll call you when it's over and I get back to my place. See you tomorrow." Conrad Dooley was all business now as he turned to leave the office.

Boyette sat in his office for a long while reviewing his plan, assuring himself it was foolproof and his new associate could handle it without difficulty. Finally he turned off the light and locked the door. At home he poured a large glass of Jack Daniels and sat to watch television while he waited for word. He had an uneasy feeling about all the bodies being created in such a small area. This would not go unnoticed by the local trooper detachment.

David Haskins had been at his desk all day and felt he needed to get out of the office. He checked the time and was surprised to see how late it was getting. It was nearly quitting time and he hadn't been out of the office all day. He reached for the phone and called Penny on her mobile number.

"Rossiter," a voice answered.

"Penny, it's David. Just checking in to see how your day was going?"

"Good, busy, but good. It takes me a long time to get anything done because I've been away from the law books for so long. It's frustrating, but it gets a little better each day. How is the police business?"

"You know how it is; more time spent entering stuff in the computer than catching crooks. I've been at the desk all day and need a break. How about you and I do something exciting this evening?"

"I was thinking we might drive out and check on Gus Sampson. How do you feel about doing that?" asked Penny.

"I think it's a good idea. It's a long drive and you can sit close to me. Yeah, it sounds like a really good idea. We can have dinner somewhere either going to or coming from Gus' place. Would you like to do that?" asked David.

"You bet, I'll call and tell Julia not to fix dinner for me tonight."

"What time should I pick you up?"

"Six," she said, looking forward to the evening with him.

"See you then. Oh wait, I almost forgot, one of the road troopers thinks he found that PA-12 you were looking for once upon a time. I'll bring you the tail numbers when I see you tonight. Do you still need that information?"

She was excited, "Yes I do, David. Those numbers are from an aircraft seen at the Hope airport at the time those women were murdered and the boys disappeared. Are there any other new developments in that case?"

"I haven't heard of anything, but I'll call Ray Finlay and ask," said Haskins.

"Thanks, David, I'll see you later."

The two spent about an hour with Gus. He greeted them like old friends and offered them coffee which they politely refused. They told the old man they were going to dinner and had just wanted to come by and check on his welfare.

"Have you seen anyone out near old Will Goodson's cabin," Penny asked.

"Nary a soul," said Gus, shaking his head, "but I go over there every couple of days to check the place. There haven't been any new tracks on the trail. I notice the troopers took down the trail cameras. Ain't seen that old Chevy pickup either, I think they gave up on using it. You guys must have made it too tough on 'em," he said directing the answer to Haskins. "It's pretty easy to tell, with all this snow on the ground."

"Just the same, Gus, you need to be careful. Those are very dangerous men. If they find you snooping around they won't hesitate to shoot you like they did Penny." Haskins showed genuine concern for the old man.

"David's right, Gus, whatever they were up to they have either quit doing it or have changed to another location. In any case they wouldn't hesitate to eliminate you if they thought you could identify them. It's a long way out here and we couldn't get help to you in time to help. Please be careful." Penny placed her small hand on his arm as she spoke.

"Don't worry about me, Kiddo, nobody sees me comin' or goin'. I don't leave tracks for 'em to follow. I sure feel good about you folks payin' so much attention to me, though. It makes me feel like a real person." Gus meant the statement to be genuine. In the beginning he had worried about the men finding him. In the past few months his concerns had waned.

"You are a real person, Gus. We just want you to be careful." Penny patted his arm again.

"Aw, heck, Penny, I like having you come out and see me. I don't get many visitors, you know."

Haskins stood up, "Just the same, Gus, we like being able to stop out here for coffee." He turned to Penny, "I think we had better be getting back to town young lady. Your mother will be sending out a search party if I don't have you back soon."

"Yes, David, we do need to get back to town." She then turned to Sampson, "please be careful, Gus."

"I will, thanks for comin' and come again." He walked them the few feet to the door where he stopped and waited while they returned to the big pickup. He waved to them as they turned around do drive away.

"I hope Gus is as cagy and sly as he thinks he is," Penny had said on the trip back to town.

It was getting late now and Penny had said she didn't want a heavy meal. They agreed to stopping at a local sports bar where she ordered Cesar salad and iced tea. David had deep fried halibut and fries with coffee. The restaurant is loud with a dozen televisions on different channels playing sporting events. It is not a place for intimate conversation. After dinner they sat in the parking lot of the restaurant with the engine running on his truck in order to heat the cab. David held her hand and spoke softly.

"I love you Penny Rossiter," he said.

"I think I'm in love with you too David, but I'm not sure I'm ready to make a commitment yet. I hope you understand. My life is a little complicated right now, what with Julia's health and me still recovering from the injuries and the new job. There are just too many things for me to cope with. If I'm going to change my life and settle down I want to do it with you. I hope you can understand," she was hanging her head now, tears filling her eyes.

"I understand, Penny, and I'll be here when you decide what you want." It wasn't true, he didn't really understand, but his feelings for the little red-headed lady were strong and genuine. "I guess I had better get you home," said David while Penny sat silently.

Julia was in the living room wearing her night gown and slippers when Penny came in. "Well, tell me all about the date," she said with a huge grin on her lips.

"I really don't want to talk about it, Mom."

"He asked you, didn't he? He asked you to marry him."

"No, Mom, he didn't, but only because I stopped him. I'm not ready for that yet. Now don't ask me any more about it. Let's have some hot cocoa."

It was after ten when Conrad Dooley called Terry. Boyette had fallen asleep on the sofa with a half a glass of Jack Daniels sitting on the coffee table. The television was turned on, but the sound muted.

"You might want to have your other hired man, that Bobby guy, go over to his house and check on him in the morning. I don't think he will be coming to work." Dooley was reporting in to his new boss.

"Any complications?" asked Terry.

"Nope, he was glad to see me when I showed him the vial. He helped himself."

"Are you certain?" asked Boyette.

"I know my business, Boss. See you tomorrow at the office." Dooley didn't want to discuss business on the telephone.

Chapter 15

David Haskins had given Penny a sheet of printed information upon delivering her home the night before. In her office now and with a slow morning ahead she read the sheet. It was the report by a road trooper of sighting a Piper PA-12, red over white with a black accent stripe. It looked as if it had received a recent re-cover job. It was parked on a private airstrip off of Robinson Loop road near Sterling. The report included the aircraft numbers, but no information on the owner.

She realized she was no longer in the investigation business, but her curiosity drove her to call the FAA office in Kenai. The registered owner information is public and the supervisor, impressed by the call from Judge Bartolis' new aide, was happy to provide the details.

"That aircraft is a Piper, PA-12, registered to Anthony Leach. His mailing address is Sterling, but there is no physical location."

"Are there any violations on his records?" she asked.

"Ah," he paused, reading the form, "No, I don't see any," said the supervisor. "Do you need anything else?"

"No, but you have been very helpful and I thank you," Penny was making notes as she spoke.

"Can I ask? Has there been a complaint about this aircraft filed with your office?" he asked.

"Oh, no, nothing like that, we're just following up on information in another matter. I appreciate your help." She said goodbye and hung up the phone. Her next call was to David Haskins.

"Trooper Haskins," he answered.

"My, don't we sound official," she greeted the voice.

"You just can't stay away from me, can you?"

"Why would you say a thing like that? This is an official phone call."

"Yeah, right. Admit it. You just wanted to hear my charming voice this morning." He was laughing now.

"That's not so, I told you this is an official call."

"Then, excuse me, let me put my badge back on and be official. What is it you need, Ma'am?" he said in a sarcastic tone.

"Don't be mean David. I need a background check on and individual."

"I'm sorry Penny. I guess this really is an official call. What's the name?"

"Anthony Leach," she gave him the registered mailing address. "This is the name the FAA gave me as the owner of the PA-12 your trooper found. That plane might be the one seen at Hope at the time those two women were killed and the two boys went missing."

"Do you think this guy could be our killer?"

"I don't know, but I think you should check him out."

Haskins thought she was correct in her suspicious assumption. "I'll check him out and get back to you with what I find. I'll also send you a copy of his rap sheet, if he has one."

"Thanks, David," she said.

"One thing, though, Honey." He cautioned.

"What's that?" she asked.

"I just want to remind you that you aren't in the investigating business any longer. You should leave it up to us now. I really don't want to see you get hurt." His concern was more than professional, it was very personal.

"I promise to do that, David, but I can't help getting involved. After all, I was involved in this case from the start." In her heart she wanted to be involved, but knew she had no business sticking her nose in it now.

Twenty minutes later he called her back, "We got some information back about Anthony Leach. He works for a trucking company in Nikiski. He's a commercial truck driver with a good record. He's fifty one years old and goes by the name of "Bud" Leach. I talked with his boss and was told he is a good employee. He never misses work. Doesn't drink or cause problems. Has an excellent work record and is liked by the bosses and the rest of the drivers, a regular 'Mr. Nice Guy'. His physical address is where the airplane is parked. He has a house on the airstrip. I'll go out there and look around a little later today."

"Thank you, David. I had two open cases when I was hurt and this was one of them, the other being the guy who shot me, of course. I can't help wanting to be involved." There was a little sadness and regret in her voice.

"I know, Penny. Be a lawyer, sit back and let me do my job. I'll keep you informed all the way, I promise."

"Thanks David, call me if you learn anything. Bye."

She had spent too much time on this today and needed to get back to her real job. She didn't know how Judge Bartolis would take her being involved in an outside investigation. She felt she had not yet established a reputation to back her up if she was reprimanded for doing private chores while being paid by the court. It was time to get back to work.

It was early when Terry Boyette called Bobby Gunther. "Hello," answered a sleepy voice.

"Wake up, Bobby I have a job for you."

"Oh, good morning, Boss, I thought it was Kenny calling. What is it you want?"

"I tried to call Kenny, but he isn't answering. I want you to go into town and wake him up. We have work to do today and I need you both. Tell him to call me when he's awake enough to talk."

"OK, Boss, but it'll take me a couple of minutes to get dressed and wash up."

It took nearly a half hour for Bobby to dress, drive to town and to knock on the door of his fellow worker. Gunther seldom became impatient, but he was on a mission from Terry and when Pierce failed to answer his knock he tried the door. It was open. He called out through the open door with no response. Bobby knew when Kenny was doing heroin he sometimes slept in and often missed work. He stepped inside the small house and called again, again with no response. He entered with the intent of going to the bedroom and waking the sleeping Pierce, but when he entered he saw Kenny sprawled and slumped on his back on the living room couch.

Bobby rushed to the unconscious Kenny, but when he was close enough he could see the man was dead. There were needle marks in his left arm and a rubber tourniquet draped above the needle tracks. It looked of Bobby as if he had shot a load into his arm and when the tourniquet was released and the heroin flooded into his heart and brain he died instantly. He had seen this happen once before to another friend who used the stuff.

Bobby was frantic and shaking so badly he could barely dial the phone. "Mr. Boyette, this is Bobby. I found Kenny and he's dead. It looks like he was doing a load of "H" and overdosed. What should I do, Boss?"

"Are you sure he's dead?" asked Terry.

"Yeah, I'm sure. He's stiff as a board and his eyes are open a little."

"Be sure you stay 'till they come. They'll know someone was there and it would look bad if they had to track you down. Just stay there and answer all their questions when they arrive. I don't like being involved in this, but if you have to, you can tell them you work for me and went to Kenny's place to get him to go to work," Boyette instructed, "Don't tell them you called me. Just say you went there to get him to go to work and you found him like that and called 911. Got that?"

"Yes, Sir, I'll do it." Bobby said as he hung up and re-dialed the emergency number.

A tall trooper in a blue uniform was on the scene within three minutes. When he arrived he asked Bobby to step outside and wait. The trooper checked the body for pulse and sign of life, but here was none. Immediately he called the office and asked for the crime scene team to come and investigate. Five minutes later there were five more troopers on the scene looking at the body and securing the house to begin searching for evidence. A cursory inspection told the story. The victim was injecting himself when he overdosed on the drug. Two paper slips and a small glass vial were on the table and all had residue inside. A small sample was dropped into a testing kit, which immediately turned color indicating the substance was heroin. When David Haskins was certain the team was taking care of collecting evidence he went outside to tell the other trooper he was free to leave. Before leaving the trooper identified Bobby, sitting in his pickup, as the caller.

Haskins walked to the side window of the truck and asked Bobby to step out. After a quick search of the young man he asked him to have a seat in his patrol car. Bobby obliged and sat in the front seat where it was warm.

Haskins took a seat behind the wheel. "What's your name, Sir?" he asked.

"Bobby, Bobby Gunther." The answer came in a nervous voice, which was understandable given the circumstances.

"Bobby, would it be alright with you if we drove over to the trooper office to do this interview? It will be more comfortable than sitting here in the car. I'll bring you back when we finish."

"Yeah, I guess so," answered Bobby.

Once at the station Haskins seated Bobby in front of a desk in the office. He offered him a cup of coffee, which Bobby accepted. "Just relax, Bobby, this is just an information gathering interview. You aren't in any trouble."

"I'm glad of that," said Bobby. "I ain't never seen nothin' like that before. I just went to get him to go to work and he didn't answer the door, so I went inside to wake him up. I found him on the couch like that. I didn't know what to do, so I called 911."

"You did the right thing, Bobby. Drink your coffee. We just need to get some information from you. Do you have your driver's license with you?" Haskins asked, entering the information into a computer on his desk.

Bobby pulled a wallet from his hip pocket and fished the license out of the plastic compartment to hand to Haskins.

The interview lasted about a half hour and was winding down when team member Lou Filson called the office to say they were finished on the scene and had bagged the body for transport. He had contacted the Anchorage office and they had asked the body be taken to the crime lab for autopsy.

Haskins ordered his men back to the office and turned back to Bobby. "You say you worked with the victim, where do you work? We work for Mr. Terry Boyette. He owns a lot of property and we do all sorts of jobs for him. I have his phone number if you want it."

There were a few more question and discussion before letting Bobby Gunther be driven back to his vehicle by another trooper. As Bobby was leaving the crime scene team returned to the office carrying bags and boxes of evidence, which had to be marked, identified and cataloged for placement in the evidence storage locker. This process took more time than gathering the evidence took. After a short meeting with Lou and the team Haskins decided to have a meeting with the boss of these two handymen. He called Boyette's number to set a meeting with the boss.

"Mr. Boyette, I am Trooper Haskins and I am investigating an incident involving a person who I'm told works for you. Is it possible to meet with you and discuss this?"

"Certainly, Trooper Haskins, I'm in my office on Warehouse Street if you want to come by this morning." He gave the exact address to David.

The office was located in one end of a large warehouse on a back street in Soldotna. The area surrounding the warehouse was neat and clean. The parking lot was plowed and sanded. The office was in the front of the building and the lights were on inside. Boyette saw the trooper car park in front of the office and motioned through the window for the trooper to come inside.

The inside of the building seemed to be cold and without heating, but the office was warm and well-lit. Boyette was a slightly rotund man with a pleasant smile. He dressed in warm and expensive wool shirt and pants. His office was filled with file cabinets and shelves with Alaska Native art displayed on them. The desk was an expensive wood roll-top style and his chair was leather. The two chairs as well as the large sofa in the office were also done in cordovan color leather. It appeared this was the office of a successful businessman.

Boyette offered a seat to the trooper in one of the chairs arranged at the side of the tall desk. Terry held out his hand to shake that of the trooper.

"Terry Boyette, we've never met."

"David Haskins, Alaska State Troopers. It's a pleasure, Sir."

"You said there was an incident involving one of my employees. Can you tell me what the incident was?"

"I am sorry to be the one to have to tell you this, Sir, but does Kenny Pierce work for you?"

"Why, yes he does. I own several rental properties and he and another man, Bobby Gunther are my laborers. They keep the properties clean and painted and other such chores. He and Bobby were supposed to come here today to plow some snow at a property I just rented out." Boyette was being helpful and friendly. "Is Kenny in some sort of trouble?" he asked.

"I'm sorry to be the one to tell you, but Mr. Pierce is dead," said Haskins.

"Dead! Good Lord. How did it happen?" Boyette seemed surprised and shocked.

"Did you know he was a drug user, Sir?"

"I suspected, but I never saw him using it."

"Your other employee, Bobby Gunther, called this morning to report that Mr. Pierce had been found in his home, dead. It looks like an accidental overdose of what appears to be heroin. He said he went there to get him up to go to work and found him. Was he a good employee? By that I mean was he in the habit of showing up late or not at all?"

"Sometimes he was late, but always came to work. He was a good man when he was working." Boyette seemed to have another thought, "You say Bobby found him. Is Bobby all right?"

"Yes, I interviewed him and let him go home." Haskins pulled a pad from his pocket and placed it on the edge of the desk. "Would you mind answering a few questions?"

Boyette agreed and was interviewed for almost an hour before the trooper ended his efforts and went back to his office.

Chapter 16

I t was late in the afternoon when Haskins called Penny. She had been busy in the law library all day researching cases for the judge. She was beginning to enjoy the work. It was taking a while, but she was recalling her legal training from her college days. In college she was pretty darn good at this kind of research. Now it wasn't grades she was after, but case data for real cases being heard by Judge Bartolis. The judge was happy with her performance and complimented her several times on the quality of her research.

"Do law clerks get to talk with boyfriends while working?" Haskins asked.

"I am not a law clerk, Sir. I'm a Legal Aide assigned to a Superior Court Judge. Please address me properly." Penny could dish it out as well as take the teasing.

"I've never dated a legal aide. I think I'd like to try it. How would you like to go for a ride after work?" David asked.

"Where would you like to drive?"

"I was thinking we might go to Sterling to see where that PA-12 was located, maybe talk with the owner. His boss said he gets off work around five and should be home before six. I should go out and meet him. I thought you would like to go with me. I could whisper sweet nothings in your ear on the way back to town."

"Trooper Haskins! I'm shocked! That isn't very professional of you."

"But it is sincere. How about it, do you want to go with me?" he asked while chuckling.

"I would love it. What time?" she asked.

"How about I pick you up at your place just before six? This shouldn't take more than an hour and we can have dinner on the way home. You pick the place for dinner. We can bring something for Julia when we come home, if you like."

"I think I'd like that, David. Are you going to be armed? This man could be a murderer, you know." Penny was slightly apprehensive at the thought of being out in the bush without a weapon of her own.

"I'll be armed, but there's no reason this should turn into a confrontation. I just want to see if he was the one at Hope on that day. I understand how you feel, but I promise I won't let anything happen to you. I love you too much to see that happen." David tried to allay her fears, but didn't think he had been successful.

It was 5:45 p.m. when he drove to the front of her house. She had seen him pull into the drive and opened the door for him. Julia was seated on the sofa waiting to say hello. David stepped inside and passed pleasantries with Julia, but didn't take a seat. He was in a hurry to be on the way. Penny told Julia she would bring her something for dinner and closed the door behind her. It was a long climb into the cab of his big Dodge Ram truck, but once inside it was a luxury ride. He reached out to her and squeezed her hand prior to putting the truck in gear. There was little conversation on the fifteen mile trip to Leach's airstrip and home. The two just held hands and enjoyed each other's company. Once on Robinson Loop Road Haskins slowed to read the street signs and found the side-road he wanted. He made a left turn and eased his way about a mile to where Leach lived. The little Piper was in a lean-to style hangar at the end of the airstrip near the house. The house was neat, probably about 1500 square feet, with a detached garage. A Ford pickup was parked in front of the garage.

David parked behind the Ford and turned off the engine. He opened the door and stepped to the ground as the front door opened and a pleasant-looking man stepped out. He was dressed in gray coveralls and wearing a baseball cap with the logo of one of the oil companies embroidered on the front.

"Hello," said David, "I'm with the Alaska State Troopers," he said, displaying his badge and identification. "Are you Bud Leach?"

"Yes, I am, what can I do for you?" he said in a friendly tone.

"I'm investigating an incident that took place some time ago in the vicinity of Hope. I have witnesses who identified your airplane as being in the area at the time this incident occurred. Have you flown to Hope recently?"

"I go there quite often," said Leach. "I like to go up there and pan for gold. Recreational, you understand. Not commercially. When do they say I was up there?"

David checked his notebook for the exact date. He read it off to Leach, who took off his cap and ran his fingers through his hair. "You know, that was a while ago, but I may have been there. I can check my log book to be sure. I have a friend who lives there and when I go up to go panning, he leaves a pickup for me at the airstrip. His name is Don Bergman. He would know the dates I was there. What kind of incident are we talking about?"

"I really don't want to say, it's an ongoing investigation, you understand. I'm just checking out some of the information we received." Haskins wanted to change the topic, "Boy that's a nice PA-12. Did you have it recovered recently?"

"Sure did. I did it myself. I added a set of flaps and Cub landing gear with large axles and tires as well as six inch disc brakes. I had a new 160 horse Lycoming built for it. It sure is sweet to fly. Are you a pilot?"

"No, but my lady friend is. She would be interested in all the whistles and bells you added to the plane. Would you mind showing it to her?" asked Haskins.

"Not at all, I'm really proud of this bird."

Penny had heard the conversation and stepped out of the truck. "Hello, Mr. Leach, I'm Penny Rossiter. I love what you've done with the Piper. It's gorgeous, can I look?"

"Sure, come on and I'll show you. I have it on skis right now, but you can see the improvements." Leach led her to the little hangar and pointed out all the modifications he had made to Mr. Piper's Super Cruiser. Penny was impressed with the craftsmanship. This 1948 aircraft looked like it had just come from the factory. The fabric was synthetic instead of the original cotton. The paint was new poly aircraft paint rather than the original aircraft dope. She saw new style navigation lights and strobes. She noted a modern King radio as well as a GPS navigation system. The cockpit had a plastic ceiling, commonly referred to as a greenhouse. There was an extended baggage compartment and all new upholstery in the interior. The new larger engine and addition of wing flaps would surely improve the performance of both takeoff and landing. It was not only a pretty airplane it was undoubtedly a fantastic performer.

"I don't have much time in a PA-12, but I would give my eye teeth to fly this one. I congratulate you on your workmanship." Penny paid him a genuine compliment, but wondered if he was the one who had met and murdered the two sisters on Resurrection Trail.

"Come back sometime and I'll let you take her for a ride," Bud Leach was a modest man with a talent for working on aircraft. She wondered if all the modifications were signed off by FAA inspectors or if he had just done the work and ignored getting proper certification.

"I would like to do that, Mr. Leach," she confided.

"I have just a couple of things to discuss with you before we leave, Bud." Haskins was trying to get the conversation back on track.

"Sure, what do you want to know?" he asked.

"You say you have a friend who loans you a vehicle when you go gold panning. Would you give me his name and address? I may want to verify this with him."

Leach gave the information along with his telephone number and mailing address.

"You asked about our investigation. I can't tell you much, but I would like to ask if you saw two young, blond, ladies with two small boys while you were in the area?"

Leach rubbed his chin and thought a moment, "No, I don't recall anyone of that description. Is that what this is all about, some missing families?"

"Like I said, Mr. Leach, I can't explain to you right now, I'm sorry."

"That's alright, I understand your position. If there is anything I can do to help please let me know." Mr. Leach was being very helpful.

The two said goodbye and climbed back into their truck, waved and drove away from the house. "That went well, don't you think?" commented David.

"I don't know why, but he's still on my suspect list. I just thought he was a little too close to the mark when he asked about 'missing families'. You hadn't said anything about the boys being missing."

"How can you be impartial as a judge's assistant when you have suspicions like that?" asked David with a grin and patting her on the left knee.

"Perhaps I just had a flashback to my old trooper investigation days. I think there's enough to warrant a trip to Hope and talk with his friend," said Penny.

"Whoa, Lady, this isn't your investigation any longer. But, I do understand that when the bell rings the old fire horse wants go to the fire. I'll be going to Hope and talking with the witness, but I'll take Finlay with me. You can't be involved. You know that." David had known from the start it was a bad idea to take her with him when he talked to Bud Leach, but it had been a chance to be with her. "You are a wonderful and beautiful woman, and I love you, but we're going to have to keep our professional lives and our private lives separate. It was a bad idea to bring you out here and I'm sorry, but that's just the way it works."

"I know, David, I get carried away. I think you'd better take me home. I need to think." She didn't look at him as she spoke, but stared at the floorboards.

David wanted to say something, but knew there was nothing he could say that could repair her hurt. "If that's what you want," he said.

Earlier in the afternoon Terry Boyette called Connie Dooley. "Come on down to the office. We need to load some stuff and make a trip to Sterling. I'll call Bobby and see if he can make it to help us. I think the troopers bought his story. One of the troopers was here this morning and talked to me about Kenny. I gathered from the conversation they're considering this an accidental overdose."

"OK, Boss. I'll be there in a few."

Boyette had summoned Bobby Gunther and ordered him to meet them at the warehouse. In spite of what had happened there was still work that must be done. Once the supplies had been loaded into Bobby's pickup he was ordered to go to the barn and wait. Dooley would ride with Terry in his truck. On the way the two men discussed exactly how Kenny had met his end. Dooley assured Boyette it had been a clean hit and there was no reason for anyone to think it had been anything but self-inflicted. Terry thought Dooley was a competent man to put in charge of at least some of the collections and deliveries. This could free him to spend more time with his real estate dealings. There was a big boom coming in the oil business and Boyette wanted to be in on the ground floor when the deals began to be made. He wanted to be there with land for sale and warehouses to rent. When the oil and gas companies began to invest there would be a feeding frenzy. Terry planned to be one of the big sharks in the water when it took place. It would all be legal and very profitable. It was essential he could never be tied to the illicit drug trade that had made him the money to invest in his future.

Boyette began to educate Connie Dooley in the supply side of the drug business. He wanted Dooley to take over the manufacturing and distribution of meth. He warned Dooley of the hazards, both physical from the toxin he would be dealing in and legal from the diligent efforts of the Alaska State Troopers. He warned his new foreman not to underestimate the abilities of these cops. "They know their business," he had said.

At the barn he began to educate Dooley about the formulas and methods of manufacturing methamphetamines. There were cookbooks and measuring devices at the lab. He was instructed on keeping the generators and heaters properly fueled as well as controlling the vapors emitting from the operation. He cautioned the new man about tracks and footprints on the trail. Excessive traffic would bring suspicion and investigation. Caution and precaution were always the foremost concern.

Dooley was an apt pupil and had an interest in this business. It was his chance to become a rich businessman. He had already proven his worth as an enforcer to Boyette and now he would be running the show. He liked the way this was working out for him.

Chapter 17

Bobby Gunther took pleasure in working with Dooley. The young man had never been a thinker, but enjoyed being a doer. He liked the feeling of accomplishment when a job was finished and he could admire what he had done. Dooley, on the other hand, was a hard worker but prided himself on being a leader. Connie was a good organizer and leader. Bobby was a good follower, which made this a perfect relationship. The afternoon and evening was spent with Dooley re-arranging the storage area and cleaning out the lab. Bobby jumped to every command given by his new foreman. Bobby was working hard to impress Dooley with his energy and it was working. By late afternoon the place had a completely new look. Chemicals were stored in neat and orderly rows. Fuel containers were stacked near the door. Dooley had made a plan to eliminate the storage of fuel cans inside the little barn by putting a large fuel tank outside and piping the heating oil to the small stove with copper tubing.

He had also built a wall and cut a vent hole to the outside where he had moved the volatile chemical storage. This should reduce the chance of an explosion in the area where the chemicals were stored. Keeping them in an unheated portion of the shed would also reduce the danger of accidental ignition. The reorganizing went well and by late in the afternoon Conrad Dooley surveyed his labors and was satisfied with the efforts. The new wall reduced the amount of space in the front of the small barn, but made it a perfect little office. He made a note to acquire a small desk and a couple of chairs. A better light would be nice, too, an LED fixture, he thought.

One final item caught his attention. Fumes from the lab were seeping into the new office. This was neither healthy nor safe. He made a note to buy some weather stripping to insulate the cracks around the door. Yes, he thought, this will do.

Dooley rode back to town with Bobby in his old pickup. As conversation he asked, "Too bad about your old partner, Bobby. How was he to work with?"

"Not very good," said Bobby. "And he was crazy. He's done some real crazy stuff. I hated to be around him when he done that stuff."

The comment drew curiosity from Dooley, "What do you mean, Bobby, what kind of stuff?"

"He's dead now so I guess it won't hurt for you to know. I was with him when he killed two different people and he shot a trooper. He was a crazy guy."

"He shot a trooper?"

"Yeah, Mr. Boyette was trying to buy a piece of acreage up Funny River Road and the guy didn't want to sell. The three of us went out there and Mr. Boyette had a paper for the old man to sign, but he wouldn't sign it. Mr. Boyette told Kenny to make him sign and went back to town. Kenny liked beating on people and he took a big birch stick and beat the guy while I held him. He beat him and beat him, but he still wouldn't sign the paper. Kenny just kept beating him and beating him. I told him to stop, but he kept it up after I let the old guy go. The old man died. I didn't like that."

"Wow! That must have been hard on you. You said he killed two people. Who was the other one?" asked Connie.

"Yeah, a couple of days ago, Mr. Boyette had us go out to North Kenai and collect some money from a mechanic who worked for a trucking company in Nikiski. We waited outside the garage until the mechanic came outside for a smoke. Kenny asked him for the money and he said he didn't have it. Kenny asked him a couple of more times and then hit him with the fish bonker from his pickup. He really smacked the guy. He kept saying he didn't have the money and Kenny kept beating him. I told him to stop, but he just kept hitting the guy. He was a bloody mess and I told Kenny we had to get out of there and we left. Mr. Boyette was really mad about that one too."

Dooley was now getting a better picture of his new boss. Warning signs were going up. He was going to have to be careful about dealings with his new boss, Terry Boyette. Connie didn't mind doing a killing for the boss, but this one was in the habit of leaving a lot of bodies lying around. That habit could bring down a lot of jail time for anyone associated with him.

"Well, you can relax now, Bobby. I don't do that kind of thing. You won't have to do it any more either." Dooley was trying to build some loyalty with his new employee. "You said Kenny shot a trooper, I think I heard about that. Were you there when it happened?

"No, I was out fixing a rental property for Mr. Boyette. He had sent Kenny out to that place where we beat up the old man. Mr. Boyette was getting ready to buy the property and wanted Kenny to clear some land behind the cabin and to keep people off the place. Kenny was out there when a lady trooper came out to check on the place. Kenny heard her coming and waited for her by the cabin. When she got to the edge of the clearing he shot her with a 12 gauge shotgun. I don't know how she done it, but she lived. She must have been a real tough lady. Kenny was a good shot. Anyway, there was somebody with her and he called for help, so Kenny sneaked out the back way and through the woods before any help came. Mr. Boyette was really mad about that one and didn't buy the property after all. He gave Kenny heck something awful over that one."

By now the two were back in Soldotna where Connie's vehicle was parked in the lot on Warehouse Street. He stepped out of the pickup and turned to speak to the driver. "You and I are going to get along just fine, Bobby. Thanks for your help today." With that he waved and closed the door. As Bobby drove away Connie entered the boss' office.

"How did it go, Connie?" asked Terry.

"I made some changes out at the barn. Nothing drastic, but it needed to be reorganized. I need to stop at the hardware store and get a couple of things. By the way, do you know where I can get my hands on a 300 gallon fuel tank? I want to get the stove fuel out of the building." Dooley described the modifications he had made at the barn.

"It sounds like you're making progress. How're you getting along with Bobby?" asked the boss.

"I think we're going to work good together. He tries hard and wants to do a good job. He has the right attitude for this job and he keeps his mouth shut. He'll work out."

"Glad to hear it. About the fuel tank, I think I have one here in the warehouse. Let's go take a look."

Connie followed his boss to the open warehouse where stacks of material and parts were piled along both walls. An old Chevy pickup was parked inside. Near the front of the pickup was a large metal tank painted black. Markings on the end said it was a 500 gallon tank. Dooley looked it over and was satisfied it was just what he needed. He wrote a short list of parts he would need to plumb the fuel tank into the heater inside the building.

"Can I use this old truck to haul the tank to Sterling?" Connie asked his boss.

"Yes, but I don't want it to be seen more than necessary, so do the hauling in the dark if you can. Bobby can help you." Boyette pointed to the other end of the warehouse. "There is a large tool box on the floor by those lockers. You should find everything you need to do the job in it."

"Thanks, I'll try to have it ready to go by tomorrow afternoon when it gets dark," said Dooley.

"Good, do whatever you need," Terry said, reaching inside his pocket for a key. "Here's a key to the warehouse. You can come and go as you like. I have to leave now. I have a meeting in Kenai about some property in North Kenai. You have my cell phone number. Call me if you need anything. Do you have enough cash to buy the parts you need?"

"I think I could use another hundred or so for parts to get the tank ready."

Boyette reached inside a pocket and came out with a roll of bills. He peeled off two crisp $100 bills and gave them to Connie.

Dooley walked down the street to the hardware store to buy the parts he needed. He found all the fittings for the tank as well as the weather stripping to seal the interior door. He also found a new ceiling light fixture for the newly built office area. He carried the two large plastic bags back to the warehouse and went to work. It didn't take long to install the new fittings on the tank and screw a new locking cap on the filler pipe. When finished he stepped back to survey his work. Everything looked like it would work as planned, but it struck him they needed a more efficient means of filling the fuel oil tank. Tomorrow, he thought, he would go to the industrial hardware store in Kenai to buy a large fuel tank with an electric pump, hose and nozzle. He gathered some tools and put them in the old pickup for morning before turning out the lights and locking the shop.

David Haskins had gone to the office to finish some work, but could not concentrate. He was worried about Penny and what he had said to her. The more he tried to work the more distracted he became until he was compelled to call her.

Julia answered the telephone. He heard her call for Penny when she learned who was calling. "She says she doesn't want to talk to you right now," said the mother.

"Tell her I can't leave it like this and I'm coming over to see her." He didn't wait for an answer, but hung up and walked to his truck. On the way to her house he stopped at the Safeway store and bought a dozen red roses.

When he arrived she was bundled in a heavy jacket and standing on the front porch. Obviously she didn't want to have this conversation in front of her mother. David stopped the truck and opened the door. "Come on and get inside where we can talk, please."

She walked slowly to the passenger side of the truck and climbed into the seat. When she shut the door he gave her the flowers. She held them to her face and smelled the roses. There were tears in her eyes.

"I'm sorry, David, I shouldn't have acted like that. You were right. If it were me investigating this case I would have done the same thing. It's just that I feel I'm still a part of it. I don't want to sit by and leave all the investigation to you and others. Please forgive me." She held back the sobs, but the tears betrayed her efforts.

"I'm the one who's sorry, Penny. If Leach is the one who killed the two women and abducted the boys, he's a dangerous man. You were almost killed once and I don't want anyone else trying to do the job. I love you too much." He reached for her hand, "If this is going to be our first fight, how about we just kiss and make up now?"

She was sobbing now and reached out with both arms to grasp his neck. She held him tightly, sobbing. "Oh, David, I'm so sorry. I'll try to do better. Please forgive me."

He hugged her, "Would you like some dinner now?" he asked.

She pulled the mirror around to inspect her tear-stained face. "Yes," she said as she took a small handkerchief from her pocket to wipe her cheeks. "Let's not fight any more," she said, I don't like it very much."

Chapter 18

Before leaving the warehouse Dooley called Bobby and told him to meet him there at 6 a.m. Bobby was punctual and the two men went inside to manhandle the large tank into the bed of the old Chevy and secured the load with a single cloth strap to prevent it from sliding rearward. He ordered Bobby to drive it to the little barn while he followed in his own truck.

At the work site Dooley had noted there was some small spruce poles stacked near the barn. He used those to fashion a stand of sorts to support the tank. Once the tank was on the stand he noted it was about daylight. This prompted him to have Bobby take the Chevy back to the warehouse and come back in his own pickup. Dooley stayed at the little barn to secure the tank on the makeshift stand and hook up the fuel lines to the heaters inside the building.

He had just finished with the tank when Bobby returned. "You should have waited and I could have helped you," he said.

"It's OK, Bobby, I managed. Come inside and I'll re-light the heater. We have to keep this place warm and I'm finished out here."

The two men went inside to re-light the small oil heater in the outer part of the building. A fan had been devised to circulate heated air to the lab section of the barn. A small squirrel-cage type fan was attached to the eight inch pipe, which vented the fumes from the lab to the outside. It was a crude system, but it worked. The lab stayed warm and without the vapors which were vented out through the roof to keep from contacting the heat source and igniting an explosion. This was a dangerous business. The air volume was sufficient to dilute the density of the fumes and helped in keeping the locals from noticing.

Unlike the marijuana growing business, which required large banks of lights and water pumps, electricity was generated on site by a small portable gasoline powered generator. The entire operation was off the main road and concealed on the wooded lot. Few curious visitors came to the spot. 'No Trespassing' signs at the end of the trail discouraged most of them from investigating the property. Dooley knew that sooner or later someone would snoop around and guess what was being done here. Like Boyette, he knew they needed an alternate location for when that occurred. He would discuss it with his boss and start looking for another spot to build another lab.

Heat was up to the normal and the two men sat at the makeshift desk enjoying the luxury.

"The cops came to my place again last night," mentioned Bobby.

"Yeah, what did they want?"

"They had a bunch more questions about Kenny, 'cause you know, I found him dead."

"I know, that must have been awful for you," said Connie.

"Yeah, it was. Kenny and me weren't really friends. We worked together a lot, but I never did like him much. He was really crazy. He liked to hurt people. He liked it too much."

"Did you tell the police about that?" asked Dooley.

"Oh, heck no, I was with him when he did some of that stuff and I don't want anybody to know about it."

"You're a good man, Bobby. I'll talk to Mr. Boyette about getting you a raise. You deserve it." Dooley had learned long ago that a small pat on the back of a flunky went a long way toward loyalty. "I think we're finished here for now. Go on home and I'll call you when I need you. I don't know what the boss has on his mind, but he went to a meeting last night and I haven't seen him this morning."

"When you see him, tell him I could use a little more grass. I'm out of smoke." Gunther was a little too open about his habit, thought Dooley.

On his way back into town Dooley stopped at Buckets, a local sports bar, to try their early morning breakfast. As it turned out it was exceptionally good. He was sipping the last of a tall glass of orange juice when Boyette called, summoning him to the office.

Penny had become accustomed to the routine in the judge's office. When a trial was in session she would have little to do but wait for a recess when the judge would give her a list of things to research during the next part of the hearing. She spent many hours in the law library, on the computer and reading legal journals. Judge Bartolis was a demanding taskmaster. A stickler for details and tolerated no errors. He was also fair and good natured when not at his desk. Penny had learned to appreciate his professionalism and admired his ethic.

The auburn haired Legal Aide sat at her desk waiting for the judge to bring her a list of duties when she decided to call Julia. "Hi, Mom, how are you doing today?"

"Just fine, Dear," she answered. "I was hoping you would call. I was thinking how nice it would be to have David come over for dinner tonight. What do you think?"

"I can call him and ask if he's free to come. What are you fixing?"

"I was thinking some kind of pasta dish. How does that sound to you?" asked Julia.

"I think if you keep feeding me like this I'm going to have to go on a diet. I don't work out as much as I used to and you'll be putting pounds on me. I know David likes that shrimp and pasta dish you make and that I always eat too much of when you fix it. I'll call him and get back to you."

David and Ray Finlay were riding together on the way to Hope when the phone jingled. David explained he was unable to speak freely right now, telling Penny what he was doing. He said he would call her when they returned. In the past he had never realized how inconvenient his work had been to his personal life, a personal life that had now suddenly become very important to him.

He and Finlay were able to locate the friend of Leach without difficulty. They asked if he had loaned Bud Leach a truck on the date of the murders. He looked at a calendar on the kitchen wall and confirmed he had. David made notes of the conversation in his book. Finlay had the man's driver's license in his hand, writing that information in his notebook. The man said he had not seen Leach on that trip, but Bud had left an envelope with a hundred dollar bill in the glove box when he left it at the airport. He had done the same in the past.

When the questions ended the two troopers thanked him and were about to leave when David asked, "Did you notice anything different about the truck when you got it back?"

"Now that you mention it, I did. He's usually alone when he comes, but there were mud and tracks on the passenger side floor mats when I picked it up. It looked like he had a kid with him."

Haskins looked at Finlay. Both men asked at the same time, "Can we take a look at the truck?"

The man nodded and led them to an old shed behind the house. A fence bordered the property on the east side, a fence entirely overgrown with raspberry vines. The owner found a shovel and scooped snow away from in front of the door. He opened the door enough to let the men enter. Finlay inspected the bed of the truck while David shone a small flashlight inside the cab of the truck. The pickup was old, but looked in almost new condition. There was nothing to be seen inside the cab of the truck.

"You must have cleaned it up after he used it," Haskins commented to the owner.

"Yeah, there isn't much to do here in Hope and I spend a lot of time messing with this old pickup."

"It's a beauty, all right." He stepped back to speak with Findley, "Find anything, Ray?"

"Nope, she's spotless."

The troopers helped the man close the garage door and walked back to the front of the house. "Sorry to take up your time, Sir. We just needed to check out what Mr. Leach had told us. Thank you."

Back in the patrol car with Finlay driving, David was reviewing his notes. "I think we may have stumbled onto something, Ray. This guy was pretty specific about seeing what he described as child's footprints on the floor mats. Do you suppose Leach killed the mothers and took the boys back to his airplane in the truck?"

"That same thought occurred to me, too, David," Finlay commented. "You've seen Leach's plane, is it big enough to transport three people?"

"The PA-12 is configured to accommodate three. The rear seat is almost double width and has two seatbelts." David wanted to take another look at the inside of the little Piper. Leach would be at work when he reached Sterling and thought it would be a good idea to take a look at the plane without Leach as a guide.

After getting into his own patrol car in Cooper Landing and saying goodbye to Finlay he called Captain Meadows to ask if he would need a search warrant. Meadows said he could look from the outside, but not open the door or get inside. This complicated things, but he wanted to look anyway.

When he reached Leach's property he drove directly to the hangar where he stepped out of the snow into the small lean-to covering the plane. He shined his flashlight into the cabin through the Plexiglas side windows to the floor of the rear seating area. Like the pickup it was spotless. Leach had cleaned the airplane with as much care as his friend had cleaned the pickup he used. Haskins looked around the open hangar, peering into cans and bins, desperate to find some indication the two boys had been in the hangar. He found nothing. Before leaving he took a business card from his wallet and placed it in the edge of the door where Leach was sure to find it.

It was late afternoon and the sun was low in the sky. The temperature was dropping quickly. Tugging his coat collar up around his ears he made his way the short distance to his patrol car and stepped inside behind the wheel.

He sat there a few moments before putting the car in gear and driving away toward Soldotna.

He was still driving on Robinson Loop Road when his phone rang. He pulled off the road and stopped to answer it. The caller was the lieutenant at the crime lab in Anchorage.

"How ya doin' Haskins?" asked a friendly voice.

"Winning some and losing some, how are you getting along with the dead guys I've been sending you?"

"That's the reason I called you, David. The last one, Kenneth Pierce, the drug OD…we finished him up today and found something strange. How many needles did he have when you found him?"

"Just one and it was still in his hand. I have the photos of the scene to verify it, but needles are one of our priorities when we visit a drug scene. Why do you ask?" The lieutenant had peaked Haskins curiosity.

"One of the new techs noticed two sizes of fresh needle tracks, both done within minutes of his death. The angle of insertion on one of those holes was entirely different from the other and it didn't seem probable it was done by the same hand. The first needle was much shorter and smaller, like an insulin needle. The second one was much larger and at least an inch longer. The larger needle had been inserted from the opposite side of the arm. It appears he had some help with the second one." The Lieutenant was reading from a report.

"I'm on the road right now, Lieutenant, but I'll need a copy of the report. It looks like I'll have to pay another visit to the one who found him. Thanks for the up-date." Haskins noted the time and made notes in his book.

"Say, David, how's that lady trooper that was shot a few months ago? Did she ever go back to work?"

"No, sorry to say, the department retired her out. She had some internal injuries they said might cause her to be injured or killed if she was struck in the same area. I miss her too. She was a good investigator and easy on the eyes."

"You lecherous old man, gets back to work. I'll send this report to you right away. Be seeing you, David.'"

David was finishing the last of his notes when his telephone rang again. It was Penny.

"Julia wants me to ask you to come to dinner tonight," she began.

"Sounds great, what time?" he asked.

"Is seven good for you?"

"Yes, I'm headed to the office now. I'll have to finish up on a couple of things and go home to change clothes, but I'll be there. I suppose a bottle of wine is out of the question?" he asked.

"You know it is, David, just bring yourself and be on time." She chided him for even mentioning wine for Julia.

"What are we having?" he asked.

"Julia is fixing the shrimp Alfredo dish you liked so well."

"I may show up early. See you." he said, looking forward to the evening with Penny.

Chapter 19

When Dooley came to Terry's office the previous morning he was given a list of small errands to perform. He was to make several rental collections and take the money to the bank. When he finished he was given the rest of the day off.

"Tomorrow will be busy," Terry had informed him.

Today Dooley came to the warehouse early. He let himself inside and waited for Boyette who came into the office a little before seven. He was surprised to see Dooley waiting for him.

"Anxious to get to work, I see," commented Boyette.

"I'm an early riser," Dooley replied.

"I'm putting a land deal together and I want you to take over the manufacturing and distribution business. I'll give you a percentage of the take in addition to your salary. Bobby will continue to work for you. If you don't want to work in the lab, you can hire another man. I'll leave that up to you; however I must impress on you the importance of the operation in Sterling. That little business is what allows me to finance the land acquisitions and rental business. As always, I don't want any of the drug sales to lead back to me. I have a reputation to maintain in this small community." Terry handed Connie Dooley a small notebook, "This is a list of customers and accounts. Supplying the product and collecting from the customers will be your responsibility. You'll see there's a note by each name. Those numbers represent the maximum amount of product that person is allowed to get without cash. Bobby knows these people and can help you until you get your feet on the ground. Bobby is a nice kid, but he isn't capable of making decisions on his own. Enforcement will also be your responsibility. If someone doesn't pay on time, I want him hurt. Hurt, you understand, not killed like Kenny liked to do. He left too many bodies around. Sooner or later that kind of thing will lead an investigation to us and I don't want that to happen. Do you think you can handle the job?"

"Sure, but I have one question."

"And what is that?"

"What kind of percentage are we talking about?" asked Dooley.

"Five percent of the gross in addition to the salary," Terry said, then added, "Don't get greedy, Connie. I'm warning you, this is my operation and it will remain my operation. You work for me and don't forget who's the boss, got it?"

"What about supplies? I don't have any suppliers for the chemicals we need," mentioned Dooley, thumbing through the notebook Terry had given him.

"You let me know what you need and I'll have it delivered to the warehouse. Anything else?"

"Nope, sounds good to me. Thanks for the promotion, Boss. I'll get started this morning." He started to leave, but stopped to ask, "What about the old Chevy? Can I use it to take supplies out to the lab?"

"Yes, but be careful. Kenny used it to do some of his work and it may be recognized. I've been thinking of selling it and getting another one."

"What if I painted it?" asked Dooley.

Terry thought a moment, "That would be cheaper than trading. Go ahead and do it."

"I'll try to get by with just me and Bobby for now. If it gets busy I'll hire someone."

"That's up to you now," said Boyette.

Connie sat in his truck reading the notebook. There were timetables for rental collection and a list of drug dealers with regular orders. Terry had also included a list of supplies, which had been ordered. At the back of the booklet were several names with amounts owed and dates of payment. The list wasn't long, but Bobby would have to point them out to him.

Dooley called his employee, "We've got work to do, meet me at the lab."

"I'll be right there, Connie," Bobby replied cheerfully.

While waiting for Bobby to come into town Connie made a list of materials he would need to build a small paint booth in a far corner of the warehouse. When Bobby arrived Connie gave the list to him and asked him to go to the hardware for the items. He would go to the auto supply store for the paint and primer, sandpaper and air filtration masks they would need for the work. While the paint was being mixed he made a stop at the Fred Meyer store for a two foot square box fan and some furnace filters as a ventilation system for his new paint shop.

He met Bobby back at the warehouse and began construction on the framework for his paint booth. It would be framed of plastic conduit pipe. It was easy to work with and cheap to construct. The framework was wrapped in plastic tarps and taped in place with duct tape. The box fan was placed on the window ledge and a cardboard baffle made to fit above it to keep out the cold. Furnace filters were placed over the back to the fan to keep paint dust from exiting the booth. A hole was cut in the plastic on the opposite end of the plastic booth and a large electric space heater to it with some make-shift ducting. When the chore was completed Dooley stood back to admire his handiwork. It had been annoying to work around the old Chevy while they built the structure around it, but the two could now do their sanding and painting in a clean, warm area. The finished product would look professionally done. The missing tailgate worried Dooley, but he surmised he could order a replacement from the internet. Other than the tailgate the old pickup was in pretty good shape and, with a decent paint job, would be admired by auto nuts in the area.

"I have some things to do for Mr. Boyette, Bobby. It's still early and this thing has to be sanded down before we paint. I'd like to have you take that palm sander," he pointed to a small box near the tool chest, "and start sanding the entire truck. It doesn't need to be down to the metal, but it does have to be smooth. Do you think you can handle that?" asked Connie.

"Sure, Connie," said Bobby energetically, "I took auto shop when I was in high school. I like doing that stuff. I'll try to get it done today."

"Thanks Bobby, do you want me to bring you a coke or something?" Connie asked.

"No, I'm good," he said, adjusting the filtration mask to his head.

"Lock up when you leave. I'll see you here in the morning."

It was late afternoon and dark outside when Dooley left the warehouse. He was to deliver some product and meet with three different drug dealers tonight. Boyette had said he would call the dealers to tell them what to expect. Dooley expected the meetings to take extra time because he would have to introduce himself and get acquainted with the dealers he was about to meet.

Hours later Dooley had finished his 'business' meetings. After introducing himself and explaining that he would now be the contact person and supplier for all drugs on the Kenai Peninsula he had given the impression he was a no-nonsense player and would tolerate no late payments or attention by police. "Keep our business private or get out," he had said. At the conclusion of each of the meetings the customer was left with no doubt about who was running the show from now on. It was late when he returned to the warehouse.

Inside, the lights were still on and Bobby was busy inside the little plastic enclosure. As he approached he could see the truck was nearly stripped of paint and looking clean. He pushed the curtain aside and stepped inside. "Great job, Bobby, this old bucket looks like it could use some paint."

"Thanks, Connie, I just finished wiping it down with Prepsol. I think she's ready for primer," Bobby said proudly.

Dooley walked all the way around the pickup, inspecting the sanding task. It looked good, especially good for this old truck. "Man, you did a good job, Bobby. Are you too tired to help me spray a coat of primer on it tonight?"

"No, I'm OK, it won't take long to paint it and I got nothin' else to do."

The two men set about mixing the paint and testing the new spray gun. Satisfied everything was working well Dooley asked Bobby to wait outside the paint booth while he sprayed primer on the entire vehicle. Once done he walked around the truck to inspect his work. Satisfied he stepped out of the paint booth with the spray gun in his hand.

"I think we can clean the gun and quit for tonight. In the morning I'll wipe it down again and spray the color coat." Dooley spoke like an autobody craftsman and had, in fact done this work for a couple of years when he was young.

"What time do you want to start?" asked Bobby. "I'll come in and get things ready."

"Meet me here at six. I'll buy breakfast when we finish."

The two men cleaned the equipment and checked the heater and fan to be sure everything was working properly before turning out the lights and leaving the warehouse.

David Haskins and Penny Rossiter were sitting in the living room while Julia was in the kitchen cleaning up the dinner dishes.

"She seems to be slowing down," commented David.

"You noticed," said Penny. I'm beginning to worry about her. She can't even sweep the floors any longer. The doctors say she'll continue to go downhill. I've been looking around for an assisted living place for her for when the time comes. I like the new one over by the river. The staff is nice and the place is super. I think the time is coming soon when she'll be unable to care for herself while I'm at work and it'll be necessary to get some kind of help for her. I hate to think about it, but the time is fast approaching, whether I want it to or not."

"Have you talked with her about it?" asked David. "How does she feel about going to assisted living?"

"We've talked about it and she's agreeable. I'm the one who doesn't want to see her go."

"I understand, Penny. This will be a tough decision for you. Whatever you decide, I'm with you."

They sat on the sofa. David put his arm around her and held her close. When Julia finished in the kitchen she pushed her walker into the living room, tailing the hose from the oxygen generator behind her.

"I'm tired, kids. I'm going to bed." Julia was struggling for breath.

"OK, Mom, I'll come say good night in a little while."

"I see what you mean," said Haskins. "I had better go and let you help her. I'll talk with you tomorrow." He kissed her and stood to leave.

The following morning at the warehouse Bobby Gunther was waiting in the parking lot when Conrad Dooley arrived. A light snow was falling, but the lot was plowed. The two men entered to find the fresh coat of primer had dried perfectly. The finish coat was mixed and readied. Bobby admired the Forest Green color Dooley had selected. This old truck was about to become a work of art. An hour later the truck was dark green and shining like an emerald. The two men cleaned the spray gun and left to go eat some breakfast.

"I looked on the internet last night and found a new tailgate for the pickup," said Dooley over his hot coffee. I ordered it and they said it would be here in two days, UPS. When it comes we will have to paint it before we put it on. I think the old rig will do a good job for us."

"Kenny used to drive the Chevy when he was doing a job and didn't want to be recognized. I never liked going in it 'cause I thought too many people had seen it at too many bad scenes. I like it now. It looks neat and nobody will think this is the same old truck." Bobby was becoming an admirer of Conrad Dooley and his varied skills.

"I bought some thin, gold striping tapes to go on the green paint. Do you want to help me pinstripe it in the morning?" Dooley was beginning to like the kid. He was quite intelligent, though uneducated. Dooley remembered when he started in this business, many years ago, he was exactly the same, but he learned.

Chapter 20

The days were getting longer, slowly, minute by minute, but they were gaining daylight hours. It was still dark outside and light snow was falling when David Haskins met with his Crime Scene Team in a small conference room at detachment headquarters. There were several items on his agenda, but two stood out. The first was the call from the lieutenant in charge of the crime lab.

"OK, guys, let's get down to business. Lou, who's doing the follow-up on the heroin OD in Soldotna?" asked Haskins.

Filson pointed a finger to the man at the end of the table, "That one belongs to Don Winston."

Haskins directed his next statement to the tall trooper with wavy dark hair seated at the end of the table. "Don, I received a call from the LT at the crime lab last night. He is sending a full report, but told me on the phone that your victim, Kenny Pierce, probably had help with his last injection. He said two different needles were used and the second one was much larger and at an angle not possible by the victim himself. I'll give you a copy of the report as soon as it arrives, but this morning I want you to take one of the other guys and go back to the house and go over it again. This time we're not looking at a suicide or accidental OD, we may have a murder. Do a full forensics retrieval, you know the drill. If you need additional help you can take one of the other troopers, just let me know who you want.

Winston had been busy taking notes and never looked up as he said, "OK, Boss. I'll use Lee and Paul." He continued to write as he spoke.

"Good. Lou I have something I want you to look at. Finlay and I went to Hope to interview a man who loaned a pickup to the owner of the PA-12 seen at the Hope Airport on the day of the killings on Resurrection Trail. We tracked the plane to a man by the name of Anthony Leach, he uses the nickname Bud. I don't know how, but we need a search warrant for the inside of the airplane and his house. The two boys are still missing and may be alive. If they are we have to find them quickly. This killer has murdered at least two women and could harm the boys. This is important. Come to my office when we finish here and I'll give you what I know."

"OK, David, but we really don't have any evidence to justify a search," said Lou.

"I know, and we can discuss it in my office." He cut off the conversation making Filson shake his head in wonderment.

"One last item. Who is following up on the Will Goodson case?" asked Haskins.

Filson raised his hand, "We don't have anyone assigned to it because we ran out of leads to follow. His pal Gus calls every couple of days to ask about the case. We all take turns driving out to check on him, but nothing new has come up."

"I've been looking at these cases and one thing hit me. The OD victim, Pierce, bares a close resemblance to one of the men described as being at the Goodson property. You remember, the three men in the old pickup. It seems strange to me no one has seen the truck again. Have Wilson or one of his men take a picture out Funny River Road and ask some of those witnesses if he is one of the three they saw in the truck. Gus Sampson may recognize the picture also. I know it's a long shot, but we don't have anything else right now."

"Anything else, Boss?" asked Filson.

"I guess not, let's go to work. Lou, I want to have you meet me in my office." Haskins gathered his papers and files to return to his little office where he added the papers to the clutter on his desktop. His team had been fortunate that no other big cases had crossed his desk in recent days, but it still baffled him as to why there was no answer to who shot Penny and killed Will Goodson. Additionally there was nothing new on the killing of the two women on the trail above Hope. He was stewing about the problem when Lou entered.

"You're letting this get personal, David. That was the first lesson you taught me when I came over to this side, 'don't let it become personal,' you said. Take a step back and above all don't let it get to be personal. Those are your words, Boss." Lou thought it was time for a reality check for Haskins.

"Yeah, Lou, you're right. I am taking it too personally. I'm going to have to be the administrator on this one. That's why I'm asking you to follow up on the search warrants for Leach's place. These were Penny's cases and I just can't think properly about them. You and the team will have to forgive me this time. It will mean extra work for all of you, but that's the way it will have to be for now. If I do it any other way the Captain will take me off the team and I don't want that to happen."

"OK, then, with that out of the way, do you have any ideas about getting a search warrant for Leach's property?" asked Lou.

"Only one, Lou, and it will be stretching the limits a bit." David slid a file folder with several sheets of printed material inside. "This is the information Finlay and I gathered from the pickup owner in Hope naming Leach as the one who rented the pickup from him at the time of the murders. There isn't any solid information to link him to the murders, but he was in the area and we're still looking for the missing boys. The judge may be a little more receptive if he knows the boys may still be alive and time is of the essence. Like I said it will be stretching a little."

"Do you think the Judge's new aide might help us out?" asked a smirking Filson.

"Get out of here and go to work," Haskins chided. "And thanks for understanding."

Don Winston and his partner made the trip twelve miles up Funny River Road to interview the people who had seen the three men in the old pickup. The first witness wasn't home and neighbors said he would be gone to his second home in Arizona until May. The second witness looked at the pictures of the late Kenny Pierce. He studied them for several minutes, but finally said he could be one of the men, but he couldn't be sure. The third witness said he was pretty sure Pierce was one of the men in the truck, but couldn't be positive.

With his frustration mounting the two men drove to Gus Sampson's home in the woods. Gus was in the shed splitting firewood when the troopers arrived. When he saw it was troopers he stuck the axe in the block and stepped out of the shed.

"Come on in, boys, and I'll put the coffee on." The two troopers followed Gus into the house. It was warm inside and it felt good. Gus was a neat housekeeper by the look of his house. After starting the pot to perking he returned to the living room to see what the troopers had on their minds.

"I would like you to look at some pictures, Gus. One of them could be part of the bunch you saw in that old Chevy pickup when Will was killed. We want you to be sure, so take a good look." He handed the groups of photos to the older man.

Gus studied the dozen or so photos for a long time. "There's only one of these that are of the men I saw." He was tapping his finger on the picture of Kenny Pierce. "He was one of the bunch, in fact he was the driver of the truck. Did you catch him?"

"We have him, Gus, but unfortunately he's dead from a drug overdose. But if you're certain he was one of the men we can question his associates. We really thank you Gus. This is the first real lead we've had."

"It's him alright. I'm glad he's dead and I hope you catch the others." The coffee was finished perking and Gus returned to the kitchen to pour three cups. When he returned the living room he asked. "How is Penny, I she doing OK?"

"Yes she is, Gus. She's working as legal aide to Judge Bartolis in Kenai. She seems to be healing up nicely. She and David Haskins have a thing going which none of us are supposed to know about." Looking over the rim of his coffee cup he gave Gus a sly wink.

"Good for her," Gus said, nodding his head.

When they left the house and were driving back down Funny River Road Don called Lou on the radio to ask him to meet them in the office. The men met to decide how to approach Bobby Gunther. After much discussion it was agreed it would be more likely to get Gunther to talk if he was to come to the trooper office. It was also agreed they would not pressure him, but try to get the young man to implicate Pierce in Goodson's death and Penny Rossiter's shooting. A short strategy was arrived at and, once done, Filson called Bobby on the phone to ask if he would come to the office for a short meeting. Bobby said he would be there in an hour. That time was spent making a list of questions to be asked. It was also determined they would not put much pressure on the young man as it could stop his cooperation. At this point he could ask for a lawyer and stop the questioning. This was always a delicate dance.

"Would you like a soda or some coffee?" asked Lou when Bobby was seated in his small office.

"I might drink a Coke, if you have one," replied Bobby.

Winston went for the drink while Filson began the questions. "Bobby, we have learned your old friend may have been involved in some serious criminal activity. We don't have any reason to believe you were involved, but we thought you might be able to confirm or dispel the word of our witnesses."

Winston entered the office with a can of Coke in his hand to give to the nervous Bobby.

"What kind of crimes do they say he done?" asked Bobby, sipping on the soda.

Filson opened a file folder and ran a finger down an imaginary list of crimes, "Let's see, we have assault, burglary, possible robbery, murder, attempted murder, it seems he is a suspect in a lot of bad things. Since the two of you worked together we thought you might know if he could have been present at the scene of some of these crimes."

"I didn't do none a that stuff," blurted Bobby. "Kenney was crazy. He liked to hurt people, but I didn't do none of it."

"Calm down, Bobby. We aren't accusing you of anything. We want to find out if Kenny was the one who did them. Were you with him when some of these crimes were committed?"

"Like what crimes?" Bobby put the soda can on the desk and clasped his hands between his knees.

"Let's start with the old man on Funny River Road. Did Kenny beat the old man up?" asked Filson.

Bobby was shaking his head, "He was crazy, he was supposed to get the old man to sell the property to us and move out. He didn't want to sell and Kenny started to beat him up. He went outside and got a big club and came back inside and hit the old man in the legs. The old man went down and started screaming, but he still wouldn't sign the sale papers. Kenny stabbed him in the gut with the end of the club and almost knocked the old guy out. Then he stomped on his arm and hand." Bobby had tears in his eyes now. "I think he broke his arm. Kenny kept hitting him until he passed out. I tried to stop him, but Kenny was having too much fun hurting the old man. After he passed out I went outside to get away from Kenny. I think he hit him again, just for the fun of it, and it killed the old man." Bobby was sobbing now. "Am I going to go to jail?" he asked.

"I don't know, Bobby, possibly, that isn't up to me. If you continue to cooperate with us it will help you a great deal, but again, that isn't up to me." Filson paused his questioning for a few moments for Bobby to regain his composure. "Do you feel like answering a few more questions?"

"I don't know. I said too much already." Again Bobby was sobbing.

"Will you tell me why you wanted to buy Will Goodson's property?"

"Our boss wanted it and told Kenny to get the old man to sign the sale papers."

"You say your boss wanted the property, for what purpose and who is he?" pressed Filson.

"I can't tell you that. He'd kill me." Bobby suddenly realized how much he had said, "I can't tell you anymore. I think I need a lawyer. I gotta have a lawyer."

Filson turned to Don Winston, "I think it's time to take Mr. Gunther to jail at Wildwood. Tell the Correctional Officers to allow him to call his attorney." He turned back to Bobby, "After you speak with your attorney we will be back to talk with you. My advice is that it will be easier on you if you cooperate with us. You can have your attorney call me." Filson gave Bobby one of his business cards.

With the sobbing Bobby taken out of the office in handcuffs and notes made in his log, Filson walked down the hall to brief his supervisor on the events.

Haskins was elated. After Filson went back to his own office David called Penny. "I think we finally caught a break in the case," he began. He gave Penny all the information he knew and said he would pass along the rest as soon as he knew the story.

112

Chapter 21

After Bobby Gunther was booked into Wildwood Pretrial Facility he was placed in an attorney visiting room where he could use a telephone without being monitored. The officer provided him with a phone book and stepped out of the room to wait. Bobby watched him go before dialing the number. He called Terry Boyette.

"Boyette," answered the voice, not recognizing the number on his caller ID.

"Mr. Boyette, it's Bobby, I been arrested and put in jail. I need a lawyer."

"You what?" Boyette shouted into the phone.

"I know... I can't believe it either. The troopers wanted to talk to me about Kenny again. I went to their office and they said someone told them I was seen with Kenny. I told them Kenny and me worked together doing jobs for you. They said I was seen with Kenny when he went to beat up that Goodson guy. I told them I didn't beat the old man up, but they said I helped and they arrested me. Please Mr. Boyette, I need your help. I gotta have a lawyer."

"Did you tell them you were working for me when you and Kenny went to Goodson's place?" asked Terry.

"No, sir, Mr. Boyette, I wouldn't do that. I didn't tell them anything about why we went there except we wanted Goodson to sign some papers and he wouldn't sign. I told them how Kenny went crazy and kept beating the old man. I didn't say nothin' about you."

"OK, Bobby, I'll send a lawyer to see you. He will be there in about an hour. Tell him everything he asks you. He works for me, too. Don't tell anyone else anything. You got me? Keep your mouth shut. We'll try to get everything laid off on Kenny. He's dead and can't deny anything. Now just sit back and wait and keep quiet. Got that?" Boyette was mapping his strategy and hoping it would hold up.

"I can do that, Mr. Boyette, but I want to get out of here." Bobby hung up the phone and waited for the officer to come back. He told the officer his lawyer would be here soon.

With that information the guard placed Bobby in a holding cell to await the arrival of the barrister. It was less than an hour, but to Bobby it seemed an eternity. After speaking with the lawyer he was disappointed to learn he would spend the night in jail and go to court in the morning. The lawyer said he would try to get him released when he went to court. Bobby spent the night in his cell, avoiding conversation with other inmates.

Later, after speaking with the attorney, Boyette called Connie Dooley to advise him of the arrest. Dooley felt Bobby would remain loyal, but his mental agility was no match for lawyers and troopers. The situation was out of his control, which made Dooley nervous. All he could do was wait for the lawyer to get the young man out of custody and back on the street. What to do next would depend on what happened at court.

Next morning in Judge Bartolis' chambers the clerk was reviewing cases appearing on the calendar this morning. When she read the report on Bobby Gunther she immediately went to Penny's office.

Without knocking she entered the office with a file in her hand. "Penny, you have to see this." Nancy Riddle was not one to be influenced or excited by anything coming across her desk, but this was different. "You were working on the Will Goodson murder case when you were shot, weren't you?"

"Yes. Why?" Penny inquired.

"They've arrested someone in connection with that case. A Bobby Gunther, he's some kind of handyman who works for a big property owner in Soldotna. It says here he was seen in the area with the man who probably killed Goodson. I know you'll want to get involved in this one, but I don't think the judge will allow it. I'll make a note on the file for the judge to read, but you are going to get a call from Judge Bartolis."

"Thanks, Nancy, I've been wondering how long it would be before this happened. I think you're right, the judge will keep me from this case." Penny handed the file back to Nancy, "Like everything else in this case, it's out of my hands."

"I'll let you know what happens," said Nancy as she turned to return to her own office.

When she was out of sight Penny called David, "You didn't tell me you arrested someone in the Will Goodson case."

"You know I can't discuss this with you, Penny. The reason for your call to me is the very reason I can't discuss it. You of all people should understand." David felt forced to defend himself.

"You could have told me, David." Penny spoke in an angry tone.

"No, I couldn't, and you know I couldn't. You know the policies as well as I do and I am not going to argue them with you. Neither of us can change them. I think you should cool off and call me back later."

His imperious attitude only enraged her more. "I don't think I have anything more to say to you." She slammed down the receiver and was immediately sorry for her words. He had been right. She was demanding what he was not allowed to share. This is where thought and feelings conflict. She knew in her mind he was correct, but in her heart she felt he should have called and let her know. It had become clear the two of them could never have a relationship as long as there were departmental lines separating them. There were always dividing lines in the criminal justice system and one of the biggest barriers was the division between law enforcement and the judicial system.

Penny could feel her emotions getting the best of her. She went to Nancy's office to inform her she was leaving for the rest of the day, 'to get her head straight' she had said. Next she checked the court calendar to learn the time set for arraignment for Bobby Gunther. It was set for 1:45 p.m. She also learned Assistant DA Stella Moore would be handling the case for the State of Alaska. At the hearing she sat in the back of the courtroom. Gunther was seated at the defense table with an attorney she recognized as Edgar Bishop. The hearing began precisely at 1:45 p.m. with Judge Bartolis the last to enter the courtroom.

The judge was introduced and everyone was allowed to be seated. The charges were read to the defendant and his attorney. The defendant was asked how he pled. He was standing as the charges were read. They were many including burglary, assault and accessory to murder.

"How do you plead?" asked the judge.

Gunther glanced at his lawyer who nodded at him to speak. "Not guilty, Your Honor," replied Bobby, his voice faltering. Bishop tugged at his arm to indicate he was time for him to be seated.

"The defense asks bail be set, Your Honor," said Bishop.

Assistant DA Stella Moore stood to say she wanted bail denied as Gunther was a flight risk.

Attorney Bishop claimed Gunther had local employment and had lived in the area most of his adult life. He had no family except an aunt and uncle in Soldotna making it unlikely he would flee, reminding the court he had pled Not Guilty to the charges.

Judge Bartolis had been advised by his clerk, Nancy, that this was the person in one of Penny Rossiter's trooper cases. The judge stared at his desktop for a long moment before looking up to give his decision. State statute demands all prisoners are entitled to bail. "Bail is set at one hundred thousand dollars, cash only. Next court date, May 15, 10 a.m."

Attorney Bishop stood. "I would like to post bail, Your Honor."

"See the clerk," said the judge, banging his gavel. With that final act he stood, gathered his files and exited the court while everyone stood.

Bobby stayed seated at the defense table while Bishop spoke to the Court Clerk. He leaned over her desk to write a check to the court.

When he returned to the table he told Bobby he would have to return to the jail with the trooper and would be released when he was processed. He said Conrad Dooley would be arriving to give him a ride home. He then recited the release instructions to Bobby and asked if he understood. He said he did.

An hour later he was seated in the entry area of the jail awaiting the arrival of Connie. He waited almost an hour for his ride to arrive, pacing, shuffling and worrying. When he heard the buzzer releasing the door he saw Dooley. He picked up his coat and said, "Get me out of here."

Penny left the courtroom to go directly home. Julia was surprised to see her. "What's wrong, dear?"

"Nothing—everything—please leave me alone for a while Mom. Please." She marched to her room to sit. She sat, she cried, she swore, she hated herself for what she had said to David. She hated the court, she hated her life, and she hated the world. Between fits of sobbing and fits of anger she became totally exhausted, falling onto the bed and going to sleep. When she awoke she went to the bathroom to wash her face and make an attempt at reestablishing her life.

It was after six when she dialed David. It rang six times before he answered. "Hello," was the short answer.

"David, its Penny, please don't hang up. I'm calling to apologize for today. You were right and I was a total fool. I guess I was just looking for someone to be mad at and you were the one I took it out on. I'm sorry. Can you forgive me?"

"Is this going to happen often?" inquired Haskins.

"Never again, I hope," said Penny. "I've been thinking about all this since I talked with you on the phone. I hate to admit it, but I was wrong. That may be the last time you ever hear me admit to it, but you were right and I had no right to put you in that position. Please forgive me?" Her voice was nearly a whisper when she finished.

"Neither you nor I make the policies, but we both have to live with them. We both know mixing professional and personal business is cause for bad decisions. How would you like to forget professional and go directly to personal? Can I take you to dinner?"

"Oh, David, you are the sweetest thing. I love you. Give me time to change clothes and I'll meet you with a kiss." Penny's spirits were buoyed and she felt happy for the first time since Nancy had broken the news about Bobby Gunther.

Connie Dooley had taken Bobby to the warehouse where they began to finish work on the old Chevy. The two men were finishing the pin striping when Terry Boyette came in and asked they meet with him in his office.

"I just came from a meeting with Edgar Bishop. Bobby, I want you to know I'm on the hook for '100 G's for you. Edgar doesn't know how strong the case against you is going to be, but he said 'don't get your hopes up.' He also said he thought the troopers were less interested in you than finding out who you work for. They know you work for me during the day and I'm OK with that, but they must never find out about my involvement in the drug business. I want you to work with Dooley and be invisible to the troopers. There's a lot of work to be done and product to be cooked. That work will keep you busy most of the time. I'll find work for you at the properties from time to time to make it look like you're still employed. The point of all this is that you cannot draw any attention." Boyette was satisfied Bobby would keep his name out of any of the illegal dealings. "If you want some weed I'll give it to you, but you can only smoke it at home at night. If you need anything else, ask Connie."

Chapter 22

Early the following morning a judge signed the search warrant for the hangar, aircraft and home of Anthony Leach. Two of the crime scene team went to the property to serve the papers, but no one was home. Lou called Leach's employer and asked to speak with him. His boss said he was on the road and couldn't be reached.

"Does he have a cell phone?" asked Filson.

"Yes," said the boss and gave the trooper the number.

Leach answered and said he was in Homer at the dock.

"This is Trooper Filson. We have a search warrant for your property in connection with a felony crime. It's necessary for us to search the inside of your airplane, your hangar and your home. I wish you were here while we do this, but since you're in Homer we are informing you of our entry."

"I don't care if you search, just don't break anything. The key to the airplane is in the tool box on the work bench. There is a key to the back door of the house on the same ring. I'm cutting my trip here short and I'll be home in two hours. I'll see you then if you're still there." Leach seemed relaxed about the search. There had been ample time for him to clean up any evidence if indeed there had been any.

"We should be finished by then, but I'll wait for you to arrive before leaving," Filson said before hanging up the phone.

There were three officers in two cars at the scene. Don Winston was given the task of searching the hangar and airplane. He set about the task with his evidence kit and a hand full of plastic evidence bags. He found nothing in the hangar, but in the airplane he used a small hand vacuum to gather particles from the floorboards of the plane. He checked for fingerprints in both the front and rear seats. He took pictures of the interior and exterior of the plane. He was both methodical and thorough.

While Winston worked in the hangar Filson and the third trooper began a systematic search of the house. It was a single story home, well-kept and tidy. Filson searched for and found the access door to the crawl space under the home. He was happy to find a light switch near the ladder and turned on a string of lights located on the center beam the entire length of the home. Filson photographed the area and looked through everything he found, but there was no sign anyone had been down here for several months. Finally he climbed up the ladder, turned off the lights and closed the access door in the floor. He and the other trooper looked inside cabinets, drawers and cupboards. They opened books and riffled the pages. They took lids off boxes and jars. It was a time consuming job and it turned up nothing. There was no sign the two missing boys had been to the property. Filson and his helper were picking up their equipment when Leach opened the back door.

"Come on in, Mr. Leach," said Filson while sitting at the kitchen table making notes. "We've finished and you can come in now."

It seemed odd, but Leach was not in the least upset by the intrusion. "Well, what did you find?"

"Not much, Mr. Leach. Not even dust bunnies under the couch."

"Call me Bud. What were you searching for?" he asked.

"We have two missing boys and your airplane was seen in the area of their disappearance. We were just following up on the information. We aren't here to arrest you, we just needed to search your place to eliminate you as a suspect."

"If that's the case then I'd appreciate it if you would get out of my house." Leach was polite but firm. "I am still working and need to get back to the job. I want to be sure the place is locked up properly."

"Thank you for your cooperation, Bud," said Filson as he picked up his bag of equipment.

Winston was sitting in his car making notes when Filson and his partner came out of the house. "I guess we're through here for now, Don. I'll meet you back at the office."

Bud Leach stood near his idling truck and watched the two trooper cars leave his property. When they had gone he walked to the hangar to check on his airplane. It seemed to be without damage. He re-locked the door and walked to the rear of the hangar and lifted a wooden crate, set it aside and lifted a board from the floor. In the cavity beneath the floor was a small, locked, metal box where his treasured souvenirs from encounters were kept. It had not been moved and he was satisfied the troopers had not discovered it. He put it back in place, covered it with the piece of wood floor and placed the wooden crate back over the spot. Feeling confident he was safe he walked back to his truck to return to the office in North Kenai.

At the courthouse Penny was forced to wait until after the morning arraignments to meet with Judge Bartolis. She was dreading the meeting after her performance yesterday. At the appointed time she walked to his office and tapped on his door.

"Come in, Penny. We're alone and don't have to be so formal. Sit down. We need to talk."

"I came to apologize for yesterday, Judge," she began. "I was wrong and I let my emotions get away from me. I was reminded how important it was to keep my personal and professional lives separate. I hope you will give me another chance to prove I can do that."

"The first time I was an acting judge, magistrate actually, I was sitting on the bench when one of the cases before me, a misdemeanor case where a young man had stolen a car from me a year before. I was angry with the young man and heard his case without listening. I had already made up my mind to punish him for stealing my car. Before delivering the sentence I began to lecture him on the error of his ways and the consequences it held. Before I could announce his sentence the court clerk, a motherly old lady whom I dearly loved, realized what I was about to do and stopped me. She said there was an emergency in my chambers and we needed to postpone sentencing for a few minutes. In my chambers she didn't say a word. She just looked at me and gave me a chance to see myself and what I was planning. She just stood by the door and looked at me for about five minutes. The last thing I wanted to do was admit I was about to make a very large mistake. I thought I was too important for this kind of remand, but she never said a word. I finally realized she was giving me a chance to undo what had not yet been done. Had I gone ahead it would have been the end of my judicial career, a career I wanted worse than anything in my life. Those few minutes she gave me changed my life and taught me the lesson you have just learned. I would remind you that King Solomon made the same error. I will make a note and put it in your file I keep in my desk. This is a private file and only to remind me of dates and times of events. You are doing a wonderful job here. I don't want to lose you. But in the future if a case come in that is of a personal nature to you I want you to, as judges say, recuse yourself from the case. I will understand when you do."

"You are far more tolerant than I deserve, Judge. I promise this will never happen again. In my trooper career I never let anything get to me like that. I am deeply sorry and I thank you for understanding. I value my position here and will keep a professional attitude from this day forward." Penny hung her head, truly sorry for creating the necessity for this meeting.

"If you ever make it to the position of Superior Court Judge, and I believe you will if you want it, you must always remember this lesson. In almost every instance the motivation is revenge…to get even for something. It will be up to you to temper revenge with wisdom. It's your calling to balance the scales of justice, not to wield the sword of punishment. You'll be criticized for many of your decisions, but if you balance the scales you will never regret them." He looked at the clock on the wall. "I have a case in five minutes. Go back to work. And when you get time thank Nancy. She had already championed your case." He was smiling broadly when she left the office.

She was making an attempt to work her way through the stack of files on her desk when the telephone rang. "Superior court," she answered.

"Penny Rossiter please," said a voice on the other end.

"This is Penny, what can I do for you?"

"This is the emergency room nurse in Soldotna. Julia Rossiter has just been admitted here by ambulance. She fell and her Life Alert went off. She is conscious and asking for you. Can you come to the hospital?" asked the nurse.

"I'll be there in ten minutes." Penny scribbled a short note for Nancy, who was in court with the judge. 'MOM FELL AND IS IN THE HOSPITAL. GONE TO BE WITH HER.' She signed it and laid it on Nancy's desk, grabbed her coat and ran to the parking lot.

A nurse met Penny in the emergency room admitting office to lead her to a small treatment room. Julia was dressed in a hospital gown with a huge bruise on her right cheek. Her eyes were glazed, but she recognized her daughter. It was a weak attempt, but she tried to smile.

"Hi, Mom," said Penny. The nurse left them alone, but returned moments later with a doctor, "Hello, I'm Doctor Bartholamew," he said.

"How is she Doctor?" she asked.

"She took a bad fall. Nothing is broken, but we are going to admit her for observation. You can see she is still pretty woozy. We haven't determined why she fell. That worries us a little." The doctor was tapping his chin with his eyeglasses, having a sober look on his face.

"Did she call for help?" asked Penny.

"No," replied Dr. Bartholamew, "I understand that when she fell, her Life Alert notified us automatically. The EMTs found her on the floor, unconscious and unresponsive. We thought at first it was a heart attack but the EKG says not. We've drawn blood for testing, but I think she's becoming weaker because her internal organs are wearing out. She isn't getting enough oxygen to sustain them even though she's using the oxygen generator. I don't want to guess as to causes until we have the tests back, but it may be time to find an assisted living home for her or hire someone to sit with her during the day while you're at work. She is a very sick lady."

"I'll have to talk it over with her when she comes around. I've been looking at a place for her, but I hate to mover her out of the house. She's always taken care of me and I love her dearly." Penny had known this day was coming, but had refused to admit her mother was in such poor health.

"I understand," said the doctor, "but it may be time. Have a seat and I'll be back when I get the test results."

Penny sat next to the bed and held her mother's hand.

"Hi, Baby," Julia finally said in a tired voice, "I heard someone say they were putting me in the hospital."

"Yes, Mom, you took a bad fall. The doctor wants to check you out."

"I hate to say this, Honey, but it may be time for me to go to a nursing home. I just can't take care of myself any longer. I'm sorry, but I just can't do it."

"You may be right, Mom, but we can talk about it later. Right now you need to rest."

Penny sat by the bed holding her mother's hand while she slept. Nearly an hour later the Doctor returned, asking her to step into the hallway to speak with her.

When they were alone and out of the room Dr. Bartholamew gave her the results of the testing. "The tests show her system shutting down. We'll give her medications to help her, but it will be a few days before she is up and around. I am admitting her right now and I think it will be at least three days before she will feel like getting up and around. I'm sorry I don't have better news for you."

Penny gave a huge sigh, "I'll stay here until they move her up to a room. I'll come back later to see her. I guess it's time to think about getting her some professional help. I'll make the arrangements and when she's released from here she can go to an assisted living home."

When they took Julia up to her hospital room Penny walked to her car where she sat for a long time, thinking. Her first call was to David to tell him what had happened. She then drove to the assisted living home she had contacted earlier to make arrangements for Julia. Next she called Nancy at the judge's office to tell her she wouldn't be back for the rest of the day.

Chapter 23

Connie Dooley and Bobby Gunther had been busy working at the little barn in Sterling. They had processed a sizable quantity of meth and were running low on supplies. It had been three days of staying out of sight and doing busy work. When the two men returned to the warehouse in Soldotna they found a new tailgate leaning against the wall outside the front door. Bobby carried it inside and began to gather what was needed to paint the metal piece. It was in good shape and had already been painted with primer. He gave it a light sanding and hung it up in the paint booth. Bobby mixed the paint for Dooley and waited outside the plastic enclosure for him to finish spraying the metal tailgate. It took only a few minutes to finish the job and for Dooley to exit the paint booth. The heat was on and the exhaust fan was running while Bobby cleaned the painting equipment and sealed the cans of paint.

"We should be able to install this new tailgate tomorrow, Bobby. It looks pretty good. We can leave the heat on tonight and pinstripe it in the morning. We need more chemicals at the barn and once we install the tailgate we can load them into the old Chevy and take them to Sterling. Nobody is going to recognize the truck now." Dooley was admiring his own handiwork.

"Yeah, Connie, it looks really good. I won't mind driving it at all. Should I gather up the supplies we need and stack 'em by the truck?" asked Bobby, wanting to be helpful.

"Give me a couple of minutes and I'll help you. I need to clean up a little before this paint becomes a second skin for me."

While waiting for his partner Bobby gathered much of the small items and placed them in the back of the newly painted Chevy. The rubber bed liner they had installed would keep the containers from marring the new paint inside the bed. When Dooley returned the two men finished loading the heavy tanks and cans into the pickup, making sure they had room to work when they installed the tailgate.

"I'll meet you here at six in the morning, Bobby," said Dooley. "I need to buy a new tarp to cover the load. I'll see you here tomorrow."

"OK, Connie, see you in the morning."

"Don't be smoking anything tonight, Bobby. I need you with a clear head in the morning.

Bobby nodded and waved from the doorway.

When he was alone Dooley called Terry Boyette. "Is there anything you want me to do tonight, Boss?"

"Not tonight, Connie. How is Bobby working out for you?"

"He isn't the brightest bulb in the chandelier, but he works hard and follows orders. He makes a great helper."

"Can we trust him to keep his mouth shut?" asked Boyette.

"Yes, but if they press him they can get him to say almost anything. He won't volunteer information, but he can be scared into admitting to the Lindberg kidnapping. We have to keep him away from the cops and out of sight."

"That's how I read him, too. Keep him close to you and keep him busy. Edgar isn't convinced he can keep him from going to jail on the charges they arrested him on. I'm worried about that. If the DA wants to make him a deal he may tell them what he knows. Right now the law doesn't know about you or me, but I worry Bobby may give them what they want if he's offered a way out on his charges."

"Do you want him to have an accident?" asked Dooley.

"Not yet, Connie, I like the kid and if we can keep him around I want to do it. Let's wait and see."

"OK, Boss. I like the kid, too. He's a good worker and he has the cooking process down pat. I'd hate to lose him."

"Take the rest of the night off and I'll call you tomorrow if I need you." Boyette was pleased with the efficiency of his new hired man. He was little too ambitious, but conscientious, thought Terry.

Early the following morning Bud Leach called his friend in Hope and asked for him to meet with him at the Hope Airport. The weather had been marginal, but without severe winds. It took a little longer to fly to Hope than expected but the clean old pickup was waiting when he arrived.

"I heard the troopers were here to see you," said Leach without greeting.

"Yeah, they came out to my place and looked at the truck. They didn't find anything and left. I don't expect them to come back."

"That's what I needed to know. They came to my place yesterday with a search warrant and looked everywhere. They didn't find anything there either.

I came up here because I didn't want to talk on the phone. You know how it is when they're looking for information."

"Well, if you have something to hide, this meeting wasn't such a good idea either. From now on don't contact me for any reason. The rental agreement for the pickup is cancelled. Keep away from me, Bud. I don't need the attention."

"That's fine with me. You know my number if there is anything in the wind." Without a goodbye Leach climbed into his little Piper and started the engine. He taxied to the upper end of the little airstrip and turned around. He gunned the engine leaving a plume of blowing snow behind him as he made his takeoff run. The pickup and driver were sitting at the side of the runway when he passed.

It was daylight with low clouds. The temperature was hovering at +20 degrees. Leach decided to take the scenic route on his way home, scouting the lakes and trails for wolves and moose. That was the beauty of flying; there was no one to bother you. Life is simple when you're in the air. It took him nearly two hours to make the 40 minute flight home. He pushed the plane into his hangar and re-fueled the tanks. It felt as though it might snow. He went into the house for a cup of hot chocolate.

About the same time Leach arrived home Penny entered the hospital and climbed the stairs to the second floor where her mother's room was located. The hospital was busy and the halls filled with nurses making their rounds. Penny found the room and entered without knocking. Julia was asleep when she arrived. Penny had brought a newspaper and went directly to the small couch near the window. She sat to read the paper and wait for her mother to awaken. She had finished reading the paper and was working the cross-word puzzle when a nurse came into the room pushing a small cart with a computer on top.

"Wake up, Julia," said the nurse, "I have to take your vitals. Your lunch will be here in a minute. How do you feel this morning?"

"Oh, I'm fine," said Julia as the nurse applied a blood pressure cuff.

"Let me listen to your heart," the nurse ordered.

It was then Julia realized her daughter was sitting near the window. She gave Penny a little wave and let the nurse finish her duties. As the nurse backed out of the room Julia turned to Penny.

"Good morning, Honey," said Julia. "You're up early this morning."

"It isn't very early, Julia. You must have been worn out. You slept late."

"Oh, my, I didn't realize the time. I don't remember them bringing me to the room. The doctor said they were going to move me up here, but I don't remember the trip. It must have been the medications."

"I wanted to talk to you about all this, Mom." Penny moved to a chair near the bed. "They say you'll be in here a few days and that you'll need some kind of help when you're released."

"I told you before, Dear, I can't be by myself any longer."

"I know, Mom, and I've made arrangements for you to go to an assisted living place when you get released. I don't want you to go there, but I have to work and you can't stay alone. I don't know what else to do." Penny had tears flowing down her cheeks.

"It's all right, dear, I've been telling you we needed to do this for a long time."

Penny slid a chair closer and held her mother's hand. She sat without speaking for a long time. During the day while she sat by the bed a tide of doctors, nurses and aides came and went. Julia remained in the bed with an oxygen tube attached to her nose. She was still weak and didn't have the energy to talk.

It was mid-afternoon when David Haskins came into the room. Julia was sleeping and Penny was seated by the window again. "Want some lunch?" he asked quietly.

"You bet," she replied as she stood and stretched aching body.

The two walked down the stairs to the cafeteria. The special was a baked chicken dish and Hungarian mushroom soup. It looked delicious and smelled marvelous. They each carried a tray and a bottle of water to a booth and slid in on opposite sides. Penny unscrewed the cap from her water and took a long drink.

"How is she doing?" asked Haskins.

"She's weak, but seems to be doing pretty well." She took a bite of her chicken, "I've made arrangements for her to go to an assisted living home when she's released. I hate it, but I can't take care of her any longer."

"She understands," said David when he had swallowed his bite of the chicken. "How are you doing at work?"

"I'm making a lot of mistakes, but the judge is keeping an eye on me."

"I have some news about the PA-12. We got a search warrant and searched the home, the hangar and the plane. We found nothing to tie him to the killings or the missing kids. Filson talked with the man when he finished the search and told me he had an uneasy feeling about the guy. Lou said Leach was too smooth and relaxed and I trust Lou's feelings."

"It sounds as if police work is going on about the same as when I was doing it." Both of them laughed and sat drinking water, trying to relax.

Gunther and Dooley were working in the warehouse readying a load of materials for delivery to the barn in Sterling. Dooley would drive his own truck and Bobby would drive the old Chevy. The load was covered with a tarp to keep the curious from seeing what was being hauled. Both men drove cautiously on the winter roadways, not wanting to attract attention to the chemicals they were hauling. At the property the two men unloaded and carried the heavy load a piece at a time to the little barn for storage. Inside, the heating and ventilation system they had devised was working perfectly. The two were dressed in hazmat suits and working on a fresh batch of product when Dooley's phone rang. He stepped out of the lab to answer it.

"Dooley," he answered.

"It's Terry, I have a delivery for you to make right away. Can you do it?"

"Sure, Boss, what are we delivering?"

It was a substantial order for meth, heroin and cocaine. It was to be delivered to a dealer in Kenai right away. "Cash only on this one," ordered Terry Boyette.

"I have the meth here, but the 'H' and coke I'll have to stop at the warehouse to pick up. I'll be there in twenty minutes." Connie hung up the phone and went back inside to tell his partner he was leaving. In the outer room he stripped off his white plastic garb and hung it in the make-shift closet. Beside the closet was a small bench concealing a small safe, which was bolted to the floor underneath. Dooley moved the bench and opened the safe to extract the amount of home-made product ordered by the Kenai dealer. He closed the safe and returned the bench to its original position, put on his coat and exited the barn. He made a stop at the warehouse where Terry was waiting with two plastic food containers filled with baggies of the specified drugs. The amount was quite large, more than a normal delivery. The size of the order was the reason for the 'cash only' terms for this delivery.

"You know the dealer, Connie. Don't let him try to scam you. Twenty five grand cash or bring back the product."

"Gotcha Boss," said Dooley, taking the containers and placing them in one of the new style cloth shopping bags now popular at all the supermarkets. "Bobby will be back here soon to return the pickup. He was finishing a batch when I left him. Tell him I'll buy his breakfast in the morning, at Buckets Sports Bar."

"Bring the cash back here. I'll be waiting for you," said Boyette, closing his office door.

Chapter 24

It was late, dark and cold when Bobby Gunther started the old Chevy to warm it up before driving back to town. He returned to the barn to take off the white plastic suit and shut down the operation for the night. He slipped his coat on, turned out the lights and locked the door. The warmth of the idling truck was pleasant. He turned on the radio and tuned it to a country music station. Lastly, before putting the truck in gear he turned up the volume on the radio until nothing else could be heard. Bobbing his head to the beat of the music he turned the truck toward town.

Traffic was light and Bobby was engrossed in the music when suddenly a moose darted across the highway. It was a large cow. Bobby applied the brakes and swerved to the left to avoid the animal. The moose made a last minute jump to avoid being hit and ran across the road, but when Bobby swerved he was squarely centered upon a young calf moose following her mother across the roadway. The slippery road made braking ineffective and the shiny green Chevy swerved into the broadside moose, killing it instantly. The moose landed on the hood of the truck and slid over the hood to make contact with and break out the windshield.

Inside the truck Bobby was slammed against the steering wheel, his face pelted with broken shards of glass from the shattered windshield. The impact damaged the radiator, stopping the engine by jamming the radiator into the fan and water pump. After the impact the sound of the crash died away and there was only the blaring sound of country music heard in the dark night.

Moments later another vehicle stopped to render aide to the injured driver. The driver of the second vehicle was able to reach past Bobby's unconscious form to turn off the key and stop the deafening music. Now the rescuer could hear Bobby moaning and choking in pain. He reached for his cell phone to report the accident and ask for an ambulance. Turning his attention back to the driver of the pickup he could see a gushing wound on the neck of the pickup driver. He reached inside, through the broken side window to put pressure on the spurting cut in an attempt to stop the flow of blood.

Other cars began to stop and their lights shone brightly on the scene. The first driver maintained his pressure on the arterial wound while others began to direct traffic around the horrific scene. Within minutes a trooper was on scene placing flares along the highway to warn oncoming drivers of the hazard.

By the time the flares were in place the ambulance had arrived and EMTs were administering aid to the victim. Two medics began treatment of and care of the bleeding neck while a third was preparing a litter on which the victim would be transported. They had determined he was in need of immediate transport and had him on the way to the hospital within two minutes. The trooper had called for assistance to clear the scene and a wrecker to tow the wrecked pickup. Dispatch would call one of the charity organizations to salvage the moose meat. In an hour there was no sign of the accident except a small puddle of anti-freeze and some broken glass on the highway to mark the spot.

Bobby had lost a significant amount of blood by the time he reached the hospital. In the emergency room there was a flurry of activity as nurses and doctors performed the many tasks of cleaning the wound and stopping the bleeding. Other nurses were pulling shards of broken glass from his skin and disinfecting his wounds. While one doctor attempted to repair the torn artery in Bobby's neck others were stitching up his other cuts. A portable X-ray machine was summoned to check for broken bones and hidden injuries. The doctors had administered sedatives to keep Bobby from awakening while they worked on him.

After almost an hour of frantic activity by the emergency room staff Bobby was stable and his bleeding stopped. Now further evaluation and blood tests were being done to determine if there were other injuries or illnesses to be dealt with. An hour after that a report of negative was returned and a general assessment was made. He was to be admitted to the hospital.

When Dooley returned to the warehouse he was surprised to find Bobby had not yet come from the lab. Connie met with Terry and gave him a report about the transaction he had just concluded. The dealer had not wanted to pay cash for the product and argued with Dooley, but when Dooley refused to leave the order without payment the dealer cursed and complained, but counted out $25,000.

"That's about what I expected," noted Boyette. "He always tries to get credit, but I don't trust the guy. He knows I'm the only one who can supply him on short notice, so he keeps coming back for another supply. He has too much contact with the law and I want cash and not much time with him."

"He struck me as that kind of dealer, too. I'll remember him. I was surprised he met me without any goons with him—him having all that cash on him and all." The observation by Dooley was warranted in this kind of business transaction.

"I don't think he has any paid employees to protect him." Boyette made the comment while placing the money in his office safe.

"Have you seen Bobby? Asked a curious Dooley. "He should have been back by now."

"No, he hasn't come back yet. His truck is still out back."

"I guess I had better go out to the barn and check on him. I'll see you in the morning." Dooley waved to his boss and walked to his pickup. It seemed strange Bobby had not come back or called to let him know where he was.

About half way to Sterling there were a mass of lights on the roadway. A wrecker was loading a wrecked damaged and another group was loading a small dead moose on a little utility trailer. Dooley recognized the truck as the one he had only recently finished repainting.

Dooley stopped and walked over to the wrecker driver to ask about the driver of the broken truck.

"He was hurt pretty bad. They took him to the hospital by ambulance. That trooper over there in his car can give you the details." The wrecker driver pointed to a patrol car with flashing lights parked a few yards behind his car-hauler.

Dooley didn't talk to the trooper. Police contact was the last thing he needed. Instead he climbed into his own truck and drove back to Soldotna. He went directly to the admitting office of the hospital emergency room to ask about Bobby. The tall blonde girl at the desk told him she could not release any information, but she would call the nurse who treated him. Dooley thanked her and waited for the nurse to come through the locked doors.

When she came into the waiting room she asked, "Are you the one asking about Bobby Gunther?"

"Yes, he and I work together and he didn't come back to the warehouse tonight. When I went looking for him they said he had been in an accident.

"Are you a relative," she asked.

"No, he doesn't have anyone but me. Is he going to be OK?"

"Probably, but it is too early to tell for sure. He is badly injured. There are no broken bones, but he has multiple facial cuts and a concussion from the impact. His worst injury is a damaged carotid artery. He would have died at the scene if not for a witness who knew how to control the blood loss. That man saved your friend's life. He has lost a lot of blood and has numerous stitches on his face and neck, but he is going to make it just fine. We sent him up to a room in the hospital and he is sedated. I would suggest you come back in the morning to visit with him."

"Thank you for the information. I'll come back in the morning."

"Is there a number where we can reach you if something happens during the night?"

Dooley gave the nurse his cell phone number and asked her to call if there was a change in his condition. She said she would be sure to let him know.

Back in his truck Dooley called Terry to let him know what had happened.

The following afternoon Lou Filson stepped into David Haskins' office. "You know that pickup they impounded when the driver hit a moose last night?" he asked David.

"Yeah, the driver is still in the hospital. I just had a call from them and they said he had no alcohol or drugs in his system. There were traces of THC, but it didn't look like he was using at the time of the accident."

"Interesting," said Lou, "the truck has traces of a lot of different chemicals, both inside and in the bed. The list matches the recipe for meth. The traces in the cab are faint, but are pure meth. I wonder why the driver didn't test positive for using methamphetamines. You don't suppose this guy was cooking the stuff without using it?"

David leaned back in his chair. "You know you might be into something. Let me show you something else, Lou." He opened a file folder lying on the top of his desk and retrieved several photos of the wrecked Chevy truck. "Take a look at these pictures. The road trooper said in his report the truck had been recently painted over the previous color of blue over white. The driver is the guy we arrested in connection with the Will Goodson killing. I've been sitting here trying to figure out how all this fits together. You may have come up with the answer, Lou."

"How do you figure?" asked Filson.

"What if this Gunther and the dead doper, Kenny Pierce, were trying to find a new place to brew their meth? Goodson's place would have been ideal: secluded, away from neighbors, off the main road far enough it wouldn't draw attention, it had power and heat. It seems to me it would be an ideal place for that kind of activity."

"You're right, David, and the pickup would match the one the witnesses said the three men were driving."

With a Cheshire cat grin on his face, Lou said, "You don't suppose we could be this lucky, do you?"

"You know the old saying, sometimes luck is better than skill. Maybe we finally got lucky. Do you want to interview the driver or do you want me to do it?" asked Haskins.

"I'll do it. I can't let you have all the fun. By the way, do you have the name of Gunther's employer? I can't find it in my notes."

Haskins took his notebook from his jacket pocket and opened it, thumbing through the last several pages, finally stopping on an item in his book. "Here it is, Terry Boyette. We checked him out, but didn't find anything on him. He's some kind of property developer, I understand."

"I'll check him out after I talk to Bobby Gunther. We talked to Bobby before and he didn't seem bright enough to be in charge of a meth lab. I think we need to slow down and try making the pieces fit together. I'll let you know what I find out." Lou stood, anxious to do the interview.

"I'll call Penny and let her know we may have a break in her shooting case. She could use some good news about now."

Penny was in her office researching several pending sentencing cases. She planned to leave work early today again. This time it would be to transport her mother to the new assisted living center. She wanted to be with Julia as she checked in and was given her new room. Penny wanted to be sure her mother was going to be comfortable in her new surroundings. She had been so engrossed in her work she was startled when her cell phone vibrated.

"Penny Rossiter," she answered without looking at the caller ID.

"Hi Penny. It's me," said David.

"Oh, hi, David, I'm glad you called. I need a break. What's going on?"

"I just wanted to be the one to tell you we may have a break in your shooting. There was a moose/car accident last night and it appears the truck could be the one identified by witnesses in your shooting. It had been recently painted, but it was blue and white prior to the new paint. The driver was connected to one of the suspects in the Goodson killing. Lou is going to the hospital to interview him now. At any rate, this may be the break we need to find the killer and your shooter. Wish us luck."

"Oh, David, that is good news." Penny was almost giddy with excitement over the news. "Who was the driver, if I may ask? Is it someone I know?"

"It sure is, Penny. Do you remember Bobby Gunther? The friend of the drug overdose person with the suspicious needle marks?"

"Yes, he was bailed out by his lawyer recently. I think he has a May court date."

"That's the one," commented David, "Filson is on the way over to the hospital to get a statement. I'll let you know how it goes. Oh, I have to go. The captain is calling. Can I see you tonight?"

"Yes, after I get Julia checked in at the new place. See you tonight. Love you."

This could turn out to be a very good day, thought Penny.

Chapter 25

A short nurse with long dark hair was tending to Bobby Gunther when Lou Filson arrived in his hospital room. Bobby was awake and talking to the nurse, answering questions for her. He sounded groggy but alert. The nurse heard Lou at the door and turned to motion him into the room.

"He's awake and you can see him when I finish with him," she said over her shoulder. A couple of minutes later she wheeled her computer out of the room.

Lou came into the room with his notebook in his hand and stood at the foot of the bed. There were bandages, cuts with stitches and a huge bandage wrapped around Bobby's throat. "It looks like you came out second best with the moose," commented Filson.

"Yeah," said Bobby, "I missed the cow, but I didn't see the calf until it was too late. They say the truck is totaled, is that true?"

"It looks like it to me. We have it at the trooper impound yard by the office. You weren't able to tell us what to do with it. That's one of the reasons I'm here. Do you feel up to talking with me for a few minutes?"

"Sure, I feel OK except for my neck. They told me my face was cut up pretty good, but my neck is what hurts." Bobby held his hand over the bandage on his throat.

"The doctor told me they were going to keep you a few days to allow the repair on your artery to heal up a little. He also said you were lucky the first guy on the scene was trained in first aid. He kept you from bleeding to death before the ambulance got there."

"Right now I don't feel too lucky, but at least I'm alive." Bobby scooted himself a little more upright in the bed. "Hey, have you got the name of the guy who helped me? I'd like to tell him thanks when I get better."

Lou wrote something on his note pad and tore it from the book. "I'll leave this here on the table for you. It's his name and phone number. I'm sure he'll be interested in hearing from you." Lou turned his notebook to a new page. "Does the truck belong to you?" he asked.

"No, my boss owns it. I was coming back from a job and hit the moose. I bet he's wondering where I am."

"Would that be Mr. Terry Boyette?" asked Lou.

"Yeah, I was supposed to put the truck back in the warehouse last night, but that didn't work too good. I'm going to call him in a little while and let him know what happened."

"I plan to go to the warehouse and speak with Mr. Boyette when I leave here. I'll be happy to take him a message if you like."

"That would be good, thanks." Bobby groaned a little.

"Are you OK? Would you prefer I came back another time?"

"No, I'm just sore and it hurts when I move. What is it you want to talk with me about?" asked Bobby.

"I just have a few questions for you, but if you start to feel bad let me know and I can come back." Filson looked at the young man for acknowledgement and received a nod from the patient. "The wreck skinned the new paint job up quite a bit and I noticed it used to be blue and white."

"Yeah, me and Connie, he's the new foreman I work for, we painted it so's it would look better when we used it on the job. We even got a new tailgate and put it on. It looked good when we got done. I'm sorry I wrecked it."

"I can see you did a nice job on it. One thing though, Bobby, that blue and white Chevy was seen by witnesses out on Funny River Road at the time a man was beaten to death in the area. The witnesses say they saw you and two other men in it. I recall you said you were out there with one other man, a Kenny Pierce. He's a suspect in the death of Will Goodson. Who was the other man in the truck with the two of you?"

Bobby answered without thinking, "That was Mr. Boyette, but he had his own truck out there and only rode with us a little ways. He was giving us orders and then went back to his own truck and left us to talk with Mr. Goodson." Bobby suddenly realized what he had just said. "Oh, Trooper Filson, please don't tell Mr. Boyette I said that. He'd kill me if he knew." There was the sound of fright in his voice.

"I won't say anything, Bobby. Was he the one who wanted to buy Will Goodson's property?"

Bobby lay silent for a moment, but finally continued, "Yeah, but I can't say any more about that. Mr. Boyette doesn't like it when I talk about his business."

"That's OK Bobby, I'll ask him about it when I see him. I won't tell him you were the one who told me about him being there. What did he want the property for, anyway?"

"I can't tell you that. I just can't. Don't ask me about that part." Bobby had become even more frightened now.

"OK, perhaps we can talk about it another time. By the way, Bobby, what were you doing out toward Sterling anyway?" Filson asked in an off-hand manner.

"Just doing some work for Mr. Boyette. He has some property out off of Scout Lake Loop. It's just a little barn where we keep supplies and stuff. You will have to talk with Terry about that."

"What about this new man, this Connie. Who is he?"

"Conrad Dooley, we call him Connie. He's kinda my new foreman. Mr. Boyette just hired him a while back. I like him he treats me good." It sounded as if Bobby admired and liked working with this new man, Dooley, but Gunther had not said what Dooley was really doing for Boyette.

"Where can I get in touch with this new man?" asked Filson.

"Mr. Boyette will give you his phone number, I don't dare." Bobby was holding his neck again, "I'm getting kinda tired now. Can we do the rest of this some other time?"

"Sure thing Bobby, thanks for the help. I'll come back another time. Get well." Filson closed his notebook and waved to the man in the hospital bed.

Filson drove directly from the hospital to the warehouse about a mile away. Three pickups were parked in the lot when he arrived. One belonged to Bobby Gunther, one belonged to Terry Boyette, but the third had only temporary license tags. It was new, large and very clean. Lou walked into the large warehouse building and found a door with a small sign reading OFFICE and knocked. The door was opened by an athletic-looking man in his early forties.

"What can I do for you, trooper?" he asked.

"I came to see Mr. Boyette. Is he in?" replied Filson.

"Yes, but he's very busy right now. Can you come back tomorrow?"

"Are you Conrad Dooley?" asked Lou.

"Yes, why do you ask?"

"I had information you had gone to work for Terry Boyette and you were the next name on my list of people to visit. Perhaps I could speak with you while I'm waiting to see Mr. Boyette."

"I'm sort of busy myself. By the way, what was your name?" asked Dooley.

"I'm Trooper Lou Filson. I'm here because one of your employees was nearly killed last night in a car/moose collision. I thought you and Mr. Boyette might be interested to know his condition."

"Oh, you mean Bobby. Let's go to my office across the hall. Mr. Boyette is on a conference call and can't be disturbed right now." Dooley stepped into the hallway and led the way to another door on the other side. He opened it to a sparsely appointed office with one file cabinet, two chairs and a desk.

There was a telephone on the desk, but no other sign the office was being used. Dooley flipped the light switch and said, "Have a seat."

Filson took the notebook from his jacket pocket and sat with it on his knee. "It appears you don't do much office work, Mr. Dooley."

Connie chuckled at the remark. "No, I spend most of my time out doing work on Mr. Boyette's rental properties. You know how rentals are, someone is always breaking something."

"I wouldn't know about that. I came to talk about your other employee, Bobby Gunther."

"Yes, we heard he was I a bad accident last night. How is he doing?" inquired Dooley.

"Quick action by a bystander saved his life last night. He's in the hospital and will be there for a few more days. The truck he was driving is at trooper headquarters across the river. We impounded it last night. It's a total loss. I was admiring the new paint job. Was that your handiwork?"

"Yes, Bobby and I painted it out in the warehouse here. I have only worked here for few days and thought we needed a work truck. The old Chevy was in good shape except for the paint so we painted it and added a tailgate. It's not a bad old truck. It made a good vehicle for hauling material, tools and fertilizer."

"You're new here, then," mentioned Filson, "Where did you work prior to coming here?"

"I had been working in Anchorage. Mr. Boyette lost an employee and needed a replacement. I was looking to move out of Anchorage and took the job. I'm glad I did, Mr. Boyette is a good man to work for."

"I'm a little curious. Bobby was nearly killed and your company truck was totaled last night and yet neither you nor Mr. Boyette has been to the hospital to check on a man who works for you. It just seems a little strange to me." Lou was writing in his notebook, but looked up for an answer.

"Mr. Boyette is in the middle of some rather large land purchases and the two of us have been very busy with the details of this purchase. As you know there is about to be a very large natural gas liquefaction plant proposed for the North Road. There are many companies competing for all available properties. Mr. Boyette is attempting to get in on the ground floor and buy up as much land as possible before the prices skyrocket. He isn't a large company and has to leverage his other properties to finance this new venture. Land like the stock market has a volatile pricing structure and missing one of his meetings could conceivably cost him a great deal of cash. Mr. Boyette cares a great deal for Bobby Gunther but his other responsibilities are demanding his time right now. You understand." Dooley was making a good case for his boss, but withholding any specific information.

"Mr. Dooley, all this is very interesting, but you still haven't told me what business ventures you are in with enough cash flow to finance this land acquisition plan. I can't imagine the low income housing market is paying enough to finance this grand plan you've explained. How does Terry Boyette make his money?" Filson was pushing Dooley a little.

"I'm sorry, but you'll have to get that information from Mr. Boyette. I'm not at liberty to give you more specific information."

"That's fine, Mr. Dooley, let's go across the hall and talk with Terry Boyette."

"I've repeatedly told you Mr. Boyette does not have time for you today. I can make an appointment for you to see him week after next, Tuesday, 11:30 a.m.," announced Dooley.

"And you don't understand, Mr. Dooley, this is an official investigation and you are about to be arrested for interfering in that investigation. Do I make myself clear?" Filson stood while delivering the message.

"I think you had better leave now. Mr. Boyette will have his lawyer contact you later this week." Dooley was maintaining his stubborn position.

"Turn around Mr. Dooley, I'm placing you under arrest for obstruction. You can call a lawyer from the jail facility."

"Hold on now, Trooper. I don't want to go to jail. Let me see if Mr. Boyette can work you in." Dooley reached for the phone to dial his boss across the hall.

"Thank you for your cooperation," said Filson.

Dooley spoke to Boyette on the telephone and hung up. "Come with me to Mr. Boyette's office," he said.

In the boss' office the desk was piled high with file folders and papers. Boyette sat behind the desk in his shirt with no coat. It appeared to Filson that Dooley had been telling the truth about his boss being busy.

"I'm a busy man, what is it you want?" asked Terry.

Without being invited Filson sat in a large overstuffed chair in front of the big man's desk. "Mr. Dooley here has been less than helpful in my attempt to find out about your man Gunther who was injured and nearly killed last night in a car wreck. Dooley thinks you're too busy to answer my question regarding your employee. It would be nice if we could talk privately for a few minutes, Mr. Boyette."

Terry heaved a huge sigh, "OK, OK, Dooley, go get some coffee or something."

Dooley nodded and left the office.

"Now," Terry began impatiently, "what do you want to know?"

Filson went through the list of questions about Bobby and his job description. Boyette provided all the information without hesitation. That is, until Filson asked what Bobby was doing that late in the day in a company pickup and supposedly working on Boyette's behalf. "Exactly where is this property in Sterling where Bobby Gunther was working so late?"

"Didn't Bobby tell you?" asked Terry.

"Bobby said he was working for you, but refused to give me the exact location of where he was working. He said I would have to ask you about that. Now I'm asking you, where is the property?" Filson asked the question in a cold and official tone.

"I think I have said all I care to say. Anything further you want to know you will have to get from my lawyer. I'm refusing to answer any more of your questions. You came in here threatening my employee and now are trying to intimidate me. Well, it won't work. Get out of here and don't come back. I'll have my attorney call you and you can ask him all the questions you want. Now get out!" Terry was nearly shouting now. He raised his voice even further now, "DOOLEY! Show this man the door."

Dooley opened the office door. Filson turned to leave, but turned back to Terry Boyette, "I'll go, but I will be back. I can't prove it yet, but I think the two of you are covering up something and I will find out what it is. When I do I'll be back to take you away to jail."

"Get him out of here," said Boyette to his hired enforcer.

Chapter 26

It was late afternoon by the time Penny finished admitting Julia into her new quarters in one of the new assisted living homes near the Kenai River. The facility is completely modern with experienced and qualified help. It offered clean, comfortable living quarters as well as ample community areas where the residents could meet and socialize. There was a gymnasium built to accommodate varied stages of health, age and agility. The staff was helpful and friendly and went the extra mile to assist the residents. Nurses were on duty 24 hours daily and doctors were on call as well. Penny had sampled the food and found it to be excellent. The residents were allowed a great deal of freedom both inside and away from the facility. Julia was satisfied with the arrangement.

Julia was tired and wanted to rest by the time her sign-in was finished. One of the nurses said she would help her get ready for bed and bring her something to eat in her room. She also said she would help her get used to the controls for the television and heat as well as the call buttons in the event she needed assistance.

"It looks like you're in good hands, Mom. I'll be by tomorrow to see if you need anything. Get some rest and behave yourself." Penny was trying to be cheerful about the move, but was a little apprehensive.

"Don't worry about me, Honey. I saw a couple of real hunks in the day-room when we came through. I'll be just fine here." Julia wanted to make light of the move and give her daughter assurance she was fine with the change. "I'll call tomorrow and let you know how I'm doing. Now you go and have some dinner."

Penny had been home only a few minutes when the door chime rang. It was David Haskins. She invited him inside out of the cold and snow.

"Well, did you get her all checked into the home?" he asked.

"Yes and she's already picking out a new boyfriend or roommate or something. She wasn't too specific, but she was cruising the crowd like a hooker on vacation. I think she'll be just fine there."

"That's a terrible way to talk about your mother, young lady. You should be ashamed of yourself." They both laughed, "How would you like me to take you to dinner?"

"I have a better idea, let's order a pizza and stay here. Do you realize we've never been alone together in all the time we have known each other?" asked Penny.

"I like your idea. You can call and order the pizza and I'll go get it. I'll stop and get a bottle of wine on the way. What do you like, red or white?"

"Red," she answered while reaching for the telephone. "What do you like on your pizza?"

"I'll eat anything you like," he replied, realizing he didn't know very much about the likes and dislikes of his new love. "If you're still worried about the calories we can have Greek pizza."

"That sounds good to me. I'm ordering it from Froso's. Hurry back to me," she said, peering over her right shoulder in a seductive manner.

It was very late when David went to his truck and drove to his home. He had considered asking to spend the night, but decided it wasn't yet time for such advances. They had spent the evening listening to music, thinking about the future and being close. The evening was casual, warm and pleasant with no thoughts of Julia, the judge or trooper cases.

As Penny readied for bed she realized she had just spent an evening like a real person in a real world: no call-outs, no fights, no shooting, no sirens, just a pleasant evening with someone she loved and who loved her back. She had even forgotten, at least for the evening, about Julia. Something she had not done in a very long time.

She visited with Julia each day over the weekend, but still took time to go for a drive to Homer for lunch with David. He had bought her a tee shirt at the Salty Dawg Saloon on the Homer Spit near the Homer Small Boat Harbor. She couldn't remember ever being so relaxed. She liked the feeling.

Monday morning Terry Boyette summoned Conrad Dooley to his office. "I've been thinking about the visit from the trooper on Friday. They know about the property in Sterling, they don't know where it is just yet, but they'll be looking. I want you to go to the hospital and see Bobby. Find out when he's going to be able to go back to work. I own a piece of land on the back side of Salamatof Lake, north of Kenai about six miles. I'm going to call a man who does dirt work for me from time to time and have him take his 966 Cat loader out to the property and clear the road. There used to be a mobile home on the property. It was a dump and I had it hauled away. But there's a nice little insulated and secure shed on the property. I think we need to move the Sterling equipment and supplies to this new location as quickly as possible. We can use the same heating system and ventilation fans and all the lab equipment. As I see it the only thing we'll have trouble moving is the five hundred gallon stove fuel tank. Jenkins, the guy who'll clear the road, has a large truck with a winch in the back. Have him pick up the fuel tank and bring it to the new property. We really need to have this done today."

Dooley wrote down Jenkins' phone number as well as the directions to the property in North Kenai. He left the office and drove directly to the hospital, stopping at the front desk to learn Bobby's room number. He found the room with little trouble and went inside. Bobby was alone, reading the morning paper.

"Mornin', Connie," said Gunther when the visitor entered.

"Good morning to you, too, Bobby. How are you feeling?"

"The doctors say I can go home tomorrow, but I can't do anything for another week. They're afraid the stitches in my neck will pull loose and I'll start spurtin' blood again." Bobby held his hand to the bandage on his throat.

"The boss and I have been worried about you. We thought for a while you were a goner. I'm glad you're doing this well. I am sort of mad about you denting the new paint job, though."

"Yeah, I'm sorry about that Connie. I couldn't help it. I missed the big old cow and ran right into the calf. I heard it really wrecked the Chevy. They told me some oil field hand stopped the bleeding in my neck until the medics got there. I guess I'm lucky to be alive."

"I need for you to get well and get back to work. I can't do all the work alone." Dooley patted the young man on the leg in reassurance. "I heard the troopers were here asking a lot of questions."

Bobby nodded, "Yeah, a trooper named Filson came here. I didn't tell him nothing, but he asked what I was doing in Sterling and I told him I was working on some property for Mr. Boyette. I didn't tell him where it was, though."

"You did great, Bobby, you did great." A CNA came into the room with a clip board in her hand. "I'll get out of here now, but I'll come back to see you. Is there anything I can bring you?"

"Nah, thanks, Connie," replied Bobby

Connie Dooley left the hospital and stopped at the Moose Is Loose bakery for a cup of coffee and an apple fritter to eat on the drive to North Kenai. The fritter was the best he had ever eaten and the coffee was wonderful. He decided this would be a regular morning stop for him. A half hour later he met Jenkins on the narrow road leading to the shed on the north side of Salamatof Lake. The big Caterpillar was plowing the road on a return trip from the property. Dooley stopped his truck and got out to converse with

Jenkins who had pulled the big loader to the side of the roadway to allow Dooley to pass.

"Howdy, I'm Jenkins. Are you Dooley?" asked the very large man wearing insulated Carhartt coveralls.

"Yes, I'm Dooley. Call me Connie." The two men shook hands. "Did you talk to Terry about hauling a fuel tank from Sterling?"

"Yup, I have to take the 966 back to the shop and get my other truck. I'll finish this job and be back in about an hour. I cleared the front of the shed and one side where the tank will be set up. The building isn't locked. You'll have to buy some locks for the place."

"Good," said Connie, "I'll see you back here in an hour."

Jenkins climbed into his loader and started the big diesel engine. He gave a small wave of his hand and resumed his plowing chore.

Dooley was impressed with the little shed. It hadn't been a woodshed as Dooley thought, but a small workshop of some kind. It was clean and had good lighting. There was nothing inside the small building, but there was a stove pipe where some kind of stove had once stood. The inside dimensions were slightly larger than the little barn in Sterling. He noted it wouldn't be difficult to build a wall to accommodate the lab area and there was already an exhaust fan built into the end wall making an excellent air flow vent for fumes generated inside the lab. He made a list of items he would need to do the job and went outside to see where the fuel tank would be located. He was finishing with his list when a large car-hauler type wrecker truck came into view. It was Jenkins. The two men discussed and agreed on the location for the tank. Jenkins said he would follow Dooley to Sterling. Several hours later the entire lab had been moved to the new location and a new copper line installed to feed the oil heater attached to the existing stove pipe. Dooley thanked Jenkins for his help before driving to the building supply store in Kenai for lumber and plywood for the new wall and new locks for all the doors.

It took him two more days to finish remodeling the shed. The new site had a more efficient air flow system than the one used at the Sterling location. This was possible because there were no close neighbors and the wind currents were much stronger here near the coastline. Dooley stocked the two lockers with fresh plastic hazmat suits and towels. He sat in the warmth of the oil fired stove and thought it was now time to begin production.

His thoughts were interrupted when his telephone vibrated. "Dooley," he answered.

"Hi, Dooley, it's me, Bobby."

"Hey, Bobby, how are you doing?"

"The doctor just said I could go home and I wondered if you'd come get me."

"Sure, Kid, happy to do it, I need your help anyway. How soon will you be ready?"

"The nurses are getting me ready now, so I guess about an hour."

"I'll be there in an hour, Bobby." Dooley hung up the phone and immediately dialed Boyette to give him the news.

"That's good news Connie. We need to get back into production right away. Is everything ready to go?" asked Terry.

"Yes, I'll trade out some gas bottles at the warehouse when I come in tomorrow morning. I like the new location, Boss. I think it will be better than the last one. More efficient, I mean."

"Good, make sure the kid has everything he needs. He should have enough grass to keep him mellow for a few days. Give him some more if he wants it. I'm going to need you for some deliveries tonight and tomorrow."

"OK, Boss. I'll take Bobby home and come back to the warehouse. I'll see you about eight o'clock." Dooley had planned a relaxing evening at home, but that now seemed to be out of the question.

Penny Rossiter had stopped to visit her mother on her way from the court. Julia was in the dining room visiting with some new friends and planning a pinochle party after dinner. It pleased Penny that her mother was settling into this new environment so quickly.

Chapter 27

Dooley spent the afternoon checking Bobby Gunther out of the hospital and getting him settled in at home. Connie offered the young helper more marijuana as Terry had ordered, but the young man said he had enough to last him a few days. Dooley checked his cupboards and made sure there was enough food and sodas to last a couple of days. He instructed Bobby to call if he ran out of anything before he came back. It was just eight o'clock when he returned to the warehouse.

"How is he doing?" asked Terry Boyette.

"He has a lot of cuts and bruises and of course, those stitches in his throat. He isn't moving very fast, but he is doing well over all."

"Did you give him some more weed?" asked Terry.

"No, he said he had enough for now. I like the kid, Boss. He isn't a quick thinker, but he's loyal and a hard worker. Too bad he got hurt." Dooley was showing uncommon compassion for the young helper. "Maybe we can give him a few extra bucks this month to make up for his missing days of work."

"I guess we can do that. How much do you want to give him as a bonus for wrecking the truck?" asked Boyette.

"Come on Boss, a couple of hundred won't break you and it would go a long way toward keeping him on our side."

"Yes, I supposed you're right. We need him." Boyette turned to face his desk, "How much do you want to give him?"

"Two or three hundred would make him happy. We don't pay him much anyway. I guess he's happy getting some free dope as a bonus once in a while, but he has expenses too. Look at it this way... it's not a pay raise, just a one-time thing."

Boyette dug a cash box out of a locked drawer and an envelope from another. He stuffed five new Ben Franklin's in the envelope and handed it to Dooley. "Here, give this to him when you see him."

Dooley was impressed with the generosity of his employer, took the envelope and placed it in an inside pocket of his jacket. "OK, Boss, what about the deliveries you want me to make tonight?"

"Do we have a good supply of meth on hand?" asked Terry.

"Yes we do. The little safe at the new shed is nearly full of product. I haven't weighed it to tell you exactly how much, but we have a good supply for our normal users and dealers."

"OK, Connie. Here's a list of deliveries I want you to make tonight. I think you've met all the ones on this list. The bottom name is the one you took the large delivery to the other night. He wants more on-hand stock. One of the items on his list is a sizable amount of our product. It seems his customers like the quality of our brand. I still don't know this guy enough to front him anything, so the rules are the same as last time; cash only." Boyette opened the safe beside his large roll top desk and took out several large packets wrapped in brown paper. "The ones with a white dot are 'H', the ones with the red dot are coke and the ones with the black dots are meth. All the wrapped packages are to go to the dealer in Nikiski and are a bulk order. The others are the usual packets and are in manila envelopes like usual. I'll meet you here at midnight and put the cash in the safe. Stop at the new property and bring me the product you have in the safe. I'm out of it here now. This order will supply the dealers for a few days until you and Bobby can start manufacturing in the new location."

"How is the new land deal going, if I may ask?" Dooley inquired out of curiosity.

"It looks like everything is on track and we're waiting for the titles to be cleared for transfer." Boyette looked into the eyes of Dooley. "Remember, this is not to be repeated outside this office."

Dooley followed his orders perfectly and delivered the small orders first. He met the new dealer in Nikiski. He was waiting in the parking lot of a notorious North Kenai bar, once the scene of a shooting where two people were killed and another shot in the leg.

"Nice to see you," said the dealer.

Dooley didn't like the meeting place. "We can't do business here, it's too public."

"That's why I picked it. I thought you might like witnesses in case there was trouble." The dealer was grinning knowing Dooley was uncomfortable with the situation.

"Halibouty Road, two miles up. The state highways department has plowed us a nice meeting place. Be there in fifteen minutes or forget the deal." Dooley didn't wait for an answer, but rolled up his window and put his truck in reverse. He watched the parking lot in his rear view mirror as he drove away. The dealer was still sitting there when Dooley went out of sight.

Dooley drove directly to the meeting spot, but parked in a driveway a hundred yards past the plowed area. He waited in the dark for the other driver to show. He was about to leave when a set of headlights came into view, slowly driving into designated area. Without headlights he drove to the other vehicle and stopped. The driver of the other car rolled down his driver side window and was about to speak when Dooley rolled down his window and ordered the man out of his car.

Both men stood in the cold night, each measuring the other. Dooley knew he had the advantage, "Don't ever try to get cute with me, Pard. If you want to do business with me you'll do it my way."

"I own the business on the North Road. If you want to supply me, fine. If not, get out of here and I'll get a new supplier. I can fly to Anchorage and be back here in less than two hours. So, don't be so sure of yourself...PARD." The dealer was flexing muscle Dooley hadn't counted on him having.

"You've obviously been in the business long enough to know the risks. I'm not willing to take on your risks. Either we do business my way or you can go ahead and fly to Anchorage. It looks like a nice night for a flight." Dooley kept the pressure on the dealer. "What'll it be? Cough up the cash or fire up the airplane?"

The dealer heaved a big sigh before deciding to admit defeat. He took the two steps to his car and brought out one of those new eco-friendly shopping bags. He turned back to Dooley, "Where's the stuff?"

Dooley stepped back one step and reached into the truck. He heard the dealer shuffling behind him. When he turned around the dealer held the money bag in one hand and a shiny Kimber semi-automatic in the other. Dooley had the packages of supplies in one hand and swung a baseball bat with the other, knocking the gun from the dealer's hand. The money fell to the ground while the dealer fell beside it. He was screaming in pain.

"I told you don't get cute with me, Pard. Keep your money and I'll keep my product. I should bash your skull in, but I'm in a good mood. Now get in that piece of crap car of yours and drive to the emergency room and have that hand looked at. I think it's broken. And don't ever call again."

The dealer was in too much pain to argue with Dooley, but was already planning vengeance. He threw the bag of cash onto his car seat and drove away. Dooley was glad to see the man go but had no idea what the boss was going to say when he heard the story. He sat in his truck for several minutes before heading back to Soldotna, thirty miles to the south.

At midnight Dooley met Terry at the office and the two men went inside the warehouse. Dooley carried a small athletic bag with the day's take inside. He followed Boyette to the small office and seated himself beside the roll top desk.

"You don't look happy, Connie. Did you have trouble?"

"A little. Your new dealer pulled a gun on me. I was ready for that and smacked his gun hand with my baseball bat. I think I broke his hand. I told him to get out of there and don't call again. But, I don't think he's the kind who listens. I think he'll try to get even somehow. Sorry for the trouble Boss, but he instigated the problem."

"I'm glad you were able to handle the situation," said Terry. "Do you think he'll try to get even with you or come here to the office?"

"I don't know for sure, but I believe he thinks he's the boss and in control. He indicated he had contacts in Anchorage and could get product there, but he wasn't specific about it. He may just get supplied somewhere else, but he struck me as someone who needs to prove a point. I may have to do something with him later."

"I'm beginning to like the way you work, Connie. You have a knack for solving problems. Try to take care of this one before it comes to the office." Boyette placed the day's take in the safe and locked the door. "How would you feel about taking control of the drug sales and manufacture part of this business?" asked Boyette. "I'm becoming so busy with the land business I don't have time for this end of the finances. I can't afford to quit because I still need the cash for purchasing the land I need. If you think you can handle the business I'll cut you in for a third of the net. You'll have to pay Bobby and any other help you may want to hire, but even so you should more than double what I pay you now. Are you interested?"

"A third of the net profits? Does that mean you still buy the supplies and furnish the lab site?" asked Dooley.

"Yes. It takes about one third to run the lab and you and I will split the rest. I need to distance myself from the drug business and this seems like a good time to take advantage of what you're doing and make the change now. I've become involved in enough land transactions that I'm becoming a public figure. I didn't plan for this, but the land business is becoming quite large and very public. I've made the local newspapers on several occasions in recent days. It's important I keep my name clean. If this all works out the way I have it planned we'll both be millionaires in a very short time."

"I really don't know what to say, Mr. Boyette. It looks like a great opportunity for me." Conrad Dooley thought this may just be the opening he had been waiting for and he liked the potential. "I guess if you have that much faith in me I should give it a try. But if I do this there'll be a few small changes."

"What kind of changes, Connie?"

"First of all I'll have to find another headquarters. You'll want to have a different image associated with your office. I'll find another small office and storage area to work out of. Somewhere on the edge of town may be better than here. If you know of a place, just let me know. Once set up I can move the containers and supplies to the new location. The gas canisters won't be a problem to move, but they need to be moved away from other businesses. It'll need to be somewhere I can come and go without a lot of eyes watching."

"I see we're working from the same page, Connie," commented Boyette. "There's a small warehouse about three miles down Kalifornsky Beach Road. It sits in the trees off the main road and it's been for sale for a long time. I'll see if I can the new location for you. Is there anything else you need?"

"I'll probably need a few things to open the office, but I don't know exactly what that will be until I get moved. Bobby will be able to help in a couple of days. By the time you find out about buying the new property we should be ready to move. Thanks for the offer, Sir." Dooley looked at this move as a giant step forward in his career.

It was three in the morning when Dooley left Boyette's office. About the same time the drug dealer from North Kenai was leaving the emergency room with a new plaster cast on his right hand and a vow of vengeance on his mind. John McGowan had been dealing drugs a long time in Nikiski without being arrested and had visions of being the head of the drug business in North Kenai. His plan now included eliminating the present North Road Supplier, Conrad Dooley, permanently.

Chapter 28

It was early the next morning when Lou Filson was seated at his desk filtering through the stack of mail on his desk. Most of it was official correspondence, which needed to be filed, but one was of particular interest. This one was a thick envelope from the crime lab in Anchorage. Inside was a report on the floor samples and sweepings he had taken from the airplane and home of Bud Leach. None of the samples were conclusive evidence of any interest, but toward the end of the report was a notation that caught Filson's attention. In the floor sweepings from the rear seat of the airplane was a tiny scrap of rubber. When tested it proved to be from an obscure type used to make a small quantity of children's athletic shoes. This particular shoe is sold by a large chain store with an outlet in Anchorage. It was the same brand of shoe worn by both boys when they had gone missing at the time of the murders on Resurrection Trail near Hope, Alaska. Lou was excited. This was a small clue, but a clue none-the-less. He read the entire report again before taking the short walk down the hall to David Haskins' office.

Filson was waving the report with his left hand as he entered the office. "Bingo!" he said as he entered. "We may have something on those missing boys."

Haskins sat upright in his desk chair, "You have? What is it?"

"It isn't much, but it's the first real evidence we have on the missing kids." Filson stepped inside the office and sat. "I just got the report from the crime lab with an analysis of the evidence we gathered with the search warrant at the Leach place. There was a small piece of rubber in the dust on the floor of the PA-12. It was in the bag taken from the rear seating area. It must have been pretty small because I didn't even see it when I bagged it up. The rubber is from the sole of the type of shoes worn by both the missing boys at the time of their disappearance. I dug out the original report and double checked the make of shoes the boys wore. They match. The lab says it's a type used by a small company and sold through an outlet in Anchorage. This material is only used on small size children's shoes. The chemical makeup and the color are the same as the soles of this brand of shoe."

"Finally, some good news. Have you talked with the DA about this yet?" asked Haskins.

"Not yet, I wanted to tell you first. I'll go call her now. I guess my next question is do you think it's enough to bring Leach in for questioning?"

"I don't know Lou, it's pretty slim. I think we'd better talk with the DA about it before we start arresting people." Haskins was thinking about Penny, "I think we'd better keep this to ourselves right now. Let me know what the District Attorney has to say. This Leach is a cool character and I doubt he'll fold up and confess when we confront him, but we certainly have something to go on now. This may be what we need to put the two boys in the airplane. The bad news is we still don't know where they are now. We don't know if they're still alive and if they are we want to keep them that way. Was there anything else in the report we can use?" Haskins was still thinking about Penny and how she was going to take the news.

"Sorry, David that was the only thing in the report we could use, at least it's all I saw there. I'll leave the report here for you to look at."

"Good work anyway, Lou. Keep me posted on your progress."

Filson took the papers back to his office and called the District Attorney.

Haskins thought about it a while before dialing Penny Rossiter at the courthouse. She was in her office and answered on the second ring.

"Hi Penny, it's David."

"Oh, hi David, how nice of you to call, I've been trying to think of an excuse to call you."

"I have some news for you. Good news I hope. Are you sitting down?" he asked.

"Yes, that's the trouble with this job, I'm always sitting down."

"Well, hang onto your hat. We may have a break in the Resurrection Trail murder case."

"Oh David, that is good news! What have you learned?" asked the excited Penny.

"You remember a few weeks ago Lou and Winston went to Bud Leach's place and served a search warrant?"

"I remember," she said.

"The report came in this morning and there is some small evidence the boys may have been in the rear seat of the airplane. I have Lou checking with the DA right now to see if we have enough to bring him in for questioning. It isn't enough to arrest him, but we might have enough to make him nervous enough to make a mistake." It was a short report, but an exciting one.

150

"Finally!" she exclaimed. "Oh, David, that is good news. Can we go out and celebrate tonight?"

"That's a good idea. Would you like to get Julia and take her to dinner with us?"

"I was thinking more along the lines of just the two of us, but it would be a good idea if we took her back early and you came to my place for a nightcap."

"Why Penny Rossiter, you're turning into such a hussy. It's shameful. What time." He laughed at his own remarks.

It was mid-morning when Dooley stopped in front of Bobby Gunther's trailer home. He was about to knock on the door when it opened and Bobby greeted him with a broad smile. Dooley was surprised to see that some of the clutter he had seen in the room on his previous visit was no longer there. The young man had taken it upon himself to attempt a lifestyle change. The inside of the mobile home was very clean. The carpet, furniture and fixtures were still old and worn, but everything had been scrubbed and cleaned. The aroma was fresh and there was a bucket on the floor where Bobby had been washing the inside of the windows. There was one other improvement, too. The smell of marijuana smoke was gone.

"Come on in, Connie," invited Bobby.

Dooley stepped inside and surveyed the new décor. "I like what you've done with the place, Bobby. What brought this on?"

"I don't mean to sound like a brown-noser, but I realized I could live better. I learned it from you. I don't want to be a bum all my life and I saw how you do it and I liked your way better. I didn't have anything better to do while I was healing up so I started cleaning the place up a little. I have a whole pickup full of stuff to take to the dump."

"I'm proud of you, Bobby. This is a good start." Dooley looked around a little more and nodded his approval. He reached inside his jacket pocket to fetch the envelope Terry had given him. "It looks like you could use some new furniture. Here. This may help a little. Mr. Boyette thought you should have a little bonus for all the trouble you've had lately." Bobby took the manila envelope and opened it. His eyes opened wide.

"Wow! How come?" asked Bobby. "I didn't do nothin' to deserve this, but thanks a lot."

"You earned it, Bobby. You've been a good employee and we appreciate it." Connie began to explain the new rules to his helper. "Mr. Boyette and I have come to an agreement and from now on I'm going to run the drug business. I want you to be my assistant. How do you feel about working for me?"

"Are you kidding me?" asked an astonished Bobby. "You and me? Working together?"

"That's what I had in mind. We're making some changes and I'd like you to be in on them. We moved the lab to a new location in North Kenai and closed the one in Sterling. I think we'll have to find another person to help in the lab. I don't know of anyone right now, but we'll find someone. I might be able to get someone down from Anchorage." Dooley was thinking out loud.

"I might know someone, Connie. A guy I know does a little dealing to pay for his own grass. He doesn't use anything else, just smokes a little grass. He's a quiet sort of guy and keeps his mouth shut. We've been friends since high school. I trust the guy. You can meet him if you think we can use him."

"You say you've known him a long time, does he have a rap sheet? I don't want someone the police are watching."

"No, he ain't never been arrested or nothin'. Do you want to meet him?"

Dooley thought for a moment before answering, "Call him and have him meet us for lunch at that little Mexican place by the Moose Club. 11:30 a.m. to beat the lunch crowd. You and I can go to the new lab and look around when we finish."

"Give me a minute to call him and see if he wants the job." Bobby found his cell phone and called. The two talked for only about a minute. "He says he's interested and he'll be there."

"Good, get your coat and you can come with me. You shouldn't be driving just yet." As the two were leaving the trailer Dooley again said, "You've done a nice job of cleaning up the place, Bobby."

Dooley made a stop at the big warehouse in Soldotna to pick up some remaining supplies and a small tool box for use at the new lab. On the way to Kenai, Dooley explained to Bobby there would be a new office for them when the deal was finalized. He impressed on his new assistant that he wanted the location to remain a secret between them, for security reasons. He said he hoped to learn the location later that day.

Bobby and Dooley arrived at the restaurant and went inside. A nicely dressed young man followed them inside and introduced himself at the table.

"Hi Bobby," he said and turned to Dooley, "I'm Danny Risso." He held out his hand, "Bobby says you're looking for a helper."

"We might be. Have a seat." Risso took a seat opposite Dooley. "The first thing I want to know is have you ever been arrested for anything at all?"

"No, never. I try to stay clear of the cops. I smoke a little grass and sell some to make enough money to pay for my smokes, but I wasn't never arrested."

"What kind of education do you have?" asked Dooley.

"I graduated from high school. I been working in the oil fields, but I ain't strong enough to keep doing it. I've been thinking about getting a job in a grocery store, maybe a produce department job. I don't need much money to live on, just rent and food and some weed once in a while."

"Bobby says you can be trusted and what Bobby says is good enough for me, but I want you to know there are rules and the penalty for violating our rules is severe. We'll pay a livable wage and take care of you, but break the rules and the consequences will be harsh. Do you understand?"

"Yes sir, Mr. Dooley. I know what you do and Bobby and I have been friends for a long time. He says I can trust you."

Dooley held out his hand across the table, "Good to have you on board, Danny. Bobby and I are having lunch, would you like to join us?"

"Sure," said a grinning Risso who reached a hand across the table to shake hands with Bobby.

John McGowan had been in Kenai to pick up some pain medications from the pharmacy and was returning to his home in Nikiski when he thought he recognized the big Dodge pickup parked at the Mexican restaurant just north of the main part of Kenai. He turned around at the next intersection and drove back to the church parking lot across a side street from the restaurant and waited to be sure this was the truck he had been looking for. A half hour later he got his answer. The driver was the same one who had broken his hand a few nights before. This was a stroke of luck. He waited and followed the truck north to a side street near Salamatof Lake. McGowan followed at a safe distance to where the big black truck turned off the main road to a wooded drive on the north side of the lake. McGowan stopped his vehicle on the main road and walked up the drive. It was quite a walk to where he found the pickup parked near a large shed. He felt it could be too dangerous for him to investigate closer at this time and returned to his own car. He decided to come back another time when no one was at the shed. He had a score to settle with this Dooley character and now knew where he could locate him. First he needed to know what was taking place inside the shed. He would learn that later today.

Chapter 29

It was nearly five in the afternoon when the three men finished work at the shed. All the equipment was now installed and operational. A small run of product to test the equipment had been done and the new system seemed to be working perfectly. Dooley stored the new product in plastic bags and placed them in the small safe bolted to the floor of the office. He was happy with the new ventilation and heating systems. The office and entry area were free from the toxic fumes created in the lab while the cooking was in progress.

"Come on boys, I'll buy you a drink to celebrate our success. Tomorrow we start production. We're going to need a lot of product in the coming days and it'll be up to the two of you to make it. I want you to stay safe while doing it. So, remember to wear your hazmat suits and masks when you're in the lab. Keep an eye on the vent stack and try to keep the fumes to a minimum. We don't want anyone investigating the new lab." They all climbed into Dooley's big black Dodge and drove toward Kenai. Bobby said he wanted to have his drink at Keen Eye Joe's, a small bar off the main street.

They each had one beer and drove back to Soldotna. They made an agreement to meet at the lab the next morning at eight o'clock.

David Haskins drove directly from work to Penny's house. He wasn't in uniform and had no need to change clothing. Penny had changed clothes and looked ravishing. She stepped out of the house as David drove into the drive. He had just enough time to reach over and open the passenger side door for her.

As she climbed into the tall truck he reached out to hold her arm. "My, don't you look wonderful this evening?" he commented.

"I'm just trying to impress my new beau. I've heard he's really fussy about whom he is seen with."

"Not any more, not any more. You're beautiful, Penny, and I'm in love with you." He was still holding her arm while gazing into her eyes.

"I think we had better go get Julia before one of us gets mushy," she said in a sarcastic tone.

Julia said she wanted the prime rib at Mykel's Restaurant, so that's where they went for dinner. It's a fine restaurant with excellent food and outstanding Prime Rib. Penny held fast to the rule of no wine for Julia, which meant the two of them, were not drinking either. It was a pleasant evening and Julia was showing signs of tiring when they drove her back to the assisted living center. Both Penny and David walked her back to her room and said good night, promising to come again soon.

On the way back to Penny's house David asked if it would be alright if he came inside for a while? He had something he wanted to discuss with her. She agreed and the two walked hand in hand to the door. Inside she shed her coat and offered David a nightcap. He said he would pass for now.

"I want to ask you something and I need a clear head to do it," he said.

"This sounds ominous," she said with a short giggle.

"Well, I guess you could call it that." He reached inside his jacket pocket and took out a small white box. He opened it to display a gold ring with one large diamond and several smaller ones.

"Oh, David, it's gorgeous," she gasped.

"I know we haven't talked about this much, but I think it's time we made this a permanent relationship. We don't have to rush into a wedding date, but I'm hoping you'll consider naming one. I love you very much and can't imagine my life without you. Please say you feel at least a little like I do."

She took the small white box in her hand. There were tears in her eyes when she looked up into his. "Oh, David, I love you, too. The answer is yes." She wiped the tears away with the back of her hand. "Do you think it will fit?" With that she wrapped both arms around him and kissed him hard.

There was little talk for the next hour while they sat on the couch holding hands and enjoying each other's company. This is the way it was meant to be, thought Penny. "Would it be OK if I called Julia and told her the news?"

It was late when David went home. It had been a long time since he felt this good about his life.

John McGowan had been checking the Salamatof property periodically all day long waiting for it to become empty allowing him the opportunity to get inside without being observed. It was early evening when the two men inside the shed finished for the day and drove away. Another vehicle, the big black Dodge belonging to the man he knew as Dooley, had come and gone several times during the day, but had not been there in the past two or three hours. McGowan drove up the wooded lane to the shed after the two workers had gone. There was a padlock on the door, but McGowan was ready for that. He reached into a small tool box in the trunk of his car to get a bolt cutter with long red handles. The padlock was sturdy, but no match for the leverage provided by the cutters. The door hardware was not locked allowing him to enter when the padlock was cut away.

Once inside the warm building he immediately recognized the odor of chemicals used in the manufacture of meth. One of the first things he spotted was the small safe near the desk in the entry room. He gave it a tug to see if it was movable. It wasn't. He looked at the row of plastic hazmat suits hanging on a rod bolted to the right hand wall. He opened the door on the opposite wall to find another small room with three chairs and a small table and a single light hanging from the ceiling. "A break room," he thought. He backed out of the room and tried the last door. It was open. Behind it was a meth lab; a fancy one at that. There was an outside heat source and a continuous flow ventilation system. Three long work benches covered with boxes and bottles lined the walls while an electric range filled the center of the small room. Several kettles, pressure cookers really, were washed and turned upside down to dry on a blanket on the floor near the electric range. There were no windows in the entire shed, but vents were cut into the walls to accommodate the air flow and heating systems.

McGowan's first thought was to set a match to the place and burn it to the ground, but he knew he needed the product produced in this little factory. He would let the men do the work and then take the product from them later. His first concern was Dooley. That man had some serious pain coming to him and it would come very soon. He left the shed, closing the door and hanging the broken padlock back on the hasp.

It was dark when Bobby and his new assistant Danny Risso arrived at the shed. When he found the lock had been cut off he called Dooley to report the entry. Connie was on the scene within fifteen minutes. Bobby had already determined there was nothing missing inside the shed and Dooley, without hesitation, began to look for tire tracks. He found them and determined they were not matching tires and therefore not the law. He double-checked the inside to be certain nothing had been disturbed. The question now was what to do? He instructed Bobby and Danny to go back to work and he would return shortly.

It was only a six mile trip into Kenai where he made a stop at the local Radio Shack store. He talked with the clerk who showed him an intruder alert that would ring on his cell phone when someone entered his property without the password. He purchased the unit and asked the clerk to show him how to operate the unit and he got a few pointers on installation.

Since there were no windows there was only one sensor to install. Power was another easy fix. Unlike the Sterling barn, there was commercial power here allowing him to plug the unit into an existing outlet. This would notify him of any future entry, but he still had the problem of whom and why was someone in here late last night. It didn't seem likely that local juveniles would be carrying a bolt cutter with them. It was also unlikely someone had just stumbled on the shed. No, this went deeper than that. He would talk with Boyette about it.

With Bobby in charge of things at the lab, Dooley called Terry and asked to come by the office for a short conference. Boyette was at his desk, which was covered with papers regarding his newest land acquisition in North Kenai.

"Come in Connie, how are things at the new lab?" asked the boss.

"That's why I came to see you. We had a break-in last night. Nothing was taken, but someone cut off the lock on the door and went inside. I found tire tracks but they didn't look like police car tires. I think it could be a competitor or a dealer looking around, but I can't imagine who it might be. I thought you had more experience in the local market and you might know who would be snooping around." There was frustration in Dooley's voice.

Boyette rubbed his chin while thinking and shook his head. "I can't think of anyone who would want to interfere with our business. Most of our customers are locals with no other source of product. I have a certain reputation here and not many of my customers want to cross me." He paused a few seconds before answering, "Hey Connie, wait a minute. What about that dealer in North Kenai, the one you had the run-in with? Is it possible he saw you somewhere and followed you to the new lab?"

Dooley slapped his own forehead, "I should have thought of him. He made a couple of threats when I took his gun away. Do you have any connections to find out who this guy is, and if he's a danger to us? I don't have a problem taking care of him, but I'd like to know it's the right one."

Terry picked a notebook from one of his desk drawers and thumbed the pages. "His name is John McGowan. He's lived in Nikiski most of his life, but was away for a couple of years. He worked for one of my associates in Anchorage for a period of time. Perhaps I can get some information from him. Come back in an hour and I'll see what I can find out."

An hour later Dooley was back in the office with Boyette. "It looks like you may have crossed a very bad dude this time, Connie. McGowan worked for one of my suppliers in Anchorage a couple of years ago. He thought he would take over the operation from my friend. It turns out McGowan is married to my friend's wife's sister. My friend let him live and he came back to Nikiski. My friend says McGowan is a ruthless individual and he's crazy. He says McGowan will kill for almost no reason at all. I told him about the run-in you had with him and he said to watch your back. McGowan will be out for revenge and he'll kill you if he gets the chance."

"I'm sure a man like that must have a lot of enemies. One of them may cause him to have an accident before I can do anything about him." Dooley knew he had to learn much more about his new foe.

"I don't want to know anything about it, Connie," said Boyette, turning back to his desk.

Dooley went to lunch before driving to Nikiski. He didn't have many resources in North Kenai, but he would generate some for this cause. A man like McGowan must have made a lot of enemies along the way. It shouldn't be too difficult to find some of them.

By late afternoon Dooley had bought drinks for a large percentage of the unemployed citizens of Nikiski. Many of them knew John McGowan and few had any good words for him. Some owed him money and were afraid of him. Some had been unable to pay him and were now disabled because of him. Dooley learned McGowan lived in an old cabin off of Miller Loop Road, had propane heat and commercial power. The old Honda he drove was his business car. He owned a big white Ford diesel F350 pickup and an aluminum commercial fishing vessel, which was covered and parked, in his yard at the cabin. Except for a few weeks of commercial fishing he didn't work, but spent a lot of money on big toys and Las Vegas trips. Few people liked him, but nearly everyone feared him.

By the end of the day he was convinced he had been asking about the right man. He had to come up with a plan to eliminate him without bringing attention to his new business venture. Given the number of people willing to talk about him it should be easy to rid the North Road of a predator, eliminate a potential competitor and make a lot of friends all at the same time.

Chapter 30

David Haskins wanted to take a day off and he wanted to spend it with his new fiancée. She was working when he called. "Hello there, Lady," he greeted.

"Who is calling, please?" she joked into the telephone.

"This is an obscene phone call, will you accept the charges?"

"Why, you dirty old man," answered Penny, a bit giddy about the call.

"Are you busy or can you talk a minute?"

"I have a minute for you. I should take the day off because I didn't sleep a wink last night thinking about us. I never thought I could be happy about being engaged, but it turns out I'm excited about it." She paused for a short second and added, "Wait a minute, you're not having second thoughts are you?"

"Not yet, are you going to try to talk me out of it now?"

"I have a ring for evidence, you're stuck with me now big boy." They both chuckled like teenagers. "What did you really call about?"

"I have some comp time coming and I thought if you could get a way we might take a drive. You know, just some time alone with each other."

"That sounds wonderful, David. The judge is in court right now, but after arraignments I think I can get away. Where would you like to go?" she asked, not caring.

"How about lunch in Seward and come back to my place for a nightcap?" David wasn't much of a drinker, but a glass of wine with his new wife-to-be sounded like a good idea.

"I would like to stop and see Julia on the way back from Seward, if you don't mind."

"Happy to oblige," David answered.

"Good, give me a half hour to see if the judge has anything for me to do then I'll be ready. I do love you, you know."

"And I love you, too. I'll see you in an hour at your house." He hated to admit, even to himself, how deeply he felt for this tiny red-headed woman. He had dated a lot of women in his career, but none of them made him feel like he felt for this one. There was no doubt in his mind this is the one he was destined to spend the rest of his life sharing his love.

An hour later he was waiting in front of Penny Rossiter's house, dressed in jeans and a flannel shirt. Nothing could go wrong on a day like this, he thought. This is the way most lovers spend an afternoon and he was intending to enjoy every minute of it.

Lou Filson was in his office when the District Attorney called him. She agreed with David Haskins about the evidence for arrest being slim and inconclusive. However, she also agreed it was enough to bring Bud Leach in for questioning regarding the murder of the two women and the missing boys. The boys were the key to the urgency of the meeting. Until there fate was known they had to assume the boys were alive. After this much time had lapsed it seemed unlikely, but Filson wanted to hold onto that last thread of hope.

Filson spent more than an hour making a list of questions to ask Anthony Leach when he came to the office. David had taken a comp day and was out of the office leaving this interrogation for Lou and Don Winston. When Winston returned Lou asked him to come to his office where they conferred in regards to the list of questions. Lou called the owner of the trucking company Leach worked for and asked when he would be available. He was told the driver would be back in the yard by 4:30 p.m. Winston and Filson agreed to meet at the trucking company yard at that time.

Filson was the officer to approach Leach when he pulled into the yard. "Hi there, Bud. Do you mind talking with us for a few minutes?" Lou asked when Bud stepped down from the cab of the tall oil tanker.

"Happy to do it, if we can do it somewhere warm," Leach answered.

"I don't want to cause you any problems here at work, Bud. Would you mind driving over to our office and meet us there?"

"Yeah, that's probably a good idea. Truckers like to gossip. Let me turn in my trip tickets and I'll follow you over there." The trucking yard was almost fourteen miles from the office.

While Leach was in the office finishing his day's paperwork Lou drove back to the Soldotna office. Before leaving he spoke with Winston and asked him to follow the driver to the office, just in case he changed his mind about talking.

Lou was in his office when Winston escorted Leach into the quiet conference room. He was offered a seat and coffee or a soda, both of which he refused.

"You said you had some questions for me, what's it all about?" Leach was still the cool customer he had been on other occasions they had met.

"Just relax, Bud, this won't take long. We need to follow up on some of the information we gathered when we did the search at your place. You remember when we did that, right?" Lou Filson sat behind his desk asking the questions. Winston stood, but was leaning on a file cabinet and not speaking.

"Yes, I came home while you were there." Leach said without hesitation. "You didn't find anything did you?"

"You're right, Bud. We didn't find much. We checked the house and the crawl space under the floor. We checked the sheds and the yard as well as the hangar. I have to say you are about the neatest housekeeper I've ever run across. I commend you for that."

"It doesn't take much to keep the place up when I'm the only one messing it up. Thanks for noticing." Leach was smiling now.

"There was one thing, though, and it's the reason we asked you to come to the office." Filson looked directly into Leach's eyes as he spoke to see if there was a flicker of guilt hiding there.

"I don't know what you could have found, there's nothing there." Leach spoke nervously.

"Like I said, Mr. Leach, we didn't find much. We sent some samples of floor sweepings to the crime lab for analysis and we just received the report. It was interesting. There was nothing in the report we would consider unusual except for the microscopic traces we swept from the rear floor of your airplane. You recall we said before that we had a witness placing your plane at the Hope Airport at the time a crime took place on the Resurrection Trail. You admitted you were there panning for gold. All that checked out."

"If it all checked out why are you asking more questions?" Leach uncrossed his legs and re-crossed them to the opposite side.

"Like I said, Bud, we sent some sweepings from the floor of your airplane to the crime lab and they found something unusual, at least for your airplane." Lou was attempting to make Leach uneasy and defensive. It seemed to be working.

"I keep my airplane clean. There couldn't be anything in there for you to find. I'll bet you didn't even find any fingerprints."

"That's a good point, Bud, but it did make us look a little closer at what we did find. We vacuumed samples of dirt from the cracks in the rear floor of your airplane and found some unusual material." Lou continued to bait Leach.

"If you found anything in the rear of the plane you had to have put it there. I always sweep my plane clean when I come back from a flight, especially if I had been prospecting." Leach's speech volume increased slightly.

"I admit it was pretty darn clean, but we have a small battery powered vacuum and used it to suck dirt from between the boards of the rear floor. We inspected the particles and didn't see anything, but the lab was able to identify some minute particles of orange color plastic. This particular plastic is used in manufacturing children's shoe soles. Only one company uses this type of material. The company is located in Indonesia. This plastic is used in only one style and one brand of shoe. It is sold in only one store in Alaska. They're not a popular brand and not many of these shoes were sold. The reason this is of interest to us is that we have two missing boys and both of them were wearing this type of shoe. They had planned to take a long hike and had these new shoes on their feet when they went missing."

Leach was speechless, "Am I under arrest?" he asked. "If I am I'm going to call my lawyer."

"You aren't under arrest, Mr. Leach, but we can't figure out how those particles came to be in the back seat of your airplane at the same time the two boys went missing. Can you answer that one question for us?" Filson had Leach squirming in his seat now. "If you can give me a satisfactory answer to that one question you can go home. If not, I would advise you to call your lawyer. Now Bud, would you like to tell us where the boys are located?"

"I'm through talking to you two. I want to see your supervisors about being treated like a criminal. You haven't even read me my rights. Now, arrest me or let me out of here!"

"Calm down, Mr. Leach," said Winston, who had said nothing up to this point. "If you want to leave you're free to do so. However I must advise you to stay in the local area and not fly your airplane until we clear this matter up. If you refuse to answer our questions we must assume you have some degree of guilt. We'll continue our investigation with or without your cooperation."

"I'm leaving right now. You two can talk to my lawyer. I won't say anything else to you without him present. Now, take me to my car." It was clear Leach had lost his cool. When taken to the back door leading to the parking lot he stormed away, spinning his wheels when backing out.

When Winston returned to Lou Filson's office he said, "I think you upset the poor man."

"He didn't say anything, but he convinced me he's guilty. Our problem now is that we have to find the boys, if they're still alive, before Leach can hurt them. We need to put a tail on him for a while to see what he does. Have two of our team keep tabs on him as long as he's not at work. I'll talk to David in the morning and we'll make some kind of plan. I think he and I will have to meet with the DA on this one. I wonder who his lawyer is?" Lou was speaking while making notes on the file atop his desk.

Filson called Stella Moore, the assistant DA. "I talked with our suspect in the abduction case."

"Good, did you learn anything new?"

"Nothing we can prove, but I'm convinced he's our guy. So sure in fact, I put a tail on him in case he decides to leave the country. At this point he's just shouting 'lawyer.' He put up a good front until we hit him with the lab report. That's when he went off. He quit talking and left the office in a huff. He was so certain he had removed any evidence he even mentioned our not finding any fingerprints, which we didn't."

"That's interesting," Stella said, "but we still have no idea where he may have taken the boys."

"He's a pilot with his own plane, they could be anywhere. In fact he may have a cabin or camp somewhere that we don't know about."

"I might be able to help you there, Lou. Cabins and camps on public land are registered and the owners pay a fee to keep them there. I'll check with BLM and the feds to see if he has one of those leases."

"It sounds like a long shot, but it's worth a try. Let me know what you find out. And if you hear from the lawyer I'd like to know about it. I expect to learn about him from the Captain. They usually come in to complain to my supervisor." Lou was chuckling about it.

David and Penny came back to Soldotna in the early evening. Their first stop was at the assisted living home to visit Julia. She was in the community room playing cards with a group of residents when they arrived. She asked to sit out a few hands while her visitors were here.

In her room she asked a direct question of her daughter. "OK, young lady, what have you been up to that has you smiling like the cat who ate the canary?"

Penny held out her left hand to display the new diamond on her finger. Julia took her hand and made a closer inspection. "Is this what I think it is?" she asked.

"It's hard to tell what you think it is, Mom, but David has asked me to marry him and I said yes. I wanted you to be the first to know. If you behave yourself we'll invite you to the wedding." Penny had a sparkle in her eyes Julia had not seen since her father died.

"I wish you all the luck in the world, David," said Julia. "I've never been able to get this girl to do anything I asked." She then put her arms around her daughter and hugged her tightly. "Congratulations, Honey, I wish the two of you all the happiness in the world."

Penny explained they'd not yet set the wedding date and agreed to ask Julia for help in planning the wedding. David had no close family of his own and was proud to be a part of this one. The discussions and promising and heckling went on for more than an hour when they let Julia go back to her card game.

"Unless you have other plans I can fix a light dinner for us at my place," Penny said when they drove away from Julia's new residence.

"I think that would be wonderful, but I have to caution you, I have to work tomorrow morning and can't stay late."

Penny slapped him on the arm and said, "Oh, You."

Chapter 31

It was early the following morning when Dooley called Bobby Gunther and asked him to meet with him in Nikiski. It was time to deal with John McGowan. He asked Bobby to go to the dealer's home and keep an eye on McGowan and to let him know when McGowen went into town. Dooley ordered Bobby to stay out of sight, but follow the dealer and to call if he decided to return to his cabin. The evening before, Dooley had made a stop at the hardware store for a few things needed to complete his task.

It was just past eight in the morning when the dealer started his old Honda sedan and drove to a local restaurant for breakfast. Bobby called Dooley to let him know where McGowan was and said it looked like he was having breakfast with a couple of other men and should be occupied for a time.

Dooley had been waiting only a mile from the cabin owned by McGowan and immediately went to the isolated home when he received the word. He drove to the front of the cabin and walked to the front door. It was locked. The common house lock proved to be no obstacle for the experienced Dooley. Inside he looked for the line furnishing propane gas to the cooking and heating stoves. He found them and located a flexible line with a brass fitting connecting the line to the appliances. Dooley taped a mouse trap to the wall near the door. He had already attached one wire of a lamp cord to the spring of the mouse trap and the other wire to a spot on the wooden platform where the spring would send the trap snare when it was tripped, thus completing a circuit when the trap was tripped. A short string was tied to the wire holding the trap in the set position and the other end taped to the base of the front door. With a pair of pliers he loosened the fitting connecting the two stoves to the propane line, leaving a loose line to leak its contents into the room. Finally, he plugged the lamp wire into an outlet in the wall. He made a quick survey of the room to see if he had left anything out of place. Satisfied he had not; he made a final check of the loose propane line and exited through the rear door of the cabin.

Dooley had just entered his own truck when his phone rang. It was Bobby saying McGowan was leaving the restaurant. Dooley told Bobby to pick up Danny Risso and to meet him at the new lab. An hour later the trio was busy with a new batch of product when they heard the sirens from the fire trucks leaving the nearby station. None of the men paid much attention to the distraction, but inside his plastic protective suit Dooley was smiling. The men worked all day, stepping outside for a breath of fresh air from time to time. It was after seven in the evening when the equipment was cleaned and the new product stored in the safe.

With work done for the day Dooley offered to buy dinner and beer at a nice little restaurant and bar on Kalifornsky Road on the return trip to Soldotna. Dooley picked up the tab for dinner and thanked the men for a good days work. He would have to wait until morning and read the paper to learn if the mousetrap had caught a rat.

Davin Haskins and Lou Filson had worked all day in the office expecting to hear from Stella Moore at any time. It was the end of the day when she called with information about Anthony Leach.

"It took all day to come up with the information, but I finally got it," she sounded frustrated.

"What did you learn?" asked Filson.

"Leach has two leases with the feds. One is a hunting camp over near Lake Illiamna. He's owned the lease for fifteen years. Wildlife troopers stop and check the camp from time to time, but there has never been a complaint filed about the camp."

"That would be nearly 300 miles from here and require a refueling stop to get back," said Filson. What about the other one?"

"That one is closer. He owns a small cabin with an airstrip at the base of the mountains where the McArthur River makes a turn to the north. I have the GPS coordinates. I talked with one of the federal Fish and Wildlife Officers who patrol the area and he says it's a nice cabin. The airstrip is really short, so not many planes land there. He did tell me that Leach uses the cabin all year long. He also said there was another cabin about a half mile west of the main house that Leach uses for a meat house when he's moose hunting over there. He says there are a couple of outbuildings at the cabin, a woodshed and a smoker. He said he flies over the camp regularly and Leach is there a lot. He also said Leach is usually alone when he goes to the cabin. That's about it." Stella had finished her summary.

"I think we should have one of our pilots go over there and take a look. It's too late in the day today, we're out of daylight." Filson said as he thumbed through his notes. "Can you give me those coordinates?"

Once he was off the telephone he turned to David, "It may not mean anything, but we have a cabin on federal land registered to Bud Leach. Do you want me to take the Super Cub over there in the morning?"

"Sure, you can do that. You need a day out of the office," commented Haskins.

Lou was about to make a rude comment back to his boss when his intercom phone rang. He answered for a long while, making notes while he listened. When he finished he just said, "Thanks" and hung up the telephone.

"That was the fire chief from Nikiski. They have a suspicious fire on Miller Loop, one man dead and questionable circumstances. Do you want to ride out there with me?"

"You bet," answered Haskins, "when did this happen?"

"Sometime this morning; the Fire Marshal has been on the scene all day. The Chief says they found some kind of booby trap device on the front door of the cabin. They want us to take a look at it."

"I'll get my coat and meet you at the car."

When they arrived at the scene it was plain to see there had been some kind of explosion. The front portion of the roof had been lifted up and all the glass in the house was blown outward. The snow close to the cabin had melted from the heat of the fire. Debris from the blast had broken the windshield of the old Honda parked in front of the cabin. A body was on the front porch and would have been blown into the parking area but for one of the posts supporting the porch roof stopping it. He may have died when he struck the large wooden post.

Nikiski Fire Marshal Keith Stilson met the two troopers when they arrived.

"What'cha got?" asked Haskins

"At first we thought it was just a gas leak, but come take a look at this." Firemen were setting up large banks of floodlights in the yard, but they were not yet operational. The fire marshal had a large battery powered light he held to show the troopers the device that had been attached to the front door. "Have you ever seen a trigger like this one?"

Both troopers studied the mousetrap trigger. "Can't say as I have," said Haskins. "Bag it all up and we'll send it to the crime lab. Kind of ingenious, though. Was the gas line tampered with?"

"It looks like it was. The fitting at the tee where it splits inside the house was loose. It was probably done to create the gas leak."

"Did you see any tire tracks or footprints when you arrived?"

"No, we saw the body on the front porch, but the fire was so hot we had to deal with that before we started looking around. At first we thought there might be more victims."

"Do you have an ID on the victim yet?" Haskins was asking the questions.

"Unofficially, yes, we all knew the guy. He's a local dope dealer. Everybody knew it, but no one ever proved it. He was a suspect in a couple of bad beatings that took place out here in the past few months. I don't know if it's his real name, but he went by the name of John McGowan." The fire marshal had done a good job of gathering evidence and assessing the situation in a short time.

"We need to bag him and take him to the crime lab for fingerprinting and identification. The techs up there will check to see if he was using drugs."

"We'll do that," said Stilson.

"Just one more thing, Keith, do you have any suspects?"

"Yeah; half the residents of Nikiski." He was laughing as he walked away to help with the lights.

When they returned to the office Filson went inside to do the report, but Haskins drove to Penny Rossiter's house to give her the news about the cabin on McArthur River. She answered the door and invited him inside.

"What brings you here this time of night?" she asked, her eyes twinkling with love.

"I came to ask what your day looks like tomorrow morning?" We have a lead on a cabin owned by Bud Leach and I'm going to send the Cub over there to take a look. I thought you might be interested in going along, as an observer of course."

"Front seat or back?" she asked, referring to the front seat as being the pilot.

"Your name is still on the authorized list of state pilots, so it's your choice." Before she could respond he continued, "On second thought just take the front seat. I know you will anyway. Besides the airstrip is short and you're the best pilot to land there if we need to do that. Besides, if you are flying I'll be able to go."

"You're going to make a good husband, David. You know how to avoid an argument. I'll call Nancy right now and let her know. I'd call the judge, but he'd tell me not to go because we may be involved in a later court hearing. I'd rather go investigate now than write an opinion about it later." She was snickering about her deceit as she spoke.

"You still have the old fire-horse in you, don't you? When the bell goes off you want to pull the wagon." He reached out to hold and hug her, "That's one of the things I love about you."

"I'll see you in the morning, and thank you for asking me, David."

"I'll see you at the office in the morning. Daylight will be around eight, so I'll meet you in my office at seven; you bring the coffee." He gave a little wave as he went out the door.

Early the next morning Dooley was at the Caribou Restaurant where he ordered a hamburger steak and eggs with whole wheat toast and coffee. He had purchased a copy of the local newspaper and opened it to read the front page when the waitress had gone to place the order. The lead story on the front page was about a gas explosion and fire causing the death of a Nikiski resident, John McGowan. He read the entire article but there were no particulars about the fire. The only fact included was a note that the cause of the explosion and fire were still being investigated. That only meant they found the booby trap and were investigating, concluded Dooley.

He was finishing his second cup of coffee when his cell phone rang. It was Boyette. "Sad thing about John McGowan; tragic, him dying in a house fire like that. He was such a nice fella', too."

"We all gotta go sometime. It must have been his time," said Dooley, sarcastically.

"What do you have on your schedule today, Connie?"

"I have to get the boys started on another run of product this morning. Once I have them lined out I can get away if you need me."

There are a couple of things I would like you to do for me today, if you have the time. Come by the office when you're done instructing your crew. I'd like to see you before noon." Boyette would never say anything incriminating on the telephone.

"I have a run of product on hand, will I need to bring it with me?" asked Dooley.

"I think that would be a good idea. See you before noon." Boyette didn't say goodbye, just hung up the phone.

Dooley met Gunther and Risso at the shed. He had opened the little office by the time they arrived and taken the package of new product from the safe and stowed it in the console of his Dodge truck.

He supervised the two young men as they put on the protective clothing and assembled the chemicals needed to make the valuable product they produced. Dooley was adamant about the precise use of the formula and timing of the brew. Following the formula was the key to making a quality product and the last thing they needed was for some user to die of poisoning from a bad batch of their brand of product.

Satisfied all the systems were at the correct temperatures and the ingredients were being measured correctly Dooley climbed into his truck for the drive to Soldotna to meet with Terry Boyette. He expected Boyette to order him to make more deliveries for him today.

The death of the dealer from Nikiski was still on the front page of the papers, but, thought Dooley, "it pays well."

Chapter 32

It felt like old times when Penny parked in the trooper parking area at the office. She was admitted like she had always been and found her way to the little office occupied by David Haskins. David was on the telephone when she entered, but he pointed to a chair and she sat. He was making notes on a pad while listening to the voice on the phone. Finally he hung up and smiled at her.

"That was the weather report. Clear and cold, no wind, a perfect day for flying. Did you bring the picnic lunch?" he asked jokingly.

"Nope, but I did bring the coffee, like any good minion would do; good morning to you, too."

"The Cub is in the hangar and warm. The emergency pack is on the desk at the hangar. The plane is fueled up and I put a phone book on the front seat so you will be able to see out over the instrument panel."

"You're so kind and considerate. Next you'll be trying to tell me there'll be no aerobatics on this flight."

"As a matter of fact that was the next thing on my list. Come on, let's go to work." They drove the trooper car to the airport and parked behind the big blue hangar. Inside David turned on the lights and they did a thorough pre-flight inspection. Making sure the magnetos were in the off position, David pulled the propeller through to be sure everything was free and working properly. He pressed the button and opened the tall door on the front of the building. He only opened it partially, just enough to allow the small plane to be pushed outside. Once outside he closed the huge door again to conserve heat in the cavernous hangar. While he turned out the lights and locked the man-door Penny strapped into the pilot seat and started the engine, idling it to warm the oil.

David maneuvered into the rear seat and strapped in. Penny closed the clam-shell-type door and heat began to be felt from the heater vents. With headsets in place and the intercom working they could now speak to each other.

"Are you ready back there?" asked the pilot.

"Hanging on with both hands," Haskins quipped.

"I'm climbing to 5500 feet to cross the inlet, and then I'll drop back down," she informed him as they taxied to the runway. The airplane was equipped with hydraulic wheel-skis, which meant they were taxiing on wheels, but the skis could be jacked down enabling them to land in snow. The takeoff run was short and the climb-out smooth and steady as she climbed to the high altitude. The altitude was a safety measure in case the engine failed while crossing the nine miles of water to the west side of Cook Inlet. Once past the midway point she began a slow and steady descent and was at 1000 feet by the time they reached dry land on the west side. She had preset her GPS to the coordinates Stella had furnished them. It was light now and the sun was illuminating Mount Redoubt in the Alaska Range on the Alaska Peninsula. Penny was grateful to be flying to the West and not East into the rising sun. She leveled at 500 feet and found the McArthur River, following it upstream to the point where it made a sharp bend to the north. Immediately she spotted a cabin at the edge of the trees. Checking her GPS she noted it was the one leased to Bud Leach.

"There it is," she said into the mike.

"Circle a couple of times and see if there are any tracks or signs of life."

"Will do David, but I don't see any smoke from the chimney."

"I'm going to video the area, make a circle at 500 and then drop to 200 for another pass. I'd like to get pictures of the other cabin, also." He tapped her on the shoulder and pointed to the meat house a half mile away. She followed his directions while he took videos of the entire vicinity.

When he had finished filming she came around to make a pass at the small airstrip. It was actually very adequate for the Super Cub. There was a light dusting of snow since the last time someone had landed here, but the tracks were still visible as were the footprints leading to the cabin. She taxied back to the south end of the airstrip and shut down the engine. After climbing out of the plane she drug an insulated engine cover from behind the seats and threw it over the cowling to hold in as much heat as possible ensuring the engine would start without pre-heating when they were ready to leave.

Both were wearing insulated boots to keep their feet warm while walking in the snow. David led the way up the short trail to the cabin. This was a very nice remote cabin. It had a well for water. The woodshed held a generator for power to run the well pump and furnish power to the lights and appliances when the owner was here. The doors were locked, but looking through the windows David saw the cabin was kept as neatly as the home in Sterling. They checked the woodshed as well as the meat house and found nothing. They were walking back to the cabin and ducking under a clothes line behind the cabin when Penny stumbled on something in the snow. She reached down to dust off the layer of snow and was surprised to see the pattern of Spider Man exposed on the cloth in the icy ground.

"Hey David, you had better take a look at this."

He turned and came back to where she was standing. They brushed away a layer of snow and found what had been a wet pair of child's undershorts frozen to the ground. David fished a pocket knife from his pants pocket and began to chip the colorful cloth from the icy dirt. Once it was free he dropped the lump into a gallon size evidence bag from his back pack.

Without a search warrant they couldn't enter the cabin, but both investigators were excited about the find. They walked back to the airplane and were about to climb inside when David had an idea. He took the cell phone from his jacket pocket and saw he had signal. He dialed a number and got an answer.

Haskins had called Ray Finlay, the Cooper Landing trooper. "Ray, David Haskins; I have a job for you."

"Does it require me to get out of bed?" Finlay answered.

"I'm sorry, but it might. This is important, Ray. Penny and I are over on the McArthur River at a cabin owned by Anthony Leach. We're heading back right now, but I need for you to call the fathers of the two missing boys and find out what kind of underwear the boys had with them. We need this information as soon as we can get it. We may have found something. We should be back at the office in an hour. Do you think you can get that info for us by then?"

"I can try," said Finlay, excited to hear there may be a break in this case. "I'll call you at the office as soon as I hear anything. Good work David."

Looking at Penny he said, "We can go now."

"Don't rush me," she said, "This thing only flies about 90 miles per hour."

"OK, just don't take any side trips for sightseeing and take a shortcut if there is one."

"Are you going to be this bossy after we're married?" she asked as she stowed the engine cover behind the back seat and wiggled into the front seat of the little blue and white Super Cub.

An hour later they were in David's office. The evidence in the plastic bag had begun to thaw. The bag was lying on Haskin's desk. Now with the ice melted it was easy to see the size of the boy's briefs. The boys were not much different in size when they were taken. Steve Baxter was nine years old and his cousin, Carl Reed, was seven. It would be difficult without confirmation from the fathers to determine which of the boys this pair of briefs belonged.

Penny waited in the little office drinking a cup of coffee while David had a short meeting with Captain Meadows. He was in the Captain's office when his telephone buzzed in his pocket.

"I have to take this, Cap." He said as he reached for the phone. It was Ray Finlay.

Finlay was excited when David answered. "I was able to get the information, David. The shorts belong to the younger boy, Carl Reed. His dad bought them the day before they went to Hope. They were purchased at the Fred Meyer store on Diamond Avenue in Anchorage. Tom Reed, the boy's father, said if you look inside the waistband he had written Carl's name with a magic marker in black ink."

"The shorts haven't completely thawed out yet, but when they do I'll look for the marking. We're going to need the father's statement about purchasing them. Will you be able to go to town and get it for us?"

"Already done, I had a trooper from headquarters meet with him and take the statement. He'll fax a copy to you as soon as it's available." Finlay had been a busy man in the last hour.

"That sounds great, Ray. You're getting pretty good at this investigating business. Do you want to move to Soldotna and make it a career?"

"No thanks, David, I like the country life up here in Cooper Landing. Glad to be able to help, though. Call me if you need anything further," said Finlay, "I'll be happy to see this one in jail."

Haskins relayed the story to the Captain before returning to his office to check for the markings. Without opening the evidence bag he moved the cloth around until he found the name printed inside the elastic waistband. Both he and Penny were relieved when they saw the printing. They were also sad because it also meant the boys were likely both dead.

"I guess our next move is to get an arrest warrant for Leach. I'll call Stella right now and get that started. You had better go home for now. I'll take Filson and Don Winston with me when we go to make the arrest. We can probably get him when he comes off his daily trucking runs. He shouldn't put up much of a fight if we get him at work."

"Don't be too sure, David. He's killed the mothers and probably the two boys. He's a dangerous man. He spends a lot of time in the bush and is a savvy woodsman. Don't underestimate him." Penny had apprehension in her voice as she spoke. "I don't want you getting hurt, not now."

"Don't worry, Penny, I'll take plenty of help when we go to arrest him. Now go home and I'll call you when we have him in custody."

"I don't want to sit at home, David. I think I'll go to work and try to catch up on a few things. Call me on my cell phone when you have him." She blew him a kiss for luck as she left the office and drove home to change her clothes and wash up for the office. And she continued to worry.

Filson and Haskins drove directly to the trucking company yard while Winston stopped at the courthouse for a copy of the arrest warrant. He was on his way to the trucking yard in North Kenai when he had a radio call telling him to turn around and go to Leach's home in Sterling. He had finished his rounds early today and gone home. The three troopers were to meet a mile from Leach's home. They met and formed a strategy for the approach. Haskins and Filson would drive directly to the cabin and confront Leach. Winston was to block the drive at the main road to stop an escape. The three patrol cars arrived at the home just in time to see the PA-12 lifting off the runway in a cloud of blowing snow. Leach's truck was parked near the hangar, the lights still burning. He had left in a hurry. Someone at the trucking company had obviously tipped him off and he was making a run for it, but to where was the question.

Haskins alerted the captain and asked to have one of the pilots use the Cessna 185 to find him. He also asked the captain to call the FAA in Kenai to alert them to the fugitive status of Leach and his Piper aircraft. Leach could have flown off in any direction. Penny had been right, this man was dangerous and he was woods-wise. He was going to be difficult to track down. A very good day had suddenly become a disaster. Haskins was not looking forward to telling Penny the news.

Chapter 33

The illicit drug business had always been a dangerous profession. Even in a small community like this drug dealers and users would disappear, never to be seen again. Bodies were seldom found. There was just too much area for any agency to search. On the west side of the Kenai Peninsula is Cook Inlet with its extreme tides and murky waters. On the east side of the peninsula is the Harding Ice Field and the Kenai Mountains rising to nearly eight thousand feet. There are three gigantic lakes on the Kenai Peninsula and thousands of small ones. There are few roads or trails with nearly all the population scattered along the paved highway system. The Kenai Peninsula is roughly 180 miles long and 75 miles wide with sixty thousand residents living in five established communities. It is not only the size of the area, but the inaccessibility that makes the task so difficult. Terry Boyette had managed to become a major player in the business without being publicly connected to the business.

All this was the reason he was willing to increase the profit share for Conrad Dooley. Dooley was a thinker and could be counted on to take care of business. He wasn't a greedy man, but wanted his share of the take. Terry saw this as his chance to further insulate his legitimate business interests from the drug trade he had operated to make enough money to become one of the big players in the coming natural gas boom. Boyette wasn't willing to divest himself of the drug business, but was willing to pay a significant amount to Dooley to run it for him.

Dooley sat quietly in Terry Boyette's office listening to the new business plan and the plan Boyette had for allowing Dooley to operate the drug business without interference from the new land baron. "You'll have to set up an office of your own, Connie. You will have to invest in a large safe in which to store your product and the shipments of other drugs you will be distributing locally. Over the years I've found it more profitable to leave the local sales to dealers and handle only wholesale marketing. This system will keep a layer of faces between you and the law. As you've learned, I will not tolerate dealers who will not pay on time. I suggest you adopt the same policy."

"I'm still learning the ropes and the territory. I value your experience and admire the fact you've never been scrutinized by the police. I like the way you keep a layer of people between you and the dealers. Unfortunately I haven't built that kind of organization yet, but I intend to follow your example. Bobby and the new guy, Risso, are both good workers, but they lack the willingness to do what it takes to keep the dealers in line. I plan to keep Gunther and Risso busy making high quality meth. I'd like to expand the meth sales into the Anchorage market. Our cut of the heroin and cocaine markets is good, but the opportunity for growth is limited. I think I can control all the flow of narcotics while using the Anchorage market for meth to grow the business. And as long as we're talking about business growth, I think I'd like to become a stockholder, if only a small one, in the land business. Maybe I could take my increased percentage in shares of the land business, sort of like you've done."

"Hmmm, I'll have to think about that one. Right now I'm inclined to go along with the idea as long as your business doesn't contaminate mine. The Chamber of Commerce isn't likely to award me Man of the Year knowing you're my partner and you're dealing drugs. I'm sure you can see my point."

"Yes I do, Terry, but I see the value of your anonymity and my goal is to be able to operate roughly the same way you're doing now. I'll tell you what; let's suspend this conversation for now and if my business plan works out we can take it up again sometime down the road." Dooley didn't want to seem too pushy, but did want his boss to know he was making plans for the future.

"Good enough, Connie. Now, let's inventory the stock on hand and see where we are as we turn over the operation to you. I think I'm going to like this new arrangement." Boyette held out his hand to shake the hand of his new manager. He then turned to open the safe beside his big oak roll-top desk. The safe contained a sizable amount of narcotics and a moderate supply of meth from their own lab.

Dooley took possession of the drugs, placed them in an insulated fish shipping box and carried them to his truck. This new turn had moved more quickly than he had anticipated and he was forced to stop at the local Sportsman's Warehouse to purchase a fireproof gun safe. The huge metal safe weighed almost 1000 pounds making it necessary for Dooley to hire someone to deliver it. The clerk at the sporting goods store was more than happy to contact and hire someone to move the safe to Dooley's home. The clerk assured Dooley it would fit through a standard thirty six inch entry door. It did fit and the moving men had no trouble getting the safe into the room, which was now his office. Dooley tipped the men and once they had gone from the house he followed the manual to open the safe. He placed the large insulated fish box inside and closed and locked the door.

It was now time to check on his workers at Salamatof Lake. When he arrived at the lab the two young men were changing out of the protective plastic suits. The lab had been cleaned, the ventilation system set and the heat control turned to the proper setting. The run for the day had been measured and packaged and placed in the small safe in the office. Dooley looked at the tally sheet Bobby had given him and was impressed with the total. If he was going to be able to produce this amount of their brand it would be easy to establish a market in Anchorage. He would talk with his former boss about doing just that.

"We're runnin' outta chemicals for the recipe, Connie. We can't run another batch tomorrow without gettin' more." Bobby handed Connie a list of the things they were running short on. Connie read the list and nodded.

"We'll get what you need in the morning, Bobby. You guys did a heck of a job today. I think I need to move you up to foreman and give you a little raise. Good job, man." Dooley knew the promotion was going to be good for morale and loyalty.

"Gosh, thanks, Connie." Bobby had never had a promotion in his entire life and it felt good.

"I'll call you in the morning when I need you to go with me to haul the supplies." Dooley wanted one more thing from Bobby. Checking to see if Risso was within earshot he spoke softly to his new foreman, "Keep an eye on Danny for me. I don't need another user like Kenny Pierce. If he uses anything besides a little weed we'll need to get a different man. Can you handle that for me?"

"Sure, Connie, but I known Danny for a long time and he don't even use weed any more. He got it scared out of him." Bobby was speaking softly also.

"OK, Bobby, I trust you, but I need to know."

"I'll watch him, Connie."

Dooley watched the two men drive away, made a final check of the lab and locked the door. It was time to contact his more lucrative dealers and let them know about the new change of command. It was nearly midnight when he returned home after a productive evening of meetings with local dealers. He decided he would have to find some sort of small office in an out of the way place to house his new office. He wanted his residence to remain off the radar to both dealers and the police in case they began nosing around and asking questions.

Dooley was finishing breakfast, a bowl of cold cereal, when his telephone rang. It was the lawyer, Edgar Bishop.

"Good morning, Mr. Dooley. I understand Bobby Gunther now works for you."

"Yes, he does, what can I do for you?"

"I don't know if you're aware, but I'm his defense attorney in a case where he's been charged with some serious crimes…felonies. In any case, I am preparing for his court dates, which are coming up soon. I would rather not discuss this matter on the telephone. My office is in Anchorage, but I can come down there to meet with you if you like. I think you and I have some mutual interests in the outcome of these cases." Bishop was speaking like a lawyer, uttering a lot and saying nothing, but getting his point across just the same.

"Would it be convenient to meet with you at your office this afternoon? I have some business in Anchorage and could have both meetings today, if you're free at say four this afternoon?"

Dooley made plans for Bobby to pick up the supplies he needed at the warehouse in Soldotna. He had decided to drive to Anchorage rather than fly by commercial airline. This would allow him to haul some much needed chemicals from the supplier in Anchorage while simultaneously moving the warehouse from the one owned by Boyette to one of his own. Rented, but his.

His first meeting was with the attorney, Bishop. Dooley didn't know what Bishop had on his mind, but knew if it was not safe to discuss it on the telephone it was serious and needed to be dealt with. He met Bishop in his office; an old house off Spenard Road. It wasn't much of an office, but his clientele didn't seem to mind. Dooley refused the coffee offered by the lawyer.

"Alright, Mr. Bishop, what's on your mind?" Dooley wanted to get right to the point.

"Call me Edgar. The point is that the DA in Kenai has contacted me in regard to Bobby Gunther's case. He says his calendar is full and wants to make a deal."

"What kind of deal?" asked Dooley, having no idea what to expect.

"A good deal for Bobby, not so good for you or Terry; that's why I needed to see you in person." Bishop was a large man and the heat in his office was very warm. He was beginning to perspire and took off his suit coat in an effort to cool off a little. "Kevin Darby, the DA down there in Kenai, said if Bobby tells him who his bosses are he'll make a deal for a probation only sentence. Bobby is looking at a lot of years if he's convicted on his charges. I think he'll be very tempted to take the deal."

"What do you think the chances are of him being convicted?" asked Dooley.

"The troopers have witnesses who can identify Bobby as one of the men with Kenny Pierce when they beat Will Goodson to death. They have a description of the vehicle they were driving, and one Bobby later wrecked. There are a few lesser things, but the point is that I think the jury will convict him. I also think that if the DA contacts him directly he'll take the deal. I know all this happened before you came to work for Terry, but your name will surely come up sometime during the deal. I also know Terry will never allow Bobby to talk to the DA, if you get my meaning. Bobby's out on bail, which I put up for him. I don't want to lose my investment, so to speak."

"I see your point, Edgar, let me think about this and I'll get back to you as soon as I can. How much time do you think we have to find a solution?"

"Not much, a few days at most. Darby wants to get this one off his calendar and figures he has a lot of leverage. As he sees it it's a win/win for him. He was a partner with Pierce. Pierce beat the old guy Will Goodson to death and shot the lady trooper, Penny Rossiter. Darby would like to come out of this with the name of the big boss who ordered the killing. The real killer is already dead. If Bobby Gunther gets out with only probation and gives up the name of a major drug dealer, Darby wins. If it goes to court, Darby will probably win. You remember the old saw about a rock and a hard place? Well this is it."

Dooley was beginning to recant his initial impression of the defense attorney. The man was a realist, if not an optimist. "I'll have a talk with Mr. Boyette and get back to you tomorrow afternoon. In the meantime if the DA contacts you, you'd better call me and let me know what he's doing." What Dooley wasn't saying to the lawyer is that it would be a bad time for him to lose Bobby.

"Try to make it as early as you can. Even if you come up with a plan it will have to be implemented. This will require me to adjust my strategy. Thanks for coming. I'll be expecting your call tomorrow."

Conrad Dooley was worried when he left the little office. He would have to finish his business with his old boss here in town and get back to meet with Terry Boyette.

The meeting with his old boss in Anchorage was rather uneventful, but very productive. He made arrangements for all the supplies to keep him in the meth manufacturing business to come to him. The delivery address was left open until Dooley completed negotiations for a warehouse of his own. He had one in mind, but it was for sale and he didn't have the cash for a purchase, leading him to the conclusion he would have to seek financing from Terry Boyette. He thought Terry would back him because it further insulated him from the drug business and allowed him to show a legitimate land transaction he could defend and make a little money in the process.

The problem of what to do about Bobby and the District Attorney was another situation altogether. Boyette's solutions always seemed to end in the death of someone. Dooley wasn't entirely against that as a solution, but wanted to find another way to resolve this. Bobby had become a key part of Dooley's new organization, he could be replaced, but not without consequences. Loyalty was not one of the things listed on an employment application.

Chapter 34

Upon his return to Soldotna, Dooley called Boyette asking for an immediate meeting. It was very late, nearly midnight, when Dooley called and said this couldn't wait until morning. They met at the warehouse owned by Boyette.

"Just what's so important it couldn't wait until morning," Boyette demanded. "I turned the drug sales over to you and gave you a larger percentage to run it. If you're going to find a need to call me out in the middle of the night, for whatever reason, I don't need you. There won't be a second chance, Dooley." Anger had taken over the normally placid nature of Terry Boyette.

"Don't give me that crap, Terry. This is a problem you and your management created. I can deal with it, but I thought you might want a say in the matter. If you don't, fine, I'll do it on my own."

"You're getting pretty high and mighty considering you still work for me. What's the problem? Let's get this done so I can get back to bed. I have an important meeting at eight."

"I had a call this morning from Edgar Bishop. He asked me to come to his office to meet with him concerning Bobby Gunther. He said he talked with you and you referred him to me."

"That's right, Gunther is now your problem," countered Boyette.

"I'm not so sure. Edgar said the DA was offering a plea bargain to Bobby guaranteeing him probation if he gives up the name of his boss at the time Will Goodson was killed. That would be you, Terry. Do you still want to go back to bed?" Dooley was pressing his boss without mercy.

"Wh...ah...I...ah," Boyette was stammering and unsure of his answer.

"I guess we can always kill him. That seems to be your answer to most problems leading back to you." Dooley continued to goad his boss.

"OK, wise guy, you've had all afternoon to think about this, what kind of solution have you come up with?"

"You're right, I have thought about it all afternoon. There are several solutions, but not many of them resolve the finality of the issue. We can send Bobby away, but that doesn't mean he won't turn up again sometime in the future or be arrested and brought back by the law. We can hide him, but in this community there's bound to be someone who recognizes him and reports it. He could have another accident or disappear without a trace. Any of those solutions will bring an investigation."

Boyette had a worried look about him, "Do you have a solution in mind, or are you waiting for me to give you one?"

"You're beginning to annoy me, Terry. You hired me to do a job and I'll do it, but I will not sit here and have you berate me because some problem you created before I came here. Until you got so righteous I would have done this as a matter of the job I was hired to do, but I need something from you and I'm willing to trade. Do you want to hear it or not?"

"OK, OK, let's hear it. What do you want from me?"

"I'll take care of the Bobby Gunther problem, but I need a warehouse, a small one to store chemicals and supplies with a small office as headquarters for my operation; somewhere off the main streets and out of the way. I thought you might help arrange that kind of place for me, since you're so anxious to help me out."

Boyette thought a moment, considering his options. He finally arrived at an answer, "OK, Connie, I'm sorry I was short with you. You're right, this is my problem. I want to know two things, one being how large a property do you need? And the other, what are you going to do about Bobby?"

"I'm glad you see it my way, Terry. All I need is a small shop building with an office space. It should be somewhere semi-private to keep the neighbors from wondering what the traffic is about."

"I think I know of a place like that. I may be able to trade another property for it and I'll make you a deal on the price—for old time sake."

"As for Bobby," said Dooley, "he may be so concerned about his up-coming court appearance that it becomes too much for him to handle and he might take his own life."

"See what you can do about Bobby and I'll look into that property for you." Boyette stood to leave, "If there's nothing else, I have an early meeting."

Dooley walked into the warehouse before going to his truck. Near the tool box he found what he was looking for, a piece of stout rope. He carried it to his truck and sat in the cab fashioning a noose on one end. He planned to tie the other end to a 4x4 beam on the front deck of the trailer where Bobby lived. It was late at night and the chances of being seen were slim. He planned to take a baggie of weed and a bottle of Jack Daniels whiskey for a late visit with Bobby to discuss the news he had learned from Edgar Bishop. When Bobby was drunk enough to handle he planned to put the rope around his neck and hoist him off the floor of the porch, placing an overturned stool under him.

Bobby was dressed in shorts and a tee shirt when he answered the door. He had been asleep and was rubbing his eyes when he answered the third knock. "Oh, hi, Connie, I was sleeping and wasn't sure I heard you. Come on in. Gimme a sec and I'll put on some pants."

Dooley entered, carrying the shopping bag containing the bottle of Jack Daniels and a large baggie of marijuana. He tossed the bag of weed on the kitchen table and went to the cupboard to find two drinking glasses. He looked in the refrigerator, but there wasn't any ice in the trays. By the time Bobby came back, wearing pants, Dooley had opened the bottle of whiskey and was pouring two large glasses full.

"What's the occasion Connie?" asked the still sleepy Bobby Gunther.

"I had a call from your defense attorney today and went to Anchorage to see him. He had some bad news for you and I've been trying to figure out what to do about it." Dooley started by building a lie.

"What kind of bad news?" asked Bobby.

"Your lawyer said the DA had called him and wanted to talk to you. He told your lawyer he was going to throw the book at you unless you tell him who your boss was when you and Pierce went out Funny River and beat up on old Will Goodson. He said if you tell him who you worked for he would recommend a twenty year sentence and if not he was going for murder one and a ninety-nine year sentence. Edgar said your defense was pretty weak and would probably make it stick. I thought I would bring over a bottle and some weed and we could get drunk and talk about it."

"Oh, man, Connie, I can't go to jail for twenty years and I ain't goin' to tell who my boss was. Oh man… oh man, this is bad." Dooley handed him the large glass of Jack. Bobby took it and drank down half on the first drink. After regaining regular breathing he reached for the bag of smoke and rolled a hefty reefer. Once the weed was burning properly and he had taken a couple drags he drank half the remaining whiskey in his glass.

Dooley sipped on his own glass and refilled Bobby's for him. It was only minutes before Bobby began to show the effects of the drugs and alcohol. Dooley sympathized with his drinking partner who was soon crying and asking what he should do.

Dooley poured more whiskey in Bobby's glass. "I have an idea, Bobby. It sounds crazy, but it just might work."

Bobby's speech was now very slurred, "What's yer idea, Con..(hic).. Connie?"

"I'm willing to help you pay for an escape, but they'll just come looking for you. How about you write a suicide note and leave it here on the table. After we finish the bottle I'll take you to Anchorage to catch a plane to somewhere safe for you." Dooley feigned drunken speech.

"I like it, Connie. Get me a paper and pencil out of that end drawer, there," said Bobby, pointing. "You tell me what to say and I'll write it down."

Dooley topped off Bobby's glass again and began to dictate a suicide note for him to write on the notepad. When it was finished he shoved it over for Dooley to read. He read it without picking up the pad, "I think it's perfect, Bobby, let's have one more for the road. I have to make a place in the truck for you to sit. I have some stuff in the seat to move. Drink up and I'll be right back."

Bobby was now unsteady as he picked up the glass and toasted his friend's gesture, taking another toke on the now short and stubby joint and finishing the last of his glass of whiskey. "I gotta pack a bag," he slurred.

"Naw, Bobby, you can't take anything with you 'cause your note says you're just going to kill yourself, so you won't need any of your stuff. Just to make it all look good."

"You're right, Connie, I'm leaving all my treasures here. You can have it all. Hee hee hee. Be sure I get a nice funeral. Hee hee hee."

"I'll do that, Bobby. Finish the bottle and I'll be right back." Dooley went to his truck to get the rope he had prepared. He came back to the porch and arranged the rope over the beam letting the noose lay on the porch floor. Back inside the trailer Bobby was nearly unconscious. Dooley offered to help him out the door to the truck.

Gunther said something unintelligible that sounded like 'thanks'. He leaned on Dooley as they went out the door. Dooley faked a fall and the two of them lay on the porch laughing. Dooley got up, but Bobby lay there nearly asleep. Dooley watched him a moment and judged it was safe to finish the job. Both ends of the porch were closed in and only the front was open to view by passers-by. Dooley slipped the noose around Gunther's neck and moved to the other end of the rope. It was a heavy chore, but Dooley was able to pull the heavy body off the floor of the porch. Bobby was so drunk he never realized what was happening until his lungs would no longer pull air into his body. In his drunken condition he only kicked a few times before he lost all consciousness. Conrad Dooley tied the other end of the rope to the next roof support leaving the body hanging nearly two feet off the floor. He went inside and got a chair suitable to look like Bobby had used it to stand on while he affixed the rope to his neck.

He went back inside the trailer to retrieve the bottle and wipe his fingerprints from it, then back outside where he imprinted the bottle with Bobby's hands. He replaced the bottle on the kitchen table and did the same routine with the baggie of marijuana. He returned the plastic bag to the table and looked around to see if he had missed anything. He had not. He picked up the glass he had been drinking from and took it to the truck with him. He left the lights on and the door unlocked as he left.

Dooley felt bad about what he had done to Bobby, but this time it had been self-preservation. It had also insured he was about to become the owner of a new office and warehouse. He wondered if he should hire someone to move the large gun safe from his house to the new office.

It had been a long night and he was hungry. He went to the Caribou Restaurant for breakfast. It was too early to call his old boss in Anchorage to find another man to take Bobby's place and it was too early to call Risso about working today. The final thing it was too early to do was call Terry Boyette to let him know the problem had been solved. On second thought, it wasn't too early for that.

Chapter 35

Little eleven year old Trudy Wheaton, dressed in snow boots, heavy coat, stocking cap and a scarf wrapped around her face to protect her face and lungs from the winter cold, was walking on the road in front of Bobby Gunther's mobile home. Singing a ditty her mother had taught her, she was on her way to the bus stop near the edge of the trailer park. She could see other children at the bus stop waiting for the school bus, which was due to arrive within minutes. Trudy was the only grade school pupil living on the frontage road that was catching the bus. She sang and skipped down the road in a happy mood.

As she passed the front of Bobby's home she glanced toward the porch. Suddenly her singing stopped and she issued a shrill, frightening scream. Two doors up her mother was standing on the front porch watching her walk to the bus.

Terrified for her daughter she ran from the house, down the icy street to where Trudy was standing in the middle of the narrow drive screaming and crying. As her mother approached she pointed to the front porch of Bobby Gunther's trailer. There, in the early morning dusky light was Bobby hanging from a beam on the porch. Trudy's mother saw the awful sight and covered her daughter's face with her hands to block the view. She picked up the girl and carried her back toward her own home.

By now the other children were running toward Bobby's house. As they gathered at the front and saw the body hanging there they all ran away, most toward their own homes, but two ran back to the bus stop. Trudy's mother was now inside her home dialing 911 and trying to comfort her frightened daughter. The bus stopped and the two remaining children ran inside to give the driver an account of what they had seen as only frightened children can tell it.

The driver told the children to be seated and picked up his radio mic to report the incident to his dispatcher. Meanwhile he drove away from the site to remove the children from any potential dangers remaining in the neighborhood.

Troopers patrol the school bus routes on a regular basis. When dispatch notified the road troopers of the incident it took less than two minutes for a trooper to arrive and take command. His first order was to have all the onlookers moved back from the scene. The onlookers were mostly the parents of children who had run from the scene only moments before. Within minutes, more troopers arrived to control the gathering crowd. The trooper in charge called Captain Meadows to inform him of an apparent suicide and to ask for the crime investigation team to come out and take over the investigation. The victim was frozen stiff and very obviously dead; EMTs would not be necessary.

Haskins, Filson and Winston arrived within minutes. Haskins asked the road troopers to stay on scene and keep the spectators back while the investigators did their work. Filson was first to look at the body and he, too initially read the scene as a suicide. But some little things didn't add up in his suspicious mind. The first was the position of the chair the victim supposedly used when he placed the noose around his neck. It wasn't kicked away, only tipped over. The second thing he noticed was the chair was far too short to allow the victim to get his head inside the noose and still hang this far off the front porch. And he noticed the knot tying the anchoring end of rope to the next post. There was a double wrap around the post using a half-hitch knot to keep it from sliding and another double wrap and half-hitch below to secure the rope. The top knot and half-hitch were taut, pulled tight by the weight of the body. The second set of knots were fairly loose and holding nothing as if put there as an afterthought.

Filson called to Haskins, "David, I think you need to take a look at this," he said.

Haskins walked toward the scene and up the steps to the porch. Immediately red flags went up in his mind. "We need to keep everyone away from the front of the scene until we can check for tire tracks in the snow. We may already be too late, but let's try."

Filson stepped off the porch and gathered the other four troopers around to give them the word. Winston was given the task of searching for suspicious tire tracks in the snowy parking area. The road troopers were tasked with keeping everyone away from the scene. Haskins had finished filming the area of the front porch when Filson returned with a large leather case containing evidence gathering kits as well as two sets of paper booties for their feet to keep the inside of the trailer from being contaminated by the officers. It was nearly noon by the time the team finished at the scene and the body removed and sent to crime lab in Anchorage.

When he finally sat at this desk Haskins dialed Penny Rossiter. "I have some news, Penny," he announced when she answered.

"I hope its good news, I could use some today," was her reply.

"I guess it depends on how you look at it. You remember Bobby Gunther, the young man who admitted to being with Kenny Pierce when they beat Will Goodson to death and when they beat that mechanic in North Kenai to death?"

"Oh, sure, in fact he has a court date coming up sometime soon. What about him?"

"He won't make his court date. Someone murdered him last night and set it up to look like a suicide. A school girl on her way to the bus stop found him hanging from the front porch roof of his mobile home." David showed no compassion in his announcement.

"No kidding?" she said with amazement. "Are you sure it was murder?"

"Whoever did it was clever and did a good job of hiding the evidence, but it wasn't a suicide." David was silent for a moment, "Does this resemble another death we had recently that was made to look like a suicide or accident?"

"Yes, as a matter of fact, that Kenny Pierce guy. Oh my gosh, he's the one who shot me. And Gunther was his partner."

"Now you get it. I think someone's eliminating witnesses. Someone doesn't want the DA to start asking about who they worked for. At least that's my guess, someone with a lot to lose. I think it was whoever they worked for. I don't see any other reason for these killings, especially the manner in which they were done. I think it all goes back to the case you were working when you were shot."

"Oh, that's exciting, David. Do you have any suspects?" asked Penny with anticipation.

"We only just now got back to the office, but the team and I will be having a meeting in a few minutes and we're going to discuss that very question. I'll let you know if we come up with any answers. I'll talk with you later."

Haskins hung up the phone and dialed a pizza shop for a delivery of three large pizzas with a lot of things on top. It was going to be a busy afternoon.

The five members of the investigating team spent the afternoon in the office piecing together evidence from this and other recent unsolved murder cases in an effort to find some common thread. The team made lists of possibilities as well as lists of names of people connected with the cases. It was a good old fashioned brain-storming session. A new name on the list was the lawyer, Edgar Bishop. He had a reputation for representing clients involved in the drug industry. He also had a reputation of being very expensive. It was supposed, by team consensus, the reason he commanded such high fees was his rate of success in representing drug dealers.

Bishop's office was in Anchorage but he was representing Bobby Gunther. Gunther was neither wealthy nor a successful drug dealer. "Do you suppose Bishop was hired by someone Gunther worked for, someone wishing to keep his identity hidden and capable of hiring someone to eliminate him if it looked as if his name could come up in an investigation?" These questions were posed by Don Winston.

Filson sat up straight in his chair, "I think Don may be onto something, boss. Think about it, we've been beating our heads against the wall for months wondering why Kenny Pierce and Bobby Gunther killed Will Goodson. Remember the way they did it was strange. Is it possible they wanted him to sign his property over to them or the man they worked for? We never did find a motive for that killing. How about this? Pierce and Gunther worked for the same guy, Terry Boyette. Boyette is heavy into buying up property around the peninsula, mostly industrial type properties. What if he was the one who wanted the old man's property? Not for industrial use or resale, but for a drug lab. What if he's financing his real estate business with drug money? Goodson's property would have been a prime location for that sort of use. Remember the mechanic in North Kenai Pierce and Gunther killed was a druggie. What if he owed Pierce's boss money for drugs? I don't have all the pieces put together yet, but it would give us motive for most of the unsolved killings. The big question is can we tie Boyette into any of the illegal enterprises in the local area?"

"You could be right, Lou. Perhaps we didn't see it before because Boyette has gone to great lengths to keep his name off our list of associates." Winston was mentally arranging the facts to see if they would fit the scenario when he suddenly thought of something. "Wait a minute guys, Boyette has a new man working for him," he looked in his notebook for a name, "Yeah, Conrad Dooley. He said he worked in Anchorage before coming here to work for Boyette. We've had at least three murders since he came to town; Pierce, Gunther and that drug dealer in Nikiski," again he referred to his notebook, "John McGowan."

David Haskins had been listening to this conversation and made note of how the logic was taking a turn toward reality. "All this is interesting, but we have no proof for any of it. If you're all in agreement about this being a possibility I think we need to get busy and find the proof. Remember, Terry Boyette is a prominent businessman in this town. We can't be running around accusing him of anything without something concrete to make it stick. Lou, I want you and Don to do a background and financial check on Boyette. Find out where he gets his money. I also want you to find out what you can about this Conrad Dooley." The men had been writing while David was talking.

The other two members of the team were the newest members. It was time for them to get their feet wet. "Lee," David pointed at Lee Stein and Paul Gorman, "I want you and Paul to drive out to Nikiski and talk with the Fire Marshal. He seems to have a handle on what's happening in North Kenai. Find out what you can about the victim in the bombing of the cabin. His name was John McGowan; Don can give you what we have on him. We can't waste any time finding these answers. We have three dead victims and one wounded cop. It's time to come up with answers. For lack of another motive we'll assume Don is correct for the moment and assume the head of this snake is Terry Boyette. Let's go to work. I'll go in and let the Captain know what we're doing. Good luck, Guys."

By quitting time none of the officers on the team had checked in. David was an hour past his shift and decided to call it a day. He picked up the phone and dialed Penny.

"It's about time you called me," she answered.

"What time can I come to your house for dinner?" he replied.

"You seem to take a lot for granted, mister."

"Sorry, I didn't mean to be pushy. What time do you want me to pick you up for dinner?"

"That's better. Is there any of that pizza left over?" she asked.

"As a matter of fact there is. I'll bring it with me. I have to go home and change clothes first."

"That will give me time to go by and see Julia a minute on my way home. Do you want to go with me tonight?"

"I'd better not, Penny. I have my crew out gathering information and none of them was back when I left the office. I think I should stick close to my phone until they check in. I'll see you in about an hour and a half at your place. I'll heat the pizza."

He was still sitting in his truck when the first team checked in. It was Don and Lou. They had some new information, but no proof. They would start again in the morning. The message was essentially the same from Lee and Paul. David went into his house and changed into a flannel shirt and blue jeans.

When he was ready to leave the house he went to the hall closet to get a pair of slippers he wanted to take to Penny's house and leave in her hall closet. He hoped this gesture would not seem too presumptuous.

The two sat in the living room watching a football game and eating pizza. Seattle beat the Steelers by three. Penny was elated and David was forced to pay his 25 cent bet before going home for the night.

Chapter 36

Dooley stopped on the way to the lab to pick up Danny Risso, the new man who was working for Bobby Gunther. News of Gunther's death had not yet made the papers, but Dooley said Bobby would be late coming to work this morning. The two men chatted on the drive to Salamatof Lake. Dooley was impressed with the new man. He was led to believe he was slow thinking and dim witted. This was far from the truth. Danny Risso was none of that. He was small of stature and extremely shy. He had said he was constantly picked on by others wherever he worked. He also said he had never been able to defend himself from the bullies he met, making him an even bigger target for them. He possessed an Associate Degree in Petroleum Engineering. By the time they reached the lab Dooley was convinced Risso could run the lab and follow the formula precisely. He would test his judgement by letting him run a batch of product today.

Dooley stayed with the new man while he suited up and prepared the equipment and measured the chemicals. An hour later Conrad Dooley was convinced he had made the correct decision and left the meth lab in Risso's care.

Dooley was listening to the local radio station on the drive toward Soldotna when the station read the news item about a possible suicide at a trailer park east of Soldotna. This happened sometime during the night, but was not discovered until the body was found by a passing schoolgirl. No further information was available from the Alaska State Troopers office.

He was more relaxed now. Had there been a question about the suicide the station would have said so. Sensational journalism was as important in a small town as it was in the big city. He checked the time and decided to have breakfast before contacting Terry Boyette. He had read the morning paper for the second time; drank three cups of coffee and worked the crossword puzzle. It was time to call Boyette about the property he was looking at for

Dooley's new headquarters/office/warehouse. Things are working out well, thought Conrad Dooley.

He dialed Terry's number. He answered after several rings. Without saying hello, Boyette said, "Can you call me later? I have someone in the office right now. Thank You." The line went dead.

Thinking this was an unusual response from his old boss he decided to drive by the office to see if he could tell what was happening. As he drove slowly up the street he saw two State Trooper cars parked near the front door of the warehouse. He didn't stop, but drove on by and went to his own house to wait.

At noon Boyette called back. "Sorry I couldn't talk before. I had the troopers here asking about Bobby Gunther. He committed suicide last night. They wanted to know what Bobby did for me and how long he had worked for me, that sort of information. They also asked about Kenny Pierce. Somehow they've linked Bobby and Kenny to some felony crimes and wanted to know if I hired them to run drugs and kill people. They were trying to get me to say something to incriminate myself, but they failed. They asked if I could think of a reason Bobby killed himself. I said yes, he had an upcoming court date on a list of felonies. I told the cops I only kept Bobby around here because I felt sorry for him and he did a lot of odd jobs for me. I don't know if they bought it, but they left here without arresting me."

"It sounds as if you've had a busy morning, Terry," commented Dooley.

"Yes I have, as a matter of fact. I haven't had time to check on that little shop I told you about. Give me an hour and come by the office. I should have something by then."

David Haskins was in his office with all the files from the related cases spread over an eight foot table he had set up for this purpose. The more he studied the cases the more Lou Filson's theory made sense. He also noted it was after Penny's shooting when Conrad Dooley came to town. Immediately the rate of bodies being reported skyrocketed. The problem with the entire theory was there was no proof of any kind. It was all conjecture.

David was feeling particularly low this morning. He wished Penny would set a date for the wedding and put an end to this suspense. Sometime during his wedding fantasies he had a wild thought. What was he going to give Penny for a wedding gift, besides himself, of course? That's when his grand plan came into being. After they were married he would move into Penny's house. It was larger, had one more bedroom and a small office space. It also had a basement, which his own house lacked because of the shallow depth of the water table in his neighborhood. He suddenly thought, he could sell the house. It would give him a sizable lump of free cash he could invest in a wedding gift for Penny.

He picked up the phone and called an old friend, Hal Anderson. Hal was a pilot and was known to buy and sell airplanes from time to time.

"Anderson Aircraft Sales," said a high-pitched voice on the other end.

"Hal, you old horse trader, how the heck are you?"

"David, good to hear from you! Are you still out there chasing crooks?" asked the old friend.

"Still chasing 'em, but not catching many," was his reply.

"I heard you had a strange ringing in your ears that sounded like wedding bells, is that true?"

"You heard right, my friend. In fact that's why I'm calling. I think I would like to find a nice airplane for her as a wedding gift. Do you think you could come up with something suitable?"

"Conventional or tail-dragger?" Anderson asked, referring to the landing gear configuration.

"Tail-dragger, I think. I'd like to find a nice Cessna 185 in good shape and not too expensive."

"You never did finish your flight instruction, did you, David?"

"No, never did, but with a pilot and an airplane in the family I might consider getting back into it." The truth was that he always regretted not finishing flight school.

"I think I have just the plane you're looking for." Anderson never even hesitated, sort of like a used car salesman. "I just finished a total re-do on my 185, new engine, new paint, new panel, new tires, tundra tires, that is, and new upholstery. She's shiny and new from prop to rudder."

"It sounds expensive. Remember, I'm just a lowly government worker." David was setting the table for negotiations.

"You and I have been friends for more than twenty years, David. I owe you a lot, and you know why. For you, my best friend, for your wedding present to your new wife, I'll make you a deal you can't refuse. I'll fill the tanks and let you use my hangar, where it's parked now. I have it listed and the price is published as firm. You can have it for the published price and I'll refund $50,000 as a wedding gift."

Haskins was stunned. "Are you sure you want to do that, Hal?"

"Only for you, old buddy. Are you interested?"

"Interested, I'll take it, contingent on two things." David was afraid Hal would back out when he heard the provisos. "Penny will have to say she likes the plane and I will have to sell my house for the cash to buy it. I wasn't thinking you would have one on hand and ready to go."

"Agreed, and I might be interested in taking your house in trade. I've done it before and always came out all right. Bring your fiancée by and look at the plane. I want to meet her anyway. I can't believe anyone agreed to marry you unless she weighs over 200 pounds and talks with a middle-east accent."

"You'll like her, Hal. She's great." David had lost his bluster and was speaking as if he was in love.

"OK, David, let me know when you want to come out and take a look."

Haskins hung up the telephone, elated with the deal he had just made with Hal Anderson. He was about to call Penny when Lou Filson and Don Winston came into his office.

"This guy Boyette is one slick customer, David. He could sell silk to a Chinaman." Filson was talking when he came through the door, followed by his partner. "According to Boyette, Bobby Gunther only worked for him when he was called and only did menial tasks around his rental properties." Filson was making waving motions with his hands, "He magically appeared and disappeared whenever Boyette summoned him," Filson was laughing now, "Sort of like you do with me, boss."

"Sometimes I wish I could make you disappear, Lou." Both men laughed, "How about the other guy Kenny Pierce, did he have the same kind of relationship with him?"

"That's what he claims, but someone paid those two and everything points to Boyette. Don and I are headed to the department of labor to see if Boyette paid payroll taxes or benefits for either or both of them. We also asked if the new man, Dooley, worked for him. He says no. He claims he knew Dooley through a mutual friend in Anchorage and he came down here as a private contractor. What kind of contractor we can't find out, but we will."

"It sounds like the two of you are on the right track. I'll bet he used each of their wages as tax deductions. There will be something to show what he paid them. I'd also check to see if his income was enough to pay for all the properties he has been buying recently. It would take a huge cash flow to allow all the investments he has acquired in recent months. There has to be a paper trail somewhere."

"We're already making electronic inquiries of the Department of Labor and the IRS." Lou turned to leave, then came back, "There is one interesting turn, David. So far Conrad Dooley is invisible. He has no past that we can find."

"It'd be nice if we could tie him to the murders of the other two employees. Keep at it, boys." When Filson and Winston had gone he went back to the telephone.

Penny had read the caller ID on her phone, "The future Mrs. Haskins here, who is calling, please?"

"You're turning into a real smarty, young lady. Be nice to me or I won't tell you what I'm getting you for a wedding present."

"Are you always going to blackmail me into telling you what you want to hear?" she asked.

"If it works this time I sure will," they both laughed. "You'll have to give me a date for the wedding before you get to see the gift."

"You're just awful, David. I want to be a June bride." She blurted into the telephone. "Is that close enough?"

"I guess it will have to do. Besides, I can't keep this to myself any longer."

"OK, David, I told you when now you have to tell me what you got me." She was anxious to hear what he had done.

"You remember we talked about me moving into your house when we were married?"

"Yes, I remember."

"Well, I traded my house for a gift for you," he announced.

"You what?" she shouted into the telephone. "What in the world did you trade for?"

"This is subject to your approval, but I traded for a used, but zero time, Cessna 185. Everything on it is new; engine, tires, paint, instruments and owner, if you approve. You can test fly it when you get time."

"Oh, David, it can't be true. They're so expensive especially one completely refurbished. Where did you find it?"

"It's true, and it comes with a rent-free hangar and full of fuel. I just hope you like the color." He was teasing her a little, but happy she was excited about the plane.

"When can I see it," she asked.

"We can go look at it tonight if you like, but we'd better wait until the paperwork clears the bank before we go flying."

"I can't wait, David."

"Hold on a minute, Penny, I have another call and it looks official. I'll call you back."

The other line was a call from an old friend from Talkeetna, 300 miles to the north. When both men were new in this business they worked a couple of commercial fishing cases together. David and Miles Tyler had remained friends, albeit distant friends, from that time. "Miles, it's good to hear from you."

"It's always good to talk to you, too, David, but this is official business."

"Aw, shucks, I thought you were calling to ask to be invited to the wedding."

"Wedding, what wedding?" an astonished Miles asked.

"My wedding, but we can talk about this later. What was the official call?"

"Recently your office asked us to keep an eye out for a PA-12 with a certain tail number. I ran across it today. It was parked on the ice over on the Kahiltna River. It caught my eye because I know the owner of the cabin where it was parked. The owner is a gold prospector and never goes there in the winter. I went back to check it out and wrote down the numbers of the plane. Another funny thing, it looks like someone is staying in the cabin, small footprints, maybe a woman. The tracks only go to the outhouse and to the river, probably to get water. I fly over there regularly and this is the first time I've seen the plane parked there. Is this important?"

"It sure is, Miles, hold on, let me get a map." David found the proper map in a file cabinet in his office. "OK, I have a sectional map. Tell me exactly where the cabin is located."

Miles read off the GPS coordinates. "The cabin is where the Collinsville winter trail crosses the Kahiltna River, just south of the trail crossing. It sets on the river bank on the west side of the main channel about a hundred yards up the bank above the river."

"I see it. It's marked on this map. Can you meet me there in about two hours?"

"If it's important, sure, I have to remind you it is going to be dark soon and landing on the ice in the dark might be risky."

Chapter 37

Haskins called Penny back, excited about what he had just heard from Miles Tyler. "Drop what you're doing and come to the office. We have to take a test drive in the new plane right now."

"Are you kidding me? What's going on, David?" asked a perplexed Penny Rossiter.

"I just got a call from an old friend from Talkeetna. He found Bud Leach's airplane at a cabin on the Kahiltna River. I'll call Hal and have him get the plane warmed up. C'mon, gal, we gotta go now."

Her tone changed immediately, "I'll tell Nancy I'm leaving. I'll be there in fifteen minutes."

David was checking his AR-15 in the trunk of his patrol car when Penny arrived. She climbed into the front seat as he slammed the trunk lid closed. Ten minutes later they were loading his weapons into the Cessna. Hal had the plane fueled and running. She was surprised to see metal penetration type skis on the shiny airplane.

"She's fueled up and warmed up and the new GPS will come in handy. Try not to bend her," shouted Hal to Penny over the sound of the idling engine.

Penny took a minute to familiarize herself with the new instrument panel while snapping the shoulder harness into place. Placing the new headset on her ears she spoke over the intercom to David. "Wow, this is really something. Give me the GPS coordinates and I'll put them into the navigation system.

David showed her the numbers he had written on the top of the map. She entered them and looked around to see if there was any other traffic in the area. She gave Hal a little wave and added power and taxied to the end of the runway. Without stopping she turned and added power for takeoff. The response was amazing. The ceiling was at 2800 feet and she climbed as high as the clouds would allow. She would liked to have had more altitude for crossing the open water at the forelands, but this was an emergency. Once on the other side she flew in a straight line to the Kahiltna River and followed it upstream to the spot indicated by the GPS. There was another plane sitting on the ice when they arrived, but it was one owned by U.S. Fish and Wildlife. Miles Tyler had arrived before them.

Penny circled and looked at the landing spot while pumping down the skis for landing. The landing was smooth and she parked next to the other Cessna at the cabin. Miles was waiting for them when she cut the engine. He helped her drag the engine cover from the back seat and hang it over the warm engine cowling.

"The PA-12 was gone when I got here, so I landed," said Miles as David approached.

"Miles, this is Penny, my soon-to-be bride. Have you seen anyone here?"

Tyler made a motion as if tipping his cap to Penny, "No, and with the windows covered for the winter I couldn't see inside the cabin."

David was carrying the assault rifle in his left hand. They began a slow and cautious walk toward the cabin sitting atop the river bank about a hundred yards away. As the trio reached the shore they found a hole in the ice where it looked as if someone had been keeping it ice free and drawing water. There was no sign of movement at the cabin. David turned to Penny without saying anything, pointing to the small footprints on the trail. They looked like those of a child.

Penny nodded and made a motion indicating she wanted his duty weapon. He nodded back and handed her the Glock. She pulled the slide and jacked a round into the chamber. Again the trio began the short march toward the cabin. There was still no sign of life, but there was a whiff of smoke coming from the chimney. David motioned for Miles to go around to the back of the cabin while he and Penny stepped up onto the small front porch. They two stood close to the log wall on either side of the entry door. David reached out with his right hand and knocked on the door.

"Alaska State Troopers, come out with your hands over your head." There was no response, so he tried again. "This is the Alaska State Troopers. Open the door and come out."

Slight sounds were heard from the inside and finally the click of the door lock being opened. The door opened a crack, "Don't shoot Mister," said a small voice from the inside.

Penny had a giant feeling of relief as she stood beside the door. David motioned for her to ask the child to come out. "OK, kids, we're here to help you. Come on out."

There was a momentary pause and the door began to open wider. "Please don't shoot us, please." Then from behind the door came two small boys, their skin nearly black from wood smoke and dirt, and their blond hair matted and dirty. Both were barefoot when they stepped out onto the porch with their hands held high above their heads.

Once they were outside Penny asked if there was anyone else in the house. They said no as she motioned for them to put their hands down. David ducked behind them and went inside looking to make sure there really was no one else inside the house. It took only a minute to search the small cabin and loft. Once done, Penny took the boys back inside the warm house.

The cabin was neatly kept and clean. Sadly the boys were not in the same condition. David knelt in front of the boys. "You're safe now. We've come to take you home." The boys looked at each other and began to cry. "Are you boys hurt? Do you need anything right now?"

"No, we're OK. But, Bud will be coming back soon and I don't want him to find me again." The spokesman was Steve Baxter, the eldest of the two.

"Don't you worry, boys, we're here to protect you. Will you talk to the lady a minute? Her name is Penny. I'm going to call your dads and let them know you're safe. Will you do that?"

"Sure," said the two boys in unison. The younger boy, Carl Reed asked, "Dad won't be mad at us will he? We couldn't help it, you know, not coming home and stuff."

Penny tucked the Glock into David's holster and wrapped her arms around the two boys. "You won't have to worry about that, boys. They're going to be very happy to see you. She hugged them tightly, as much for her as for the boys. She was wiping tears of joy from her face as she held them.

Miles was now in the cabin sharing the happy moments as David came back to deliver the message. "OK, boys, Penny and I will be taking the two of you to Anchorage. You fathers will meet us there at the state hangar. We're ordering an ambulance to take you to the hospital for a check-up, but your fathers can go with you."

"Yay," shouted Carl. I want to see my dad."

"Hold on a second, boys, I have to find out if you know when Bud will be back here? We want to ask him some questions."

"No," said Steve. "He just said he would be gone until tomorrow and we had to keep the fire going. He said we shouldn't use the lantern 'cause we might set the place on fire. We got plenty of food in the kitchen and plenty of firewood in the shed. Bud taught us how to take care of ourselves and he's really fussy about keeping the place clean. He gets mad if we mess it up."

"We're going to have to ask you a lot of questions about all that has happened to you, but we won't do that now. First we'll take you back to your dads and to the hospital. The worst thing you will have to do is take a bath, but you never have to worry again about what's going to happen to you." David was on the verge of tears as he spoke to the boys. Get your coats and shoes and we'll take you to meet your fathers."

David had been talking with Captain Meadows and made arrangements for another trooper to come to the cabin and do the crime scene investigation. He would be coming from Anchorage. Miles Tyler would wait for the second trooper and assist him in his tasks. Troopers had been dispatched to deliver the message of the rescue to both fathers.

David strapped the two boys into the rear seats of the Cessna and climbed into the right front seat while Penny started the engine. She turned on the landing/taxi lights and taxied back to her landing point. She made a last minute check and began to add power. The flight back to Anchorage and the Lake Hood landing strip would take less than an hour, but would seem much longer to all four passengers.

Penny landed with the skis retracted and taxied to the end of the narrow runway where an ambulance was waiting. Also waiting with the ambulance were two anxious fathers, Tim Reed and Gary Baxter. The boy's saw their fathers standing by the bright red ambulance as the plane rolled toward them. The boys began to call out, "Dad," said one, "Daddy," called the other. Penny was fearful one of the fathers, rushing to the airplane might walk into the still spinning propeller, but a waiting trooper grabbed them by coat sleeves and pulled them back. As soon as the engine went silent David jumped from the front seat and began to unbuckle the boys, Carl first, then Steve. The fathers were pushing to get at their respective sons. Everyone was crying, including the pilot, Penny.

It took several minutes of hugging, crying and more hugging until the medics were able to get close to the boys. They appeared to be in good health, but loaded them into the ambulance for the trip to the hospital to be checked. The two fathers were inside with the boys when it left the aircraft parking area. It was then David noticed the trooper on scene was Ray Finlay. When he had been notified of the boy's recovery he told Captain Meadows he wanted to be the one to deliver the message to each of the fathers. Once he had called them to give them the good news Finlay drove to Anchorage to be there when the boys arrived.

While all the greeting was in progress Penny was busy placing the engine cover over the warm cowling. She joined the reveling crowd, tears streaming down her cheeks. They were tears of joy for the happy ending at least to this part of the story, with the safe return of the young boys.

When the ambulance had left Finlay said "Hello" to David and Penny. "When the captain told me what was taking place I asked him to send one of the road troopers to Leach's place and stake it out in case he came home for some reason."

"Good thinking, Ray. How did the boys' fathers take the news?" It was David asking.

"Disbelief at first and then pandemonium. They were so excited I asked them to wait for an officer to pick them up and bring them to Lake Hood. I didn't think they were in any mental state to be driving. I'm glad I did it that way. Those two are so excited they would never have made it here. I'm afraid of the let-down when they learn what's happened to the boys and how much psychological help they'll need in the near future. Did you ask them about that aspect of their abduction?"

"No, but you could see it in their eyes when they came out of the cabin. They were afraid of us and thought we might shoot them. I'm glad Penny was there. They responded better to her than to Miles or me. I'm afraid these kids will be in therapy for a long time. They still don't know about the deaths of their mothers. That'll be another blow to the youngsters' mental state." There was a deep sadness in David's entire demeanor. He walked a short distance away and paused to compose himself. He was taking deep breaths when his cell phone rang.

"Hi David, it's Miles. I'm on the way back to Talkeetna. Your trooper said he would stay at the cabin tonight in case Leach decided to come back. I'll go out there in the morning and check on him."

"I can't thank you enough, Miles. It was a miracle you saw the plane over there. It was an even bigger miracle we found the boys alive. You should have been here when the boys and fathers got together. It was pretty emotional. I owe you big time, partner. I owe you."

"All in a day's work David. I'm glad it turned out the way it did. Say, that was a really nice 185 you were flying. When did the troopers get one that nice?"

"I guess you haven't heard, I'm getting married and this is a wedding present for my bride."

"You're getting married?" Miles asked in amazement.

"Yup, and the pilot with me tonight is the lucky girl. She wants to be married in June, but hasn't set the exact date yet. I made a deal for the plane today and when we got the call from you I called to get her to fly it and me up to the Kahiltna River. When she picks a date, you're invited to the wedding."

"I'll be there, old buddy, I'll be there. I'll call you tomorrow and we can work on the reports, and congratulations, you lucky dog."

David walked back to the plane where Ray and Penny were standing. "That was Miles on the phone. He's heading back to Talkeetna. That other trooper is staying the night in case Leach comes back." He turned to Penny, "Well, after the test drive how do you like the plane? Shall I say we'll take it?"

"Oh, David, I love it almost as much as I love you, but I'm not sure newly-weds can afford a gift like this."

"That's all I need to hear, my love. I'll sign the papers tomorrow. I'm trading my house equity for the plane and it'll be yours free and clear. By the way, there's a set of floats in the hangar. They go with the plane. The hangar is ours to use as long as we want it and he gave me a big discount on the price of the Cessna as a wedding gift."

"I think I'm going to like being married to you." She stood on tip-toes to kiss him before reaching out to take the engine cover off the plane and put into the back seat. They hardly spoke on the return trip, but love filled the cockpit.

<h1 style="text-align:center">Chapter 38</h1>

With the airplane safely back in the hangar and the lights turned out, Haskins and Rossiter climbed into the patrol car for the ten mile trip to Soldotna. Penny had given the Cessna one last look-over before leaving the hangar. She was excited beyond belief about it.

"OK David, you can buy the airplane," she said once inside the trooper car. "I like the color." She took David's hand and squeezed it hard. "I just can't believe it, thank you David. It will be ours, not just mine. You'll have to finish your flying lessons."

"I'm glad you like it. I want this marriage to begin on a happy note." He squeezed her hand. "I'm going to drop you off at home and go on to the office. This is going to be a long report and I want to get it done while the office is quiet. The office will be empty this time of night, making it easy to concentrate without interruptions. I'll call you tomorrow and see if you still work at the courthouse."

"The judge is going to scold me, but when he hears how it turned out I think he'll let me off with a letter of reprimand in my personnel file." She snickered a little, "And if he fires me you'll have to support me anyway. The upside of being fired is that I can fly the new airplane a lot more—if you buy the gas."

"Speaking of tomorrow, where do you suppose Leach went today. He couldn't possibly have known we were coming. Hell, we didn't even know."

"Take it easy, David. We'll catch him," speaking as if she was still part of the trooper team.

"I know, but we need to get this nut off the streets as soon as possible. We can't take a chance of him doing this again." He gave a huge sigh, "I hope he comes home tonight and the trooper at his place gets him." It all seemed like wishful thinking to David Haskins.

David dropped Penny off at her house and drove to the office. As he suspected the Captain had gone home for the day and the duty shift was out on the road. He sequestered himself in his tiny office and began to write his reports, including the part about using a private aircraft and pilot to fly him to the Kahiltna River cabin. He was nearly finished when the night shift came back to the office to do their reports and sign out. Haskins put the finished report on the captain's desk and went off duty. It had been a long day and he needed some rest.

David had only been gone from the office for about an hour when Lou Filson came in to begin his day. He was still sipping his first cup of coffee when Don Winston joined him.

"I might have some good news for a change," he said, sitting across from Filson and waving a copy of a report one of the other members of the Crime Scene Team had left on his desk late the prior evening.

"Let me guess, the lottery ticket we bought is a winner," muttered Filson.

"It's almost that good. You remember we had Lee and Paul take pictures and castings of the tire tracks at the suicide scene east of town the other morning?"

"I remember. What came of it?"

"You remember you and I took photos and casts of some tire tracks at the explosion on Miller Loop in North Kenai?"

"Yeah, I remember that, too."

"Those new guys looked through the books and identified them as the make, brand and size used on some new trucks. Trucks like the one that new helper for Terry Boyette drives. Same brand of tires, same wheelbase truck, same relationships to Boyette. The one out north is a different circumstance, but what if this all goes back to drugs? What if Boyette is the one in charge of the manufacture of meth and the distribution of 'H' and cocaine on the Kenai Peninsula? These tire tracks could link all these killings to Boyette. Conrad Dooley could be the connection we haven't been able to find."

"That's a lot of supposing, Don. But I have to admit, it makes sense. Let's find out which bank Boyette uses. The money has to be cleaned up somewhere and his rental business would be a good cover. I'll talk it over with the Captain. I had a note saying David wasn't coming in until after noon, so I'll try to get the Cap to let us follow up on this."

Don Winston knew the banks would never divulge the names of customers, but he had an idea. He made a stop at one of the local title companies and inquired about who would be the most likely to handle title transfers on properties in Nikiski and the entire North Kenai area. The receptionist said she couldn't give out that information, but perhaps the office manager could help. She buzzed a line on the intercom and said, "Miss Lawrence will be right with you, Sir."

Within seconds a beautiful blond woman in her mid-thirty's appeared to take him to her office where they could talk privately. Don was surprised at the size of the office, it was huge. It was also the cleanest office he had ever seen. He thought it looked more sanitized than clean. There were two pictures in frames on the desk. One was a graduation picture, probably of her daughter, and the other was of her and some young man poolside at what looked to him like some Mexican vacation resort. She looked to like she fit in rather well with the jet set crowd.

She pointed to a chair in front of her desk as she walked by to sit behind her spacious stage. "How may I help you?" she asked Winston.

"I don't mean to take up a lot of your valuable time Ms. Lawrence, but I'm working on some local felony cases and I need some information. Information that I understand is mostly confidential. I don't want you to break any rules, but I would be grateful for any help you can give me. I hope you understand what you learn from me is also confidential. Do we understand each other?"

"Of course, and please call me Deena. We aren't as stuffy as this office would lead you to believe. Our clients prefer certain level of service and this office is geared to that end. What is it you want to know?"

"Thank you for clearing that up for me. By the way my name is Don. I'm investigating a series of murders and a local businessman may be involved somehow. He's involved in buying some rather large parcels of land mostly in North Kenai. I have no way to track the financing of these properties, but I understand that's the basis of your business. I need to know if there's any way to track the money being invested in these properties. I guess what I want to know is where did this money come from? Is it leverage from other properties or cash from another business? Since I have no training or experience in this field I came here to see how it's done. Is there any way you can help me with this quest?"

The beautiful Deena showed a bright smile, "I might be able to give you some pointers, from a hypothetical view, of course. Excuse me; let me close the door so we can speak more privately." She stood and walked to the door, closed it and returned to her seat behind the desk. "Now we can talk, Don. I can't give you specific information on any deal being made, but I can give you general information on how the deals are done. Between you and me, we may have suspicions about the same local businessman. In fact if we are dealing with the same person I can start by saying I have had some of these same questions in my own mind."

"Are we completely off the record here?" asked Winston.

"We went off the record the moment I closed the office door. Let me start by asking you a blunt question that you may not be allowed to answer. Are we talking about a very large local businessman? One whose holdings are growing much faster than his cash flow could allow?" These were extremely candid questions Winston had not expected.

"It may be, but since I have no knowledge of the financial world I don't know if his investments are financed by legitimate means. Off the record, I do know there's a lot of drug business going on around here with much of it pointing back in his direction. Our man has hired a new assistant of sorts. He appears to be attempting to erase the line of cash flow between his legal public business and the drug business. We think he may be making the cash to finance his rental business and his new venture that seems to favor properties of interest to the coming oil and natural gas industry around Nikiski. That is about as clear as I can get without giving you privileged information." Don found himself being uncommonly open with this lady title broker.

"I think we're talking about the same man, Don. If any of this conversation gets out of this office I'll never be able to work in this industry again. Do you understand my position?"

"Yes I do, and I sympathize with you on your position. I want you to know that we're talking about at least four murders. I can't impress upon you enough how important this is. Rest assured I will protect your position in this conversation. I really need your help."

"Ok, here goes my job. If you're referring to Terry Boyette we are talking about the same man. He's growing at an astounding rate. At a rate his rental and real estate business can't support. But when he makes a deal he always comes up with the cash to close. It could happen once with almost anyone, but Boyette makes a habit of it. He comes up with cash by bank check from the First Bank of Alaska. This happens often. I know the bank manager is a straight arrow and would never allow any of this to go through his bank unless it was justified. I've tried to think of how he does it and I can't, unless he has an invisible trust or a corporation of investors, I don't know how he can do it."

"It would seem we share the same question, Deena." Don Winston was scratching his head, wondering where to go next. "I'll give you some confidential information, which you cannot repeat outside this meeting. In recent times, over the last couple of years, there's been a tremendous increase of meth use on the Kenai Peninsula. The experts tell me this meth is locally manufactured and the quality is some of the best they've ever seen. A small group of investigators think the meth lab is owned and operated by Terry Boyette. He's clever and we've never found a clear link between him and the meth lab. We also think he's the largest importer of hard drugs into this area. Again, we've never been able to tie Boyette to any of this. All this is particularly frustrating when we have several unsolved murders we think are related to the drug business. One of those murders was an old man with no ties with the drug trade. We think they did it to get possession of his cabin and acreage for a meth lab. Without some kind of proof we haven't been able to stop either the drug trade or solve the murders."

"I understand your concerns, Don. I sympathize with your position. I'm sorry I can't help you more." Deena Lawrence seemed as frustrated as Winston. "If it will help I'll call over to the First Bank of Alaska and see if the manager there can help you. Remember, he has rules to follow the same as me, but if there's any way he can help I'm sure he will. Would you like me to call him?"

"An introduction from you would be very helpful, I think. Thank you for being so candid with me, Deena. You've been a big help." Don put out his big hand to shake her delicate one as she reached for the telephone with the other.

Minutes later Winston climbed the stairs to the administrative offices of the First Bank of Alaska, Soldotna Branch. Don was shown to a nice corner office to meet with the man in charge of all the Kenai Peninsula branches of the bank. Leo is a large man who has spent more than thirty years directing this office. He is noted for his sense of humor and down to earth policies. Winston did his banking at a saving and loan down the street and had never had occasion to meet Leo.

"How do you do, Sir," said Don Winston, holding out his hand in introduction. "Don Winston with the Alaska State Troopers, I believe Ms. Lawrence called to say I was coming to see you."

"Call me Leo, everybody does. Yes Deena called, but I really don't know how much help I can be in your investigation. We're a tightly monitored institution regulated by the federal government and those folks don't like us talking out of school, so to speak."

"I understand your position, Leo. I have to play by essentially the same rules. I promise to not ask any questions that would violate your ethics, however, if I step over the line you tell me and I'll change my question. Fair enough?"

An hour later Winston walked out of the bank with a notebook full of notes on banking procedures and protocols. Most of the conversation was directed specifically at the methods used by Terry Boyette to finance recent large tract land purchases in Nikiski. Though the banker couldn't divulge the nature of specific transactions he pointed out that many of the cash movements were in excess of the $10,000 limit the federal government allowed without filing a form stating the deposit or withdrawal. He also said he didn't know if the feds would release that information to the troopers, but he would call and find out for him.

It was noon when he returned to the office to find Lou Filson in the office with David Haskins talking about the rescue mission the evening before. The three men sat in the office reviewing each case on their list, comparing notes and trying to make some sense of what they had learned.

Just before two in the afternoon Haskin's phone rang. It was Lee Stein, the team member staking out Bud Leach's property. Stein was parked in a grove of spruce trees several hundred yards up a small hill from the cabin. With his car partially concealed by the trees, he could watch the property without being observed from the air or the road. "David, it's Lee. I'm out at Leach's place and there's an airplane circling overhead. It's too far away to see the real colors or the tail numbers, but it looks like a PA-12. I think he's circling to see if it's safe to land. You'd better get some backup out here, just in case."

Haskins closed his phone and said, "It looks like Leach is home. Let's go boys."

Chapter 39

Three troopers in two patrol cars left the office parking area with lights and sirens running. Winter road conditions made the drive take much longer than it normally would have. They were three miles from the home of Bud Leach when the trooper on lookout came on the radio to report the airplane was slowed and on final approach. Haskins told him to stay out of sight until they arrived. A mile from the cabin the lights and sirens were turned off. Lee Stein came on the radio once again.

"He's here and out of the plane. He's going into the house."

"We'll be there in one minute, Lee. Get down there and block his plane so he can't take off." Both trooper cars sped up the slippery side road as fast as possible and arrived at the driveway just as Stein parked his patrol car close as he could to the engine of the small plane. He sat inside his car while the others drove to the site. All the troopers were puzzled by the fact Leach hadn't heard them and come outside to see what was going on. Winston parked behind the plane and stepped out of his car, leaning over the hood to cover Haskins who had driven to the back porch.

With the three troopers watching from near the airplane, David climbed the steps to the back deck of the house. He knew Leach was armed and approached the door with caution. Standing beside the door he knocked. There was no response. He knocked again and again no response. He reached for the door knob and turned. It opened. He pushed the door open and shouted inside, "State Troopers, Mr. Leach, come out with your hands raised."

Leach heard the door open and was surprised. He'd taken off his shoulder holster and a belt with the large bowie knife attached to it when he entered the bathroom. He cursed himself for being so careless. With the water running he hadn't heard them coming. He walked quietly down the hallway to where he could see the open front door. He didn't see a trooper but knew he was outside, waiting. "Give me a second, I'm coming out."

David motioned for Lou to come to his position while making quick motions with his hand indicating he wanted the other trooper to hurry. Lou ran across the open yard in a partial crouch, moving up the steps as quickly as possible. He had just stepped from being directly in front of the open door when Leach appeared in the doorway, one hand behind his left leg.

"OK I'm coming out, don't shoot!" Leach stepped out of the doorway with one hand over his head. He saw David on the right and turned toward him, raising his left hand with a large bowie knife in his grasp. He lunged through the doorway at Haskins, but Lou Filson was to the left and behind the frantic Leach. As he lunged forward at David, Lou hooked Leach's left arm. Leach had been so intent on attacking Haskins he hadn't seen Filson standing on the other side of the open door. Lou held the left arm and with the other hand reached for the wrist holding the huge knife. Leach was struggling with Filson when David jabbed the barrel of his Glock under his chin. Leach immediately dropped the knife.

"Anthony Leach, you are under arrest for kidnapping and murder." He stood silently while the troopers read him his constitutional rights and applied the handcuffs to his wrists. Lou searched him for weapons. Haskins asked, "We're going to lock the place up after we search it again. Is there anything special you want us to do when we leave here?"

"My key ring is on my belt in the hallway. Turn the heat down to 65 and lock the door. I'd appreciate it if you would put my plane in the hangar, in case we get a lot of snow."

"I want you to know the boys are safe and back with their fathers. Just in case you really care," said Haskins with as much sarcasm as he could muster.

Lou helped put Leach in the back seat of Lee Stein's car and asked Don Winston to ride with them to Wildwood Pretrial Facility for booking. "David and I will do the search of the property and move the airplane inside the little hangar. Meet us back at the office when you finish."

The first item into an evidence bag was the Bowie knife with a 10 inch blade, which was now lying on the front porch where Bud had dropped it. The two troopers searched the cabin carefully. Not much in the way of evidence was found in the cabin except some books under the mattress of his bed where several magazines containing child pornography were found. Haskins admired the cleanliness of the property, but was frustrated he hadn't found any more hard evidence. The guns, knives and pepper spray were bagged and loaded into the patrol car. When they finished in the house they locked the door after turning down the thermostat as Leach had asked.

The last place they wanted to search was the hangar. It had been recently searched leading them to believe it held little in the way of evidence. Filson was searching an area near the rear of the hangar when he moved a large wooden crate from in front of the work bench. Under the crate was a plywood patch in the floor. It seemed out of place and Filson kicked dirt from the edges to see it more clearly. Strangely it was hinged. Lou used a screwdriver from the bench to pry up the end of the cover. He shined a small flashlight from his belt inside the opening. Inside was a small metal box, like a small cash box. He called to his partner, "David, you'd better take a look at this."

David Haskins had been searching the inside of the airplane a few yards away. "What is it?" he asked as he neared the back of the hangar.

"I'm not sure, but I found a hidden container under the floor. I'm going to put on a new pair of rubber gloves to handle it. We'll need to check it for fingerprints. Do you want to take some pictures before I take it out of the hiding place?"

"I think we should, Lou. Let me get the camera."

The two men went about retrieving the small metal box, cautious of damaging any evidence it may yield. Since they already had a warrant to search they took the box from the hideaway and set it on the workbench. Haskins aimed a video camera as Filson opened the box, which was not locked. Inside were an assortment of small items, nearly all looked as if they belonged to small boys. There was Matchbox cars, toy airplanes, small superhero figures and other similar items.

"Bingo!" shouted Filson. "I'll bet you a double espresso we find some of these items in cases of missing kids from years past."

"I won't bet you on that one, Lou. I have the pictures, close the box and let's finish searching the hangar."

Nearly two hours later they moved the PA-12 inside the hangar, placed yellow police tape across the front of the hangar, loaded everything into their cars and left the scene. When they arrived at the office the other members of the team were inside. Lou and David carried all the items they had collected to a conference room with a long table where they would inventory and catalogue everything before securing them in the evidence locker.

"We left him in the booking room with the corrections officers after signing the remand slip. Leach was screaming for a phone call to his lawyer when we went out the back door." It was Don Winston giving the report. "We need to be sure to cross all our T's and dot all our I's on this one, guys. I think we're going to be meeting a high-dollar lawyer very soon."

Lou Filson made a list of the contents of the metal box they'd found and began a search of old cases with missing or abused children to see if any of the items were mentioned in those files. The first search found two cases where missing children had items matching those in the box with them when they went missing. It was beginning to look like Leach would be charged with the two recovered boys, and in at least two other cases. Both those cases were several years old and had not been solved.

It was after midnight when the initial reports were finished and all the documents readied for delivery to the District Attorney first thing in the morning. The entire crime scene team was exhausted by the time they quit for the night. David checked his watch and decided it was too late to call Penny. Not talking with her tonight left him with an empty feeling in his chest. He drove home, showered and collapsed into bed. It had, indeed, been a very long day with another one ahead.

DA Kevin Darby was on the telephone first thing in the morning. "I've been looking at these charges you filed against Anthony Leach," he said, opening the conversation with Haskins.

"What is it, Kevin? Didn't we get it right?"

"You have this guy charged with every crime in the 20th century and the 21st. The only thing on this list you missed was the bombing of the twin towers in New York and breaking Humpty Dumpty. Two counts of murder in the first, five counts of kidnapping, two new and three old ones, assaulting an officer, child pornography, child molestation; this is one heck of a list, David."

"If we find the bodies of the three missing kidnapped kids we'll add three more murder one charges. This guy is a monster, Kevin. He's a pedophile who's preyed on kids for years and gotten away with it. As a rule I don't get emotional about these crimes or the criminals, but this one is different. In this case he killed two young mothers, kidnapped the two boys and held them in total fear and abused them all this time. The fathers have suffered not knowing where the boys were or what had happened to them. We have evidence that ties him to three similar cases where the children were never found. But he kept souvenirs from those cases and we found those, along with some new ones from these boys we recovered. He abused all these kids, Kevin. Helpless, defenseless kids. It's our job, yours and mine to protect them and we failed. Now we have a chance to make up for some of that and I don't want him to escape. I don't want him to ever get out of prison."

"Take it easy David, I'm going to put him away. I was just jerking your chain. I didn't realize you felt so strongly about this case. I'm sorry."

"No, Kevin, I'm the one who's sorry. I get wound up when I feel guilty for allowing this to go on for so many years."

"Don't take it so personally, David. The system isn't perfect and some things fall through the cracks. It's your job and mine to correct the errors when we can. What you and your team did with this case is almost miraculous. You caught the offender and brought the victims back alive. Look at the record, in the past cases that didn't happen; they didn't catch him and the victims never came back, alive or otherwise. You can't blame yourself for that. You prevented it from happening again. Now it's up to me and the court. We'll do the rest. Don't worry. Good job, David." Kevin hung up the phone sorry he'd upset his friend at the trooper post. But it does show that to most cops it's more than just a job. It affects more than the victims; it gets personal.

David dialed Penny on her cell phone. "Do you still have a job?" he asked when she answered.

"Yes, but the rating on my personnel evaluation went down considerably with the letter of reprimand in my file. I'm mad at you for getting me into trouble." She was teasing him, not knowing how badly he was feeling right now.

"It was too late last night to call and let you know we got him. I just got off the phone with the DA and he is arraigning Leach today. The psychologists will begin to work with the boys today and I expect to get some pretty horrible reports about what he did to the boys. Usually the psychs try to keep the kids out of court and take testimony with interviews and depositions. I hope they can do it with these two kids. They've been through enough."

"I agree and hope for the best for them. I guess I haven't told you how much I enjoyed flying the new plane. I hated the mission, but loved the flying. The airplane is beyond belief. You should have seen Julia's face when I told her about your wedding gift. She was nearly hysterical. I can't blame her, I'm the same way. I love you David Haskins."

"I love you, too, Penny. I never thought I could feel this way about anyone, but somehow you make me feel different than I have ever felt in my life." He was speaking softly and sincerely. "Well, I'd better get back to work. Crime doesn't take a day off, you know."

"I hope I'll see you tonight. Bye-bye."

Chapter 40

The State of Alaska uses the designation of boroughs instead of counties for functions of local government within the state. The Kenai Peninsula Borough is a second class borough meaning it has the power to levy and collect taxes to run local service areas such schools, the hospital and emergency services such as fire departments and emergency medical services. The difference between this and a first class borough is it does not inherently have law enforcement powers.

Don Winston was in the Kenai Peninsula Assessing Department in the borough building in Soldotna meeting with the assessor. He wanted to learn what rental properties were owned by Terry Boyette. Phil Lenox headed the department.

"Sorry to keep you waiting Trooper, it seems we have more questions than we have people to answer them. Now, exactly what is it you want from me?" asked Phil.

"I'm gathering information in an investigation and I'd appreciate it if this inquiry was kept confidential."

"Of course, we get these requests almost daily from banks, title companies and the like. What kind of information are you looking for?"

Winston pulled a pad from his jacket pocket, "I'd like to find out how many and what the locations are of rental properties owned by Terry Boyette. I don't need all his properties, only the ones he claims as rentals. I assume he must have a business license for his rental business."

Lenox turned to his computer screen, "Let's take a look and see what we have." He began pecking away at the keyboard. "He has quite a list of property with his name on them, but only six are listed as rentals."

"Is it possible for you to give me a list of those properties? I'd like to write down the addresses of the six rentals." Winston had his notebook open now.

"Oh, heck, I can print you the partial list." He punched a few more keys and a printer began to chatter. Moments later Lenox spun around in his desk chair to retrieve three sheets of printout from the printer tray. He handed the sheets to Winston. "Will this do?" he asked.

Don scanned the list, amazed at the detail listed on the list of property. "This is wonderful, Phil, you've saved me about three day's work. Thanks."

"Always happy to help, is there anything else I can do for you?"

"Not a thing at this point. Thanks for the help. I'll get out of here and let you get back to work." He shook the hand of the assessor and left the office. His next order of business was to find each of the listed properties to determine which ones were rented and guess at the rental fee. This task took most of the rest of the day.

Two of the rentals turned out to be private residences and both looked to be occupied and located in the City of Soldotna. Two more were small business fronts, also in the city. One was in North Kenai and rented to an oil field service company. The lights were on inside the office portion and two pickups and one car were parked in front. Winston made notes on the printed sheets at each address.

The last address on the list was recently purchased by Boyette. It took a while to locate it as it was off the main road and obscured by the surrounding trees. A narrow drive led from the side street to the property. It was a small shop style metal building. When Winston drove around the last small curve in the drive he stopped. Parked in front was the same big black pickup he had seen parked at Boyette's office in Soldotna. He called for a check of the new license plate number. It was registered to Conrad Dooley, listing a Soldotna residential address. Winston backed slowly out of the drive and picked up his cell phone.

"Lou, this is Don. I was out here on Kalifornsky Beach Road checking out rental addresses on this list and came across something interesting. The last place I checked is off the road a little way and hidden in the trees. It's a small shop or warehouse. Our man Dooley? His pickup is parked at the building. What do you want me to do about him? Should I go inside and talk with him? Or should I just follow him to see where he goes?"

"Stay out of sight for now, Don. I'll check with David and see what he wants to do. I wonder why he moved his office from Terry's warehouse to this new location." Lou was puzzled by this change, but couldn't talk with David Haskins until he returned from court. He was attending the arraignment of Bud Leach. "If it gets late and you need to come to the office, I'll send Paul out to relieve you. I think we need to find out what he's up to. This may just be a business call to someone else with an office there."

"I thought about that, but his is the only vehicle parked here." Movement caught Winston's eye, "Hold it, I gotta go, he's on the move. I'll call you back when I see where he's headed." Don watched until the big black truck was nearly out of sight before following. When Dooley reached K-Beach Road he turned left toward Kenai. Winston let a couple of vehicles get between him and the truck, following at a safe and unseen distance. Dooley drove across Bridge Access Road to the Kenai Spur Highway and turned north. Winston followed as the truck drove out of Kenai toward Nikiski. When he neared the Salamatof Lake turn he slowed and drove off the main road. A short distance later he turned into a private drive with low-hanging trees shrouding the roadway. Winston stopped at the end of the road and followed on foot.

The drive meandered toward the lake, but ended in a stand of trees where there was a neatly kept shed. Dooley was just entering the shed when Don stepped out of the trees. He cautiously walked toward the shed, keeping low when he caught the odor of a strong chemical. He stopped and keyed his shoulder mike. He told the dispatcher where he was and to send Lou and the team as backup right away. Keeping low he made it to the truck, reaching inside to pull the keys from the ignition. He stepped back behind the truck and waited. He noted the heavy odor had diminished since Dooley went inside.

Minutes later, two patrol cars drove slowly down the drive. Lou Filson and Lee Stein stepped quietly out of their vehicles. Stein stayed near the patrol cars while Filson made his way to join Winston.

"I think there's someone else in the shed," said Winston. "They've been in there since I called in. They should be coming out soon. How do you want to handle it?"

"Why don't we just go knock on the door and tell Dooley he's under arrest?" said Filson, half joking.

"Good idea, let's go." With no further explanation Winston stood and walked directly to the front door with Filson a short distance behind him.

They took positions on either side of the front door. Lou did the honors, "Mr. Dooley, Alaska State Troopers. Come out with your hands above your head. This is the Troopers, Dooley. Come out with your hands up."

In the one small window in the front of the shed a head appeared quickly then disappeared again. A small voice from the inside said, "OK, I'm coming out. I have a gun, but I'm leaving it inside the shed. There are two of us. Don't shoot."

"I understand, both of you come out with your hands raised." Filson nodded to Winston. Making certain he was ready. Seconds later the door opened a crack.

"We're coming out," said a voice from the inside as the door opened wider. Dooley came out first, hands over his head. He was followed by another man neither of the troopers recognized. He was dressed in white plastic overalls similar to the ones troopers carry in the trunks of their cars for handling hazardous materials. The two men walked down the two front steps without looking right or left.

Filson stepped up behind Dooley and snapped a pair of handcuffs to his wrists while Winston did the same to the other man. Both men were searched for weapons.

"You said you had a gun. Where is it?" asked Filson.

"Inside on the table," replied Dooley. "What are you arresting us for?" His tone was angry.

"We have evidence linking you to the scenes of two murders. They were made to look like suicides, but both men were murdered. We'll talk about it at the office."

"Lock my building and my truck," ordered Dooley.

"We'll do that, Mr. Dooley. We will be getting a search warrant to search both the truck and the building. I'm going into the building to retrieve your weapon, with your permission, of course," informed Filson.

Lee Stein had walked to the aid of the others. "I want you to stay here and call a wrecker to take the truck to the impound yard. I also want you to put crime scene tape around the shed. We'll come back to search it later." Filson then turned to Dooley, "I assume you have a key to the front door."

Dooley turned to show Lou a string of keys on his belt. "Take them, I don't want anything stolen."

"We'll put one of our own locks on the door, but we don't want someone to lock us out. We may have to damage the door to get inside again."

"Let's put that guy in your car and I'll put Dooley in mine." Filson was talking to Winston, but turned to Dooley, "What is his name anyway?"

"Danny Risso," explained Dooley, "he works for me."

"OK Lee, when you get to the office take Risso to David's office and I'll take Dooley to mine."

After locking and securing the property the two patrol cars drove back to the headquarters building in Soldotna. On the trip back Dooley tried to hold a conversation with Lou Filson, but Lou ignored him. Once in the office he made an attempt to put Dooley at ease by taking off the handcuffs and offering him something to drink. Dooley rubbed his wrists and refused the offer. Lou began by gathering Dooley's statistical information; name, date of birth, place of birth, education, etc.

Dooley was becoming impatient. "When are you going to tell me what I'm charged with and let me call a lawyer?"

"I'm sorry, Mr. Dooley. I don't mean to make you uncomfortable, but I have to ask these questions. You understand. As for charges, we're still working on those, but for now we're holding you on two charges of murder in the first degree in the deaths of Kenny Pierce and Bobby Gunther. I must say you did an excellent job of setting those up to look self-inflicted, but there were some details you missed. I suspect you'll also be charged with manufacture and distribution of various drugs once the crime scene team is finished at your little shed at Salamatof Lake."

"That isn't my building," Dooley blurted, his anger numbing his judgement.

The comment surprised Lou and made him snap around to face him. "Who does own the building then, Mr. Dooley?"

"The man I work for, Terry Boyette." Dooley was angry with Boyette and mentally blaming him for this turn of events.

"Oh, you don't own the meth lab you were working at, is that correct?"

"That's right. I run it for Terry, that's all." Dooley had completely lost his cool now.

"We knew Pierce and Gunther both worked for Boyette, is that why you killed them?"

"It was Boyette's idea. Pierce was becoming too ambitious and Terry wanted him out of the way. Bobby was about to go to court and the DA wanted to make him a deal, so Terry wanted him shut up. I did the work, but none of it was my idea."

An hour later Dooley signed a statement incriminating Boyette. Captain Meadows rushed to Kenai with the statement in hand to meet with the District Attorney and the Judge to obtain a warrant for the arrest of Terry Boyette. When he returned to the office he was met by David Haskins, Don Winston and Paul Gorman. Meadows handed the warrant to David. "Bring him in," he ordered.

In another office Lee Stein was interviewing Danny Risso without much success. Risso was a new hire and had little knowledge of Boyette or Conrad Dooley for that matter. He said Dooley had taught him how to cook meth and had insisted he use the exact formula he was given. "High quality meant more money," Dooley had explained to Risso. Stein was able to get Risso to tell all he knew about his duties as a lab worker. He said Dooley treated him well and paid him on time. He liked that. Once Lee could no longer think of anything to ask he drove Risso to the jail for booking.

By the time Lee returned to the office Lou was finishing his initial interview with Conrad Dooley. Dooley was now screaming for a lawyer. Filson told Dooley he would be able to call his lawyer as soon as the booking process was completed. With that he snapped the handcuffs back on Dooley's wrists and loaded him into the patrol car for the ride to the booking facility in Kenai.

It had been a very busy afternoon. There were mountains of papers to be typed and information to be entered in the computers. Filson was pleased with himself for having irked Dooley enough to make him implicate his boss. As he drove back to the office his cell phone rang. It was David Haskins.

"Meet me at the office. Boyette wasn't at his office and we'll have to make another plan to arrest him."

"I'm headed there now," said Filson.

Chapter 41

D on Winston had a phone message when he arrived at the office. It was from the borough assessor. Winston called him back as soon as he got to the office.

The call was forwarded to Phil Lenox. "Trooper Winston, you asked me how much income some rental properties would generate and I told you I had no idea. I've been thinking about it and I can give you a formula to estimate the amount. Would that help you?"

"As a matter of fact it would, thanks. Do I need to come get a printout of the process?"

"Heck no, you have everything you need. I gave you a printout of the properties and their valuation used in the assessment process. That's all you need. Just take the estimated value of the property and multiply by .01. The average rental value is usually in the neighborhood of 1% of the appraised value. A $100,000 property should rent for around $1,000. It's the best way I know to establish rental income."

Winston had the printouts in his hand now, "Thanks, Phil, you've made my day. I have to go now, but I'll be in touch soon to let you know how this works out."

After hanging up the phone Winston hurried to the little conference room where the others were meeting. He made a thumbnail presentation of the property values and the probable rental income to the team.

Haskins smiled when he heard this bit of news. "If we can get a search warrant for the office I'll bet we can find some deposit slips and bank statements for the rental properties. We'll be able to match the figures. Good work, Don."

"My new friend, Leo the banker, told me one way money is laundered is to add cash to deposits of legitimate businesses. For instance, a rental property of Boyette's would bring $2,500, and his deposit for the property shows

$3500. No one would take notice, especially if it was on a regular basis. Leo can't give me the amounts of the deposits made by Boyette, but if we could get into his office we might find something interesting."

"I have Boyette's home address. Why don't we go over and ask him if we can see his office?" Haskins chuckled, "Aw, heck, let's just go over and arrest him for conspiracy to commit murder and ask him about his office later. We'll take three cars. Lou you ride with me. Lee, you and Don go together and cover the back in case he wants to run. Paul, you stay with your car out front in case he surprises us."

All the men nodded understanding. In an effort to save time David stopped at the office of Captain Meadows to ask him to get a warrant to search the properties and home of Terry Boyette. Meadows agreed and the team headed across town.

At Boyette's home address they found his large Cadillac sedan in the drive. Lou and David waited for Don and Lee to get into position before knocking on the front door. They heard shuffling inside. Moments later Boyette opened the door, shocked to see the troopers standing on his front porch. Boyette was a large man with the size and strength to put up a good fight. David and Lou rushed through the door, forcing Terry against the wall and snapping handcuffs to his wrists.

"What do you think you're doing?" he demanded.

"Mr. Boyette, you've been named as a conspirator in the deaths of three men. We're arresting you on those charges. You're suspect in several other felonies as well. Will you come to the office and discuss any of this with us in a peaceful manner?" David spoke loudly and clearly, but the adrenaline in his system was making him breathe hard.

"You're out of your mind," blustered Boyette. "I want to speak with my lawyer, RIGHT NOW!"

"I'm sorry Boyette, if that's going to be your attitude we'll just take you over to jail and book you in. You can call your lawyer from there." He was searched for weapons and walked to the waiting patrol car belonging to David Haskins. Lou walked to where Paul Gorman was sitting in his car and told him to get the others and return to the office.

The signed statements by Dooley were enough to arrest Boyette, but there would be additional charges when the search of his offices was finished.

The office search found rent receipts and deposit slips for all his properties. The rent receipts fell far short of the deposits, which were padded, to the tune of nearly $10,000 each week. He had laundered nearly a half million dollars a year through his rental business and financed the purchase of dozens of land parcels with the money. He had also used the same scheme to launder money through another bank across the street from First Bank of Alaska. Leo had described Boyette's scheme almost to the dollar. He would have the Colonel write a letter of gratitude to the banker.

In the following weeks, with all the participants in jail, the charges kept mounting; drug manufacture and distribution, drug sales, numerous assaults, though the shooting of Trooper Penny Rossiter was not mentioned in the charges. The death of Will Goodson was included at a later date.

Penny Rossiter was now Judge Nelson Bartolis' right hand. She had been barred from any contact with the cases being filed by the Alaska State Troopers against Terry Boyette, Conrad Dooley or Danny Risso. The judge had reprimanded her for her part in the Bud Leach case, but privately thanked her for helping to save the two young boys.

All the cases had moved through the court system in a slow and direct manner, but none of them had come to trial nor were they likely to do so in the next two months.

Penny had set June 6th as her wedding date. Julia was already buying new shoes for the occasion. They decided it would be a small civil ceremony with Judge Bartolis doing the honors. The guest list was long and would fill the gallery in the courtroom. It was only days now until the wedding and Penny was in her office daydreaming, when David came in to say hello.

"You aren't supposed to be back here, David," said Penny, wrapping her arms around his neck.

"I know, but I have a letter here for you, it came to the captain and he asked me to deliver it."

"Who's it from?" she asked.

"I don't know, but it's postmarked Disneyland."

"Oh, David, stop teasing."

"I'm not teasing, look for yourself."

She took the letter and read the postmark. "Hmm," she said while opening the colorful envelope. It was a thank you card with Mickey Mouse on the cover. The note inside was simple:

'They told us you were going to get married soon.
We wanted to wish you good luck and to thank you for helping us like you did.
The doctors say we will be good now and have you to thank.
We are having fun at Disneyland and we wish you were here with us.
We love you, Trooper Penny.
Steve and Carl'

There were tears in her eyes when she finished the note. "Oh, David, isn't that the nicest thing you ever read?"

David smiled, "I love you, Trooper Penny, I love you.

Cinch Knot:
A Multinational Plot to Nuke the Trans Alaska Pipeline

Devil's Heart:
Native American Lore and Modern Police Work

Ice Blue Eyes:
An Alaskan Story of Greed, Love and Revenge

Blue Sky, Green Grass:
Murder, Money Laundering and Winter Farming in Alaska

Poacher's Paradise:
An Alaska Wildlife Trooper Novel

Easy Come, Easy Go:
Alaska Gold Fever

Brothers of the Badge:
Alaska State Troopers, FBI Agents and US Marshals Probe an Informant's Death

Penny Files:
Alaska State Troopers Unfinished Business

Getting Even:
What Goes Around in Alaska, Comes Around in Florida

Wyatt Earp V:
Alaska Bush Guardian

Alaska Fish Wars:
Nobody Wins

Flying Blind:
Alaska Adventure and International Intrigue